My Sister
Is a
Werewolf

My Sister Is a Werewolf

KATHY LOVE

BRAVA

KENSINGTON PUBLISHING CORP.
http://www.kensingtonbooks.com

BRAVA BOOKS are published by

Kensington Publishing Corp.
850 Third Avenue
New York, NY 10022

ISBN-13: 978-0-7582-1855-1
ISBN-10: 0-7582-1855-9

First Kensington Trade Paperback Printing: July 2007
10 9 8 7 6 5 4 3 2 1

Printed in the United States of America

My Sister
Is a
Werewolf

Chapter 1

"Ouch! Dammit."

Elizabeth threw down her tweezers, blinking away the sudden blur of tears. Gradually both the pain and the blurry vision subsided, leaving her glaring at her reflection.

She swiped at her eyes and reached for the discarded tweezers. Then she changed her mind, leaving them where they'd landed in the sink. It wasn't as if getting her already well-groomed eyebrows further tamed was going to calm the restlessness building inside her. At least it hadn't worked thus far.

Edginess, as if she'd drunk about three pots of coffee in a three-hour span, wracked her body. She wanted to crawl out of her own skin. That particular feeling was usually reserved for the full moon, and she knew that auspicious time of the month was still days away.

She wandered out of her bathroom, roaming from room to room in the sprawling house. The old farmhouse she was renting was just the type of place where she'd always wanted to live. Bedrooms nestled under the eaves, a wraparound porch with a swing, a huge country kitchen. Woods, mountains. The place was perfect. So why couldn't she cast off the feeling that something wasn't right, that something was about to happen?

She started at every sound. She paced like a caged animal.

You are anxious to hear what Dr. Fowler thinks, she told herself.

At first she'd tried to attribute the anxiety to her new surroundings. But she knew that wasn't it. She'd moved a lot, stayed in places far more secluded than this, and she'd never felt nervous.

And this wasn't nerves, exactly. It was . . . as if she was being driven slowly mad, by something she couldn't see or hear or feel. An endless unsatisfied feeling—so intense she couldn't seem to concentrate on anything else.

It must be the newest serum, she considered, not for the first time. But again, she toyed with the idea. These feelings had started before her last injection. Still, what else could it be?

The idea upset her. The serum she'd prayed would finally cure her had apparently done nothing—except possibly make her an agitated, nervous wreck. Not what she'd been going for. Oh, she had seen a change in the cells, but none in her condition. Hence sending her findings to Dr. Fowler.

She paced the length of the upstairs hallway again. She had to hear from him soon. She'd been so convinced she was on the right track. So certain she'd gotten it right this time. Dammit.

A loud bang halted her train of thought, or perhaps accentuated it. She paused for a second at the top of the staircase, then hurried down, her feet silent on the worn wooden steps. Carefully, she approached the front door, pushing aside the curtain to peek out.

The sun had nearly disappeared among the mountains and trees—only faint traces of pinkish orange streaked the sky where the orb had been. But Elizabeth's eyes adjusted instantaneously to the waning light. She could see her front yard as clearly as if it were lit by the noonday sun.

Another sharp bang sounded again, causing her to freeze, her muscles tensing. Every part of her body remained motionless except for her eyes, which scanned the yard, taking in every detail.

A large barn that accompanied her house loomed to the

right, a black hulk against the evening sky. As another gust of wind blew through trees, she saw the barn door swing, then hit its frame with a sharp, resounding whack.

She shook her head, annoyed at her panicky reaction. She wasn't a person to be easily shaken—even through the years with . . .

The door slammed again, the noise startling her. She fully expected to see someone out there in the shadows, even though she knew what was causing the sound.

Something else she could add to this strange edginess: the feeling of being watched, although she'd not found any signs to validate that feeling. More unexplained weirdness.

Unless maybe he was coming for her. He hadn't contacted her in all these years, but that didn't mean it couldn't happen. Hell, she didn't even know if he'd ever looked. But she knew he would come eventually—after all, she was his. His forever.

She shivered. Why was she even thinking of Brody? She hadn't in years. Why now? She pulled in a deep breath to calm herself—as much as she could. She supposed it was everything. Her nerves. And she realized that getting closer to a cure also reminded her of him. That she could truly be free.

"You, Elizabeth," she reminded herself, saying the words out loud as if vowing them to the empty house would make them true, "are only his until you find the cure."

So stop acting like a ninny, and get back to work.

She opened the front door and headed down the steps of the porch. The breeze ruffled her hair and felt crisp on her skin. Newly fallen leaves crunched under her feet; she savored their scent, earthy and rich. A clean, natural scent.

She breathed in, taking the fresh air deep into her lungs. The distant hint of wood smoke mingled with the other smells of autumn, not tainting the scent but adding to it.

However, her enjoyment was short-lived. Even the signs of fall, her favorite season, seemed to agitate her, restlessness snaking through her limbs, pooling in her belly.

Damn, she felt like screaming. What was wrong with her? She was usually an unruffled person, having learned to control her emotions long ago, when she realized how little control she had over her new life. Her calm *was* her control. Composure, her way to manage the unmanageable.

Now she felt set adrift, like she had when she'd first realized what she'd become. Not that anyone could fault her for getting a little agitated about discovering she was a werewolf. That did tend to shake a person—just a little.

She picked up her steps, hurrying into the barn, securing the door behind her as if she could keep her anxious feelings at bay. Locked outside. If only.

Repeating her now familiar chant to *calm down* over and over in her head, she walked to the far end of the barn where she had sectioned off several of the old horse stalls and knocked down the dividers, using thick plastic to create makeshift walls and a ceiling. Her lab. Certainly not what she'd had in New York, but she liked it. And she planned to build a proper lab in there after the winter, if she still needed a lab by then. She hoped she wouldn't.

She refused to look at the stall across from her temporary lab as she parted the plastic and stepped inside, even though she could visualize the thick chains and manacles mounted to the rafters overhead. Instead, she concentrated on the creaking of the floorboards under her feet. The whistle of the wind outside. A storm was building.

Then she forced everything aside as she busied herself with taking her cell samples out of the small refrigerator and preparing slides.

After dropping her third slide in a row, she gave up.

"Damn it, damn it, damn it," she muttered. She braced herself against the edge of the table, closing her eyes, trying to get control.

"You're tired," she told herself. She hadn't slept for more than a few hours for days. *Because you know you are close.*

But she knew it wasn't just the urgency of her research that kept her awake. Sleeplessness was another issue that had arisen shortly after moving here—seemingly not in conjunction with the injection, either. She didn't understand what was causing it, but she knew the insomnia wasn't helping her anxiety.

"Calm down," she muttered to herself. "Relax. You are close."

She'd even been so sure she was only just a few genome sequences away that she'd sent her latest serum to Dr. Fowler, her mentor. He'd be able to look at the cell changes and tell her where the cure stood. She knew it was so close.

And that was probably part of her impatience and agitation. She couldn't wait to hear back from Fowler.

Opening her eyes, she still felt unsteady, but her reasoning had helped a little. For the first time, she realized her workstation was littered with test tubes, petri dishes, discarded slides. She frowned at the mess, surprised by it. Normally, she was very neat. Almost compulsively so.

"That's your problem," she said, fumbling to tidy her space. "You're rushing. You're not taking your time and thinking clearly. You are anxious to hear what Dr. Fowler thinks and it's making you careless. You need to just *calm down*."

"Who?" an eerie voice said from behind her.

Elizabeth spun; her lips curled back, her stance ready to attack. The thick plastic seemed to shiver as the wind whistled through the barn boards, but otherwise she heard no sound. Still she didn't relax her pose as she cocked her head, listening intently.

The walls creaked under another gust of the wind. She could hear the leaves rustling outside. Then she heard the ghostly question again.

"Who?"

Taking slow, precise steps, she edged closer to the entrance of the lab. The plastic rustled as another blast of wind caused the barn to moan. She hesitated for just a fraction of a second, then whipped apart the thick, draped plastic.

"Who?"

Elizabeth's head snapped upward, realizing the sound was coming from overhead. Even though the barn was dark, she could still easily see the several oval shapes lined up on the rafters. Yellow eyes blinked down at her.

She tilted her head, surprised.

"Owls?" she said, a bewildered smile touching her lips. Seven owls peered at her. When was the last time she'd seen an owl this close? In the stables of her family's Derbyshire estate, maybe?

She watched them for a moment, amused by the rare sight. Or rather, a rare sight to her. Then she took a step closer, fully expecting the animals to sense they were near something that they really shouldn't be, and fly away. But they remained still, except for the occasional blink of those impassive eyes.

Frowning, she stepped closer, until she was nearly beneath the rafter. The birds didn't shift and showed no inclination to flee. Instead they bowed their heads, watching her with those golden, unreadable eyes.

"What are you crazy birds doing?" she finally asked, with a bewildered shake of her head. The reply to her question was more incomprehensible blinks.

How very odd. It would have been odd enough for so many owls to be perched in the barn. But to stay near her? That was very strange.

Thunder rumbled in the distance, and Elizabeth wondered if the birds had decided she was a safer risk than the approaching storm. Another gust of wind hit the barn, and a draft reached her where she stood. Air played over her skin and ruffled the tendrils of her hair like unseen fingers.

She gasped at the invisible touches, something akin to desire rocketing through her, shocking and powerful. Too powerful. Overhead she heard the whoosh of wings fill the air, joining the mayhem.

Well, the owls weren't completely senseless. They had sensed the powerful change in her, and self-preservation had finally kicked in. She watched them swoop through the rafters, as she tried to suppress the strange compulsion inside herself. Finally, although she had no idea how much time had passed, she felt under control. Mostly under control.

Slowly, one by one, the owls returned to their previous perch, again watching her. She stared back, confused.

"Why are you here?" she asked.

One hooted, another blinked, and none of them answered her—of course.

Suddenly the strangeness of the past few days, the agitation within her, this new and sudden flare of restlessness that had felt strangely like arousal—even the damned owls staring down at her—were too much.

She had to be driving herself too hard. She needed a break. Surely she could spare one evening. She obviously needed it. Then she could approach all of this again in the morning, calmer, more relaxed.

She looked back up at the owls, who sat stock-still. The embodiment of tranquility.

Oh yeah, she needed to get away from here.

Chapter 2

Elizabeth heeled down the kickstand of her motorcycle just as the rain started to fall in large, cold splats around her. She'd parked the large black Harley Night Rod as close to the side of the building as she could, hoping that would shield it from some of the water. With quick steps, she approached the bar, working the chinstrap of her helmet and pulling it off just as she stepped through the door.

She glanced around, searching for her brother. She located him behind the bar, where he poured a mug of beer from the tap. The sight still gave her pause. Christian. Her brother. Her family. The family she'd believed was gone forever. The fact that the wealthy brother she remembered now tended bar in a backwoods watering hole just added to the surrealism of the scene.

"Elizabeth," he greeted her with a smile that seemed just a little amazed as well.

As she walked up to him, her boots thudding loudly on the worn floorboards, she wondered if his expression reflected his own amazement that she was alive, too. The fact that she and her brothers had been reunited for nearly three months now hadn't diminished their wonder. Her beloved brothers.

Christian's eyes left her face, dropping to her outfit for just a fraction of a second. Some of her joy fled. Maybe the amazement in his eyes had more to do with the fact that she was nothing like the little sister he remembered.

But whether he was shocked by who she was now or not, his pale eyes shone with pleasure as he came around the bar and gave her an enveloping hug.

"Hey, I'm glad you stopped by tonight," he said after he released her. "Jolee and I were thinking about coming up to your place to be sure you were all right. You've been a real recluse since you moved there."

Guilt filled her. When she'd believed her brothers were dead, she'd cried over the loss for years. She'd begged to have them back. Yet now that she finally had them, she had a hard time facing them.

"My research is keeping me very busy," she told him, feeling the excuse was lame, even though it was true. Just not the whole truth.

She feared that her brother wouldn't understand, much less like, the person she was now. She was so, so different from the young, naive girl her brother once knew. But she didn't want to be. She had her family back now, and she wanted that girl back, too. That long-gone girl.

Whereas, aside from being more handsome, stunningly so, Christian was unchanged. He looked just like the brother she believed dead in 1822. But time had no effect on vampires, except to make them more attractive. He was still the Christian she remembered.

She knew he didn't see the same arrest of time in her. She'd once been the baby of the family—nearly ten years Christian's junior—but now she'd caught up to him. In fact, she was his same age exactly. And that was just the start of the changes.

Did he wonder where the frivolous, carefree, innocent sister he'd once known had gone? And who was this older, leather-clad, toughened woman who stood in front of him now?

"You look great," he said as if he guessed what she was thinking. He hugged her again.

This time, she closed her eyes and hugged him back. God, she had missed him.

"So this is the long-lost sister, eh?"

Elizabeth glanced toward the gravelly voice that sounded behind Christian. Even though she'd only been to Christian's—or rather his mate, Jolee's—bar once or twice since moving here, she recognized the speaker. An old, thin man with a bushy beard and watchful eyes. On the same bar stool where she'd seen him last with a mug of beer in front of him and a cigarette hanging from his lips.

"Elizabeth, you remember—" Christian started, but the old man cut him off.

"Just call me Trader Vic."

Elizabeth frowned at the amused look on the old man's wizened face, then realized the joke. So this old coot knew the truth about her. Given that, she supposed it *was* hard to pass up a good Warren Zevon joke. "Werewolves of London" was like a national anthem for her kind.

She expected to be irritated that this stranger, this mortal, knew what she was, but something in the old man's eyes reassured her that her secret was safe with him.

"Hey, Vic. So I guess you know that I'm *not* Little Red Riding Hood?"

The older man chuckled, then reached for his beer.

Christian cast a puzzled look between the two, then shook his head. "Okay. Introductions have been made—I think. Take a seat here," he gestured to the stool beside the old man's, "and let me get you a drink."

Elizabeth nodded, placing her helmet on the floor next to her seat. Damn, she needed a drink. She started to ask Christian for a whiskey, straight up, then stopped.

What would her brother think of that? The baby sister who'd never had more than a few sips of watered-down punch, asking for a shot of hard liquor.

MY SISTER IS A WEREWOLF

"I'll, um, take a light beer—whatever kind you have." That was an acceptable compromise, wasn't it?

"Sure." Christian seemed fine with it as he reached for a mug.

Vic leaned toward her, his wise eyes twinkling. "That wasn't what you wanted, was it?"

Elizabeth shook her head and smiled slightly, already feeling camaraderie with the old man.

"Elizabeth," called Jolee as she came down from the back of the bar. The sound of her full name on someone's lips other than her brother's gave Elizabeth pause.

She was used to thinking of herself as Elizabeth—somehow she'd always managed that. And Christian calling her Elizabeth was just natural. But everyone else, for years and years, had called her Lizzie. Somehow that nickname had been easier, as if Elizabeth had died with her family and Lizzie had been born. But now, people wanted Elizabeth back. She was just afraid that person was gone.

She cast her thoughts aside and forced a smile at the tall, beautiful redhead. This woman was now her family, too. Another wave of guilt and anxiety coursed through her, making her shift on her bar stool. Jolee probably knew all about her. Or rather all about the "other" Elizabeth. Another person who expected her to be someone she no longer was.

"How are you?" Jolee asked, her slow, drawling accent and her wide, warm smile making it impossible to believe she was a vampire.

Elizabeth supposed a vampire with warm southern charm was as appropriate as one with aristocratic, European charm, making her brother and Jolee a well-suited match. *Charm* being the operative word to describe most vampires. *Charm* wasn't a word applied to werewolves. At least, not the ones she knew.

She refocused on her sister-in-law's question. "I'm fine," Elizabeth said automatically.

She was so far from fine, but that would require her to reveal just how far away she was from the Elizabeth of the past.

"Is the house working out?"

Elizabeth nodded, a small but real smile touching her lips. "Yes, I love it there." She really did, even if she had been edgy and tense since moving there. "West Virginia is beautiful."

Jolee grinned back, and again the room seemed to fill with warmth. It was little wonder why Christian served beer in this backwater bar. Elizabeth suspected he'd do anything Jolee wanted—just for that smile alone.

"If Jolee had her way, she'd get our whole family moved to this godforsaken place," Christian said, joining them and placing the pale beer in front of Elizabeth. Then he squeezed Jolee affectionately to temper his words. She elbowed him, but grinned at his teasing.

"Can you picture Sebastian ever leaving the city?" Jolee laughed. "That brother of y'all's is far too in love with the perks of urban living to come here. But Rhys . . ." She cocked an eyebrow like the idea of getting Rhys and his wife, Jane, to West Virginia might hold merit.

"You can work on them, then maybe Sebastian and Mina will follow." Christian leaned in to kiss his mate's cheek, more respect and love in his ribbing than teasing.

Elizabeth watched them, a pang of envy flitting through her. What was it like to have a relationship like that? But the notion was almost instantly ripped from her mind, replaced by an overwhelming swell of pure need. Sharp and breath-stealing. Just like the one she'd experienced in her barn earlier. What on earth was happening to her?

She pulled in a breath slowly through her nose, focusing on the bottles lining the wall behind the bar. Clear bottles, green bottles, brown bottles, a few blue, too. She tried to focus on anything but the attraction between her brother and his mate. And this raging need whirling through her.

"So is your research going well?" Christian asked, not

seeming to notice her agitation. That had to be good, right? She wasn't totally out of control.

Christian frowned, however, when she didn't answer. "Elizabeth? Your research?"

She pulled in one more calming breath. "Umm, yeah, it's going fine." Everything was fine. Keep saying that and maybe it would be so.

"Are you any closer, do you think?"

Elizabeth nodded again, then took a long swallow of her beer to hide her frustration with this uncontrollable agitation inside her. The golden liquid tasted bitter, but didn't have the bite she was craving.

Her family, her research, even her drink—nothing seemed to be satisfying as it should. Nothing reduced the feelings inside her. The strange restlessness that kept battering at her, wearing her down.

"Oh," Jolee said, glancing back to the booth where all her sound equipment was arranged. "This song is nearly done. Please excuse me."

She rushed back down the bar toward the karaoke system and the small stage where a woman stood at a microphone. The woman's eyes were moving from left to right as she followed words on a large teleprompter—half-reading, half-singing them—off-key and a little behind the music.

Elizabeth twisted on her seat, surprised that she hadn't even registered the singer. Now that the singing had penetrated her stressed brain, it was pretty darned hard to miss.

"And that was 'Love Is Like a Butterfly,'" Jolee announced in an impressed voice, as if she'd found the off-key rendition very enjoyable. Further proof that her sister-in-law really was a kind, kind vampire.

"Now, here is," Jolee glanced at the square of paper she held, "Jill Lewis—"

A cry of embarrassment came from a table near the stage. Elizabeth spotted the indignant woman seated with a man, who she glared at, and another couple. She continued to frown at the man as she waved her hands adamantly in the universal sign of "no." But the signal didn't work—the others at the table cajoled her to take the stage.

"Here we go again," Christian said, drawing Elizabeth's attention to him for just a moment. But before she could ask what he meant, she found herself turning back to watch the escapade.

For a second, she felt sympathy for the poor woman, who still adamantly declined to take the stage. She obviously didn't want to sing. But then the woman stood. Maybe she would get up there after all.

Reaching for her beer, Elizabeth took a sip, and, for the first time tonight, felt a little normal. The atmosphere seemed to envelop her, as if she was meant to be there. A much-needed sense of contentment filled her. The talking, the laughter, the smell of drinks and salty, roasted peanuts. It made her feel oddly better. This was a good idea—a good distraction. Tomorrow she'd return to her research more relaxed and focused.

Elizabeth smiled as Jill Lewis finally took the stage. The reluctant woman shook her head, glaring good-naturedly at her friends.

"All right!" Jolee cheered from over her microphone, and much of the audience exploded into applause. Elizabeth clapped along with them.

Jolee started the music and the woman's voice filled the room almost from the first note. Elizabeth recognized the tune as a song from the radio with a happy, contagious beat. And the woman sang it well—better than well. It was little wonder that her pals were urging her to get up there. She was great.

Elizabeth looked back to the woman's table of friends to see their reaction to the woman's fantastic singing. Two of them, a man and a woman, beamed and clapped, while the other at the table, a male, just watched. He was somehow distant from the other two. The clapping male leaned over to say something to him, and the one who only watched turned toward his friend, giving Elizabeth her first full view of his face.

Elizabeth's smile disappeared. Desire, so strong that it almost made her cry out, ripped through her, shredding any trace of calm she'd found. Every muscle in her body tensed, every sense sharpening until her whole being was centered on the man before her.

Without saying a word to Christian, she rose. Carefully, purposefully, she zigzagged through the tables, her eyes never leaving the man. Just tables away, she stopped herself, fragments of her reasonable mind taking control. She glanced back to the bar. Christian watched her, but when he saw her looking, he busied himself by taking an order from one of the patrons.

Her brother could sense her desire now. Of course he could. Vampires could sense emotions—and she knew hers ran very strong. Shame filled her, but still her gaze returned to the male at the table.

The man was beautiful—dark hair, sculpted features, perfectly shaped lips that any woman would have killed for, yet on him they were sinfully masculine. He was beyond handsome.

Elizabeth had seen many handsome men in her life, but her body had never reacted like this. Moisture pooled between her thighs, dampening her panties. Her nipples hardened, rasping the cotton of her camisole. Her mouth watered.

She swallowed. *Control yourself! What was she doing?*

But instead of walking back to her bar stool like her brain ordered her to, she took another step toward the table of friends. Then another. She sauntered slowly past the man's chair, not getting too close, not drawing attention to herself—not just yet. She had to assess, she had to watch. Stalking her prey.

She lifted her head to breathe in his scent. The hint of woodsy cologne, the freshness of soap and shampoo, the minty traces of toothpaste. And a warm, rich scent—a scent that made her want to tip back her head and howl.

She continued around the table until he was directly in her line of sight—then she sat down at an empty table. Eyes trained on him, she studied him. Oh yeah, she wanted him.

For just a moment, she closed her eyes as her rational mind took tenuous control. Why was this happening? It was as if the wolf was in control. But that didn't happen. She didn't stay in human form and think like the wolf. She didn't allow that. Some werewolves did. Brody did. He was more wolf than man at all times. She didn't allow that. She didn't.

Her eyes snapped open. The man was looking at her. She'd felt his gaze before she'd actually seen it. Their gazes met, and even in the dim light, she could see his eyes were a mixture somewhere between brown and green.

Again her body told her this was what she needed. This was what she'd been wanting. *He* was what she wanted. She continued to stare, meeting his gaze, until he looked away. Still she watched him. Unable to do otherwise. The need was in control now.

She was acting like a bitch in heat. And she didn't care.

Chapter 3

Jensen only half-listened to the conversation going on around him. He'd thought tonight would be okay. The bar was a place he'd never been, so it shouldn't conjure memories. But location wasn't the issue. Oh, it definitely was at other times, but tonight, it was the company.

He glanced at the man sitting to his right. Brian Lewis, his best friend growing up. Brian had changed very little, maybe a bit thicker in the middle, broader in the shoulders. But he still had the same easygoing nature and dry sense of humor. And he still had Jill.

He glanced to Jill, Brian's wife for . . . was it five years already? Jill looked the same, too. Maybe a little more mature, more refined.

An image of Jill and Katie immediately appeared in his mind. One brunette, the other blond, both in ponytails. They'd been as inseparable as he and Brian had once been. As all four of them had been. They'd always assumed they'd stay friends, no matter where their lives took them.

But sometimes it only takes one event to change the tide of a man's whole future. Jensen had ended up in a direction far, far different from anything he'd ever imagined. Too far to get back to the person he'd been when Brian and Jill had known him.

He hadn't seen either Brian or Jill for over three years—

not until his recent return to West Pines. And even then, he'd avoided them.

But after Brian had called him nearly a dozen times, he'd realized he couldn't sidestep them forever. Not in a town the size of West Pines. So they'd gotten together a few times. Even though Jensen quickly realized he still liked his old friends, very much, it had been difficult—so many memories revolved around these two people. Memories of . . .

"Oh, please sing, Jill."

Jensen blinked, pulled out of his thoughts by the pale blonde to his right. Melanie was the woman who Brian and Jill had invited along as his date. Although no one had said that, exactly.

Jill shook her head. "No. Not tonight."

"That's what you think," Brian said, wiggling his eyebrows. A gesture Jensen remembered well.

"What have you done, Brian Andrew Lewis?" Jill demanded.

"Nothing," he assured her, his grin in direct opposition to his denial.

"You put in a song request while I was in the ladies' room, didn't you?" Jill drilled her husband with a look that would have crumbled a weaker man.

"Maybe. Maybe not."

"Did he, Jensen? I know I can get the truth from you." She gave a pointed look to her husband. "Jensen was always the more upfront one of the two of you."

Jensen forced himself to swallow the sip of club soda he'd just taken, the carbonation hurting his throat. Upfront? Yeah, that showed how little they knew him now.

Fortunately, he was saved from having to respond by one of the bar employees announcing that Jill Lewis would be the next to sing.

"You," Jill growled at Brian, although there was no real anger in her eyes. Her cheeks did flush a bright red.

Suddenly Jensen was seeing Jill as she'd looked right before the senior talent show their high school had held every winter. She'd blushed a bright red just before taking the stage. Katie had been nervous, too, although no one would have guessed it. She'd had a way of remaining so calm, so composed. Only Jensen had known, because when he'd held her hand before she took the stage, her fingers had been ice cold and trembling.

Ice cold, trembling. He paused, his memory wandering off for a moment, to a dark place, a place he didn't want to go. He forced his memories back to that senior show. Katie had walked up onto that stage with Jill, looking like she hadn't a fear in the world. They'd sung "Everything Changes" by Kathy Troccoli. They'd won. And now, that song seemed strangely prophetic.

"Go on," Brian urged, his voice distant, becoming a part of Jensen's memory. "You know how I love to hear you sing."

Jensen recalled how he and Brian had cheered and whistled for Katie and Jill that night.

Jill stood, her movement pulling Jensen's attention back to the present. Her cheeks were an even brighter shade of pink, but she assented, walking up to the microphone with only a little trepidation in her steps.

Jensen forced a smile and applauded with the rest of the room, but it was only a reflexive reaction. In his head he was back with Katie, remembering her voice rather than Jill's.

"She's just as good as she always was, isn't she?" Brian said.

Jensen blinked, again torn from his own memories. He glanced around, for a moment almost confused by where he was.

"Yeah, she is," he agreed.

Suddenly, the hairs on the back of his neck stood up, his spine straightening. He started to glance over his shoulder, expecting to see Katie right there behind him. She'd had that effect on him, bringing his body to attention just by walking into a room. But he stopped himself. She wasn't there. He was obviously reacting to all the memories being dredged up by seeing his old friends and watching Jill sing. This was why he'd avoided them. The memories were too much.

A hint of something spicy, like an exotic mixture of vanilla and cinnamon, wafted around him, growing more and more intense until it was nearly overwhelming. He shot a look at Brian to see if he smelled the scent, but Brian's attention was locked on his wife.

Jensen then looked at Melanie—she also watched Jill until she noticed him staring at her. She smiled, nothing in the gesture indicating she smelled the heady scent surrounding them.

He was obviously hallucinating. His memories became far too real, far too tangible, although the perfume lacing the air wasn't something Katie would have worn. She'd liked light scents, floral scents. This smell was rich and earthy, reminding him again of dark, ground spices. Wild, exotic.

Suddenly Brian and Melanie were on their feet, cheering and applauding, and Jensen realized that Jill had finished her song. He rose, too, automatically clapping along with them. Still the scent enveloped him. What was it?

Jensen heard the others compliment Jill as she returned to the table. He even murmured his own praise, although he couldn't have said what his words had actually been. Obviously coming here was a bad idea—he just felt weird tonight.

"I say this calls for another round of drinks," Brian said, clapping Jensen on the back.

Jensen started at the affectionate tap.

"I don't know," he said. "I think maybe I should call it a night."

"Man, it's still early," Brian said. He sounded truly disappointed. "Hell, we have the babysitter until midnight."

Another surreal detail. Brian and Jill had children. A boy and a girl. The perfect family.

Again, Katie appeared in his mind, as they'd lazed in the grass on his grandfather's lawn, young kids planning a big future.

"I want a boy and a girl," Katie had stated, as if it was a given certainty.

"What if we get two boys or two girls?" Jensen had said. "It could happen, you know. I'm not a doctor, but I know about this type of thing."

Katie had grinned. "That would be fine, too. But I know we will have one of each."

"Jensen," Jill said, drawing him back to the present. "Please stay. We've barely seen you since you moved back."

Jensen's first instinct was to simply tell them that he had to go. This was too much. He was overwhelmed by memories tonight. He thought he could handle it, but—he just couldn't. But that might lead to topics he really didn't want to talk about.

In the brief moments he'd seen his old friend, Brian had made it clear that he thought Jensen needed to move on. But Brian didn't have all the facts. He never would.

Maybe if Jensen just stayed for one more drink, then he could escape without talking about anything too personal.

"Okay. One more."

"Sit," Brian urged him with a pleased smile. "This one is on me. Are you still sticking with club soda?"

Jensen nodded.

"I'll go with you," Jill said, joining her husband. "Wine—right, Melanie?"

"Yes," the woman at his left answered.

As Brian and Jill headed to the bar, Jensen again wished he'd just said he was calling it a night. Said he wasn't feeling well. That wouldn't be a lie. Instead he was left here with the woman they had hand-selected for him to move on with.

"So, Jill tells me that you grew up in West Pines," Melanie said, drawing his attention to her.

He nodded. "Yes."

Melanie smiled. She was a pretty woman with shoulder-length, honey-blond hair, gray-blue eyes, and a smattering of golden freckles across the bridge of her nose. It wasn't hard to tell why Brian and Jill had introduced him to her. Blond hair and fresh-faced beauty. Just like Katie. The type he would be attracted to, except he felt nothing looking at Melanie. Not a twinge of attraction.

He'd have to tell Brian that he appreciated his concern, but he wasn't interested in meeting anyone. No more setups. Period.

"And you are a veterinarian?"

He nodded again.

"Jill said that you are taking over your grandfather's business. That he was also a vet."

"Still is—although he's getting too old for some of the work. He doesn't seem to know it, though."

Melanie laughed. A nice laugh, but again he felt nothing at the sound.

He forced a smile, but the strained curve dissolved as he had that sensation again, the feeling someone was watching him. Again, he told himself to ignore it.

"I'm not from around here," she volunteered, and he realized he probably should have asked.

"I grew up in Chicago, so this was a big change for me," she continued. "But I really love it here. The area is so beautiful. The people are very warm. I teach third grade, and I enjoy my job. The children are a lot of fun."

The strange feeling persisted as he tried to follow Melanie's words. Tingles ran over his body like whispering fingers on his warmed skin. He flicked a look around the room, half expecting to see a pale blonde with wide sky-blue eyes. Instead his gaze landed on a woman seated at the table facing them, his eyes drawn right to her as if she were a lodestone.

Her head was tilted back just slightly, exposing a long, elegant neck and a billow of dark hair. A delicately pointed chin and full lips, the bottom one lusher than the top. Her eyes were closed, and those wide lips parted. For all the world, she looked like a woman right at the point of rapture.

Instantly, his cock hardened, desire coursing through him that matched the look on the woman's face.

Then her chin lowered and her eyes opened. She met his gaze unerringly as if she'd known he'd been watching her.

Their eyes met. Attraction, need tightened his muscles; his penis pressed against the unforgiving material of his jeans. Stunned, he looked away, facing Melanie, not seeing her.

A wave of something akin to nausea joined the desire in his body. What the hell? Here he was, telling himself that he wasn't interested in meeting anyone. And he wasn't. His libido had been on hiatus for a long time. But then, in the span of an instant, he was getting rock-hard over a total stranger.

"Did you like it?"

Jensen blinked, realizing that Melanie was still talking to him.

"I'm sorry," he blinked again, trying to focus, "what did you say?"

She smiled, not seeming to sense his distraction. "Jill said you went to college in New York. Did you like it there?"

"I did," he managed to say, even though he could still feel the other woman's eyes on him. His excitement spiked.

He slid a glance in her direction. She was watching him, her light blue eyes, almost eerily pale, direct and unblinking.

Who was she? Why was she staring at him?

"...I didn't know how I'd like it here, because it's so small-town. And aside from the occasional bout of loneliness, I have really liked the change. Small towns are all that people say. Everyone knows each other. And people care about each other, help each other. It's nice."

Jensen nodded again, realizing that Melanie probably thought bobbing his head up and down was the extent of his communication abilities. And at the moment, it was. Again, he caught a glimpse of the pale-eyed woman in his peripheral vision. A man approached her, and he tried to feel relief. Her boyfriend or husband—that was good. But instead he felt oddly irritated.

"Of course," Melanie said with a small, rather shy smile that still managed to show she could be interested in him, "it's always nice to have a new face in town."

He forced another smile back. This was too damned weird.

Yet he couldn't stop glancing again at the stranger. She sat, perfectly still, her attention trained on him. She didn't even seem to register the man beside her. Jensen shifted, his body reacting to that steady gaze as if it was a touch, stroking over him, teasing his burning skin.

"Here we are," Brian said, setting down another soda water in front of him. Both Brian and Jill took their seats, and the other woman was mostly blocked from his view.

Good, Jensen told himself. His reaction to the woman had to be an aberration, a response brought on by too many memories. He just wanted to have another quick drink and then go home.

"Hey there, what's a pretty lady like you doing sitting by herself?"

Elizabeth flicked a quick look at the man who braced his arms on the table, leaning toward her. Then she returned her gaze to the other man. The man with the eyes like the deepest forest.

But in that glance, she had made note of the man next to her. He was average height, muscular, good-looking in a rough sort of way. His blond hair was shaggy. His jeans were a little greasy on the thighs, like he'd been working on a vehicle of some kind and had used the denim as a wipe rag. The same engine grease lined his fingernails.

"Can I buy you a drink?" the shaggy blonde asked.

"No," she heard herself say, not looking at him. She had to watch the one with the eyes, the forest eyes. She had to study each of his moves. Tracking her prey.

"Come on, one drink won't hurt. I'm as harmless as a lamb."

Elizabeth tore her gaze from the man she wanted, meeting the blonde's eyes directly.

"But I'm not," she stated, her voice little more than a low growl.

Instead of being turned off by her warning, the blonde's interest heightened, his attraction filling the air like the musk of an animal. He wanted her. He wanted sex.

"Well, that's how I like my women. Dangerous." He grinned, and more arousal radiated from him.

Go with him. Take him back to his place, screw his brains out, and get yourself under control. One human male will serve your purpose as well as another.

No, not just any man would do. Only one.

"Go away," she stated flatly, looking back to the man at the other table, although she was irritated to see her view was blocked by his returned friends. No matter, she could still keep an eye him.

"Come on—"

"Go now," she snarled, and maybe this time there was just enough crazy in her eyes, because the shaggy blonde backed away. Then he shrugged, trying to look as if he couldn't care less that she'd rejected him. He strolled back to his friends, a table of men who all watched her with interested eyes.

She registered their attention, then moved hers back to her target. She shifted so she could see that he was taking occasional sips of a drink, listening to his friends, but talking very little himself. And he was making a concerted effort not to look at her.

Pointless. She'd have his full attention before the end of the night.

He leaned toward the pretty blonde at his side, trying to hear something she said over the off-key croon of yet another karaoke singer. The woman touched his arm as she spoke.

A shard of possessiveness ripped through her. He was *her* man. At least for tonight.

That could be his girlfriend, his wife, her reasonable mind murmured, the notion barely registering through her need.

So. She just wanted the use of his body. Then the blonde could have him back.

"I heard you weren't interested in my buddy."

A growl built in the back of her throat at yet another interruption, but some tenuous hold on her human side made her restrain the noise. Still, her only thought was that she couldn't lose sight of her prey. She didn't even glance at the new speaker. All her senses were locked on the man at the table in front of her.

"Maybe I'm more your type."

She fought back another irritated growl, but this time she did turn to the man standing very close to her.

This guy was taller than the last, more muscled, a goatee and an arrogant twist to his lips. His hair was equally as shaggy as the blonde's, but a shade darker, somewhere between blond and brown.

She let her gaze move slowly down his body. Thickly muscled arms, a broad, equally muscled chest. A noticeable bulge was outlined by his faded jeans.

"No, you're not my type," she stated, her voice low and husky with need, but not for this mortal.

Then she sensed *her* man moving.

She whipped her eyes back to him just as he rose from his chair. Tall, lean muscles moving under his blue button-down shirt, long legs encased in worn jeans carrying him smoothly across the bar. She started to rise, too. She had to follow him. But the man at her side touched her arm.

She sneered at him, registering him as little more than an annoyance, then she made to follow the other man, noting that he headed to the men's room rather than the exit.

"Now, you are hardly giving me a fair shot here," the man beside her said, catching her wrist in a large hand.

She spun back to him, this time not containing the growl that rumbled from deep in her throat. The man's eyes widened slightly at the sound, but still he didn't release her.

"Let me go," she warned, intense rage filling her. This was her chance. She had to go after her man. She couldn't allow anything to come between herself and her choice.

But instead of dropping her wrist, the man tugged her toward him. Her body hit his, her chest brought fully against his massive one. The contact enraged her more, all her instincts growling, *fight*. And she obeyed. She shoved him hard, barely controlling the strength of her overstimulated body.

The large man launched through the air, crashing down on a tabletop. The man and the table crumpled to the ground, the noise causing everyone at the bar to turn in her direction. The music, lyric-less and oddly discordant, did nothing to fill the sudden silence of the room. All eyes were on the man— then on her. Even the latest karaoke singer just gaped, his hand on the mic.

Elizabeth looked around her, then back to the man, who struggled to his feet. She backed away, stunned by what she'd done—or rather, what the wolf had done.

God, she was losing it. She was totally out of control. She had to leave now, while her rational mind had taken a brief hold on her thoughts.

"Elizabeth," Christian said, appearing at her elbow. "Are you okay?" His voice was soft and steady, as if he knew he was talking to someone who was more animal than human.

Shame filled her. What did her brother think of her now? There was no disguising that she was not the Elizabeth he remembered. Not now.

She didn't meet his eyes as she nodded.

"Is *she* okay?" the man she'd just shoved demanded. "She's the one who attacked *me*." He jabbed an angry finger in her direction. "Crazy bitch."

She opened her mouth to apologize, but only a low, angry growl escaped her throat. Christian stepped between them.

"Then maybe you should take your hands off a lady when she asks," her brother said, his voice still even but leaving no room for argument.

The man glared at them both, then called to his friends, loudly announcing what he thought of this establishment and its owners.

Once he and his buddies left, Jolee came on the micro-phone announcing that the still-gaping man at the mic was going to start his song again.

As soon as the music restarted, the bar patrons settled back into normalcy, most of them continuing their socializing, only a little more subdued than before.

"Are you sure you're okay?" Christian asked again.

"I'm okay," she assured him, even as she felt the wolf rising in her again. She had to get out of here. "I'm just going to go."

Christian looked as if he wanted to argue, but then he nodded. "Be careful." Then he smiled. "Although I think you are pretty capable of taking care of yourself."

She thought she might have seen pride in his eyes, but she was too embarrassed and too afraid to be sure.

She mumbled her farewell and rushed to the door. She needed to go back to her house, away from people. She was dangerous. She'd never acted like this. Never. Something was very, very wrong.

Rain now fell in a steady drizzle as she stepped out into the parking lot. She put distance between herself and the bar, stopping in the shadows among the parked cars to gather herself.

Raising her face toward the sky, she prayed for the cold rain to dampen down some of the heat inside her. Heat from embarrassment and from the desire still swirling inside her, unsatisfied and growing.

She had no idea how long she'd been standing there when she heard the bar door open and the crunch of footsteps on wet gravel. Her body tensed. She didn't need to open her eyes to know who was coming in her direction. She could smell him. Woodsy, clean, and so, so tempting.

She opened her eyes to see her man, walking right toward her, his tall, strong body silhouetted against the lights of the bar. And just like that, the wolf was back and in full control.

She stepped out of the shadows in front of him.

"Hi there," her voice was low, husky, and full of hunger.

"I don't suppose you'd be interested in giving me a ride."

Chapter 4

Jensen came to a halt as the figure appeared from between two parked cars, directly in front of him. It took him only a fraction of a second to recognize who the tall, slender form was. The watcher. She'd seemed to materialize out of the darkness, appearing now as quickly as she'd disappeared.

He'd noticed that she was gone as soon as he'd come out of the rest room, making an escape of his own. He'd assumed she'd left with the rough-looking giant, whom he'd noticed talking to her. He'd felt oddly disappointed, even as he told himself she, with her leather jacket and pants, appeared well-suited to the dangerous-looking man. And it wasn't as if Jensen was going to talk to her himself.

Or so he'd thought.

And now she was asking him for a ride. And he got the feeling she was talking about a ride that wouldn't necessarily get her safely home. Again, his muscles reacted, tensing with need.

Stop, he ordered his rebellious libido that had suddenly chosen tonight to decide it had been long neglected.

"Are you having a problem with your car?" he asked, managing to sound far more relaxed than he felt.

"No," she said, taking a step toward him. The movement brought her into the light.

His eyes started to move down her trim body, but he stopped himself. "Did your ride leave you?"

"No," she said again, then smiled. His pulse reacted instantly to the wide curve of her lips—his muscles vibrated with desire. She was definitely a beautiful woman.

You're not interested, he reminded himself. Despite what his body might think. And it thought being alone in a vehicle with her was a freaking fantastic idea. Still, he ignored his body's enthusiasm.

"So, if you aren't having car problems, and your ride hasn't left you, then I'm not sure why you need a ride from me."

Her smile turned indulgent as if she knew that he wasn't comfortable with the idea of being alone with her.

"I have my motorcycle," she said, tilting her head toward a silver-and-black bike parked against the bar. "Not a good night for driving on these twisty roads."

She held out her hands, palms up, as if to display the rain falling on them. "At least not on two wheels."

Jensen couldn't argue with that, but reluctance still kept him motionless. He couldn't be alone with this woman.

"But I guess if you aren't interested in helping a lady in distress . . ." Her words trailed off, and she started toward the bike. A bike that looked too big for her to handle on a dry, straight road, much less a rain-slicked, winding one.

Shit. He couldn't have her on his conscience, too.

"My truck is this way," he said, walking away from her, not waiting, not looking. Like that would stop his body from reacting to her.

Just give her a ride, then go home. No big deal.

He heard her boots on the gravel, then she was beside him. Though she was at least a couple of feet away, he swore he could feel the heat radiating off of her body.

This was not good, he told himself. His body sizzled merrily in her heat, not listening.

She didn't speak until they reached the truck; he unlocked her side first and opened the door, making sure he made no contact with her.

"Gallant," she murmured with another smile as she slid up onto the bench seat.

He laughed wryly. "I don't know about that." Not with the way he was feeling at the moment.

He crossed to the driver's side, unlocked the door, and joined her in the dark vehicle. He didn't glance at her as he slid the key into the ignition.

"I wouldn't want you to be too gallant, though," she said, her husky voice brushing over him. The desire crackling through his limbs flared.

He shot her a quick look, then shifted the truck into Drive. When they reached the road, he braked. "Which way to your house?"

"Right," she said, pointing in the correct direction, her eyes never leaving him.

He nodded, trying to concentrate on driving, which was no easy task. He could feel her eyes locked on him, studying him.

"I guess I should introduce myself," he said after a moment, the uneasy silence making him more aware of her gaze. "I'm Jensen."

She smiled. "Hi, Jensen." She didn't offer her name.

Again silence filled the vehicle, the only sound the whir of the tires, and the rhythmic swish of the wipes. Yet, his senses were overwhelmed. He could feel her just a few inches away, smell her, realizing the spicy, rich scent he'd smelled in the bar had been her—although that didn't seem possible.

"You can turn here," she said, her voice almost startling him. She pointed to a narrow dirt road that he wouldn't have even noticed if she hadn't gestured toward it.

Slowing, he made the sharp turn, and the truck was quickly encompassed by gray, nearly bare maples and oaks and thick evergreens.

"You can stop here," she said after they had driven only a few hundred feet.

"Here?" He glanced around, seeing no sign of lights in the

thick woods, no sign of a house. But he braked as she asked. He put the truck into Park, then turned to look at her. As seemed to be her way, she regarded him with those spookily pale eyes, saying nothing.

"Where is your house?"

"Close," she answered. Then she reached out her hand and brushed her fingertips over his lips, a gentle, whispering touch. His breath caught, his muscles contracting into painful alertness.

"You have a beautiful mouth. I can't take my eyes off it."

He pulled in a shallow breath. Shocks of violent need burned through him as her finger continued to trace the sensitive skin of his lips.

"You saw me watching you." Her words were a statement, but he felt the need to respond.

"Yes."

"You liked it." Her fingers grazed his cheek, his jaw, the side of his neck.

He thought to deny it, to put a stop to this right now. But the words wouldn't come.

"I wanted you from the moment I saw you," she murmured, her voice low, husky. And so sexy.

He'd wanted her, too—he couldn't refute it. He looked into her pale eyes, a blue so light they were the color of the moonstones. Her dark hair swirled around her face, adding to the feminine beauty of her features. High cheekbones, a pointed chin. And her lips. So pink and wide that they should have overpowered her delicate features. Instead they looked unbearably sexy, utterly kissable.

Before he realized what he intended to do, his mouth was on hers, tasting her with a greed he couldn't restrain. She responded in kind, her mouth opening to let him in, their tongues tangling. The kiss grew into a frenzy. He wanted to devour her, each brush of their lips, each sweep of their tongues firing his need more, until he couldn't remember wanting anything more than this woman.

Catching her under the arms, he pulled her closer. She sank willingly against him, her hands stroking his face, his chest. Wildly, they consumed each other.

She moaned, her lips leaving his to move hungrily over his throat, across his collarbone. Her fingers moved deftly on the buttons of his shirt until the fabric was undone and parted. Then she pressed open-mouthed kisses over his chest, her tongue flicking over his ignited skin, her teeth nipping.

He sucked in a sharp breath as she caught his nipple, worrying it gently. Desire needled through him, the sensation bordering on pain, like blood returning to a sleeping limb. Not an inaccurate analogy, really.

She pulled back, her eyes hooded but just as intense as earlier. "I want to fuck you."

He wouldn't have thought he could be any more turned on, but he was wrong. Her raw demand, said in that soft, almost purring voice, was the most erotic thing he could remember ever hearing. His cock pulsed and hardened further.

As he watched her, she sat back and slipped her leather jacket off to reveal the black camisole underneath. He could see, even in the faint light, she wore no bra under the tiny shirt. She didn't need one—her small breasts were perfectly rounded, tipped with hard little nipples.

Then her fingers moved to the button of her leather pants. She undid them. A few wiggles of her hips and they were down, exposing tiny black panties. She kicked them off along with her boots. Then she was watching him again with those peculiar eyes.

His fingers itched to touch her, but instead he said, "This is crazy."

She reached out and caressed him again, her fingers tracing the line of his jaw. Soothing him, encouraging him. He caught her hand and pulled her back against him, kissing her. She caught the back of his head, tasting him with greedy demand.

"Do you want to be inside me?" she murmured against his lips.

God, yes. He wanted that so badly that his whole body ached with it. Shards of biting need scored through him.

But instead of saying so, he stared into her eyes. "What do you want?"

She stilled, for the briefest moment something like uncertainty filling the pale depths. For the first time since seeing her, she broke their gaze before he did. She hesitated, and again he thought he should stop this. It was too fast, too out of control.

Then her hands moved to his jeans and worked the button open. Slowly she pulled down the zipper. She slid her fingers inside the worn material, cupping the granite hardness there.

He groaned, fighting the need to thrust himself against her palm. She smiled, a pleased, naughty smile as if she sensed his struggle. He groaned again. God, she was sexy.

"Lift your hips," she whispered, that husky voice of hers a low vibration throughout the dashboard-lit vehicle.

He did as she asked, and she worked his jeans and boxers down until his erection bobbed free.

She smiled up at him, a wide, wolfish grin. "Very, very nice."

Then she leaned forward and lapped him, her tongue a hot, velvety rasp up the length of his penis.

Shit! He was going to explode right here. Damn, he wanted this woman.

In one move, he lifted her slender body, sliding so he was on her side of the vehicle with her knees on either side of his hips.

She gasped at the sudden shift, but he didn't give her time for further response. His lips caught hers, licking their softness, nipping at her velvet skin. As he continued to assault her mouth, his fingers slipped into her panties, finding the steamy moisture there. She was so wet, so hot, for a moment, his control nearly fractured. But he focused, finding her tiny clitoris, stroking her.

Her lips left his, her head falling back. Soft, growling

moans escaped her, the sound spurring on his own desire. She ground against his hand, her sex growing slicker, hotter.

"Come for me," he growled, loving the feeling of holding her ecstasy in the palm of his hand, loving the noises she made.

She raised her head, her face mostly in shadow, her eyes somehow bright, twin moons, hypnotic, breathtaking. "Not without you."

She leaned forward, catching his lips. He took her shuddering whimpers into his mouth as she moved his hand from between her thighs and rubbed her soaked sex against his erection. At the first slide, all control dashed away.

He ripped the fragile lace from between her thighs, and braced his hands on her hips and positioned her over his throbbing erection.

In one thrust, he was deep inside her, filling her to the hilt. Her wet heat gloved him, searing hot and incredibly tight. He groaned, his head falling back against the seat. He didn't move, letting her get used to him buried inside her, letting himself gain a little restraint.

But she didn't allow him that respite. She tilted her pelvis, moving up and down in full strokes. Her fingers dug into his shoulders as she pumped, picking up speed, her movements becoming a little awkward with her need.

He caught her hips, guiding her, bringing her down onto him hard and tight, then lifting her until the head of his penis was just at her threshold. Small moans escaped her lips each time he pulled her down his length. The sound excited him, encouraging him to jerk her down harder, filling her deeper. She cried out, bucking her hips, taking him as deeply as she could.

Their movements grew wilder, more frantic. He rammed into her, his hips rising off the seat. She arched back, grinding her pelvis against him. Her hand left his shoulder, slapping onto the glass of the steamed windows, while the other moved behind her to use the dashboard as leverage. She impaled herself over and over, until he thought his whole body would implode.

Just when he was certain he couldn't hold off any longer, she cried out her violent release, the sound somewhere between a growl and a whimper. Her muscles clamped around him in hundreds of shuddering spasms, milking him.

Unable to stop it, his muscles tensed and his climax joined hers, fierce, body-shaking as her heat still held him, stroking him with tiny contractions.

Utterly dazed and drained, his head fell back against the seat, his hands still holding her hips loosely. After a few moments, he noticed she still remained upright, their bodies not touching except for where she sat on him.

He managed to crack an eye, fully expecting her to be watching him again. She wasn't. She leaned back against the dash, apparently as spent as he was. The angle jutted her chest forward, her narrow back twisted at an odd angle, cold plastic grinding into her spine.

He reached forward, looping his arms around her, pulling her toward him. She started at the touch. She opened her eyes, regarding him with those intense eyes, her thoughts unreadable.

"You don't look comfortable. Rest against me," he murmured, tugging her again.

She hesitated for a fraction of a second, her eyes locking with his again, still unreadable. But then she did, settling against his chest, her head nestled against his shoulder. He pulled her closer, amazed at how delicate she felt in his arms. He let his head fall back again, his eyes drifting shut, his body boneless. And this woman's warmth surrounding him.

He wasn't sure how long he dozed, but when he woke, the woman sat on the driver's side, one of her boots held loosely in her hand. As usual, her pale eyes were studying him, but something in addition to intensity burned in them, an emotion he hadn't seen there before. Something like melancholy, but when she realized he was awake, she smiled and whatever he thought he saw vanished.

She returned to pulling on her boot.

Glancing down at himself, he became aware that he still lounged against the seat, his jeans undone, his shirt hanging off his shoulders. As he sat up to straighten his clothing, she leaned over and pressed a kiss to his jaw.

"Thanks," she said, her voice oddly airy, given the strangeness of this situation. Then she opened the car door and hopped out into the darkness.

"Hey," Jensen called, hurrying to zip his pants. He pushed open his door, peering out into the pitch-black woods. "Hey . . ." He didn't even know her name.

He paused, listening, trying to figure out which direction she'd headed in. No sound met his ears but the patter of soft rain on the underbrush.

He stood there for several minutes. He'd have to hear her eventually, but he didn't. She had simply disappeared.

He shouted to her a few more times, but received no answer. He listened again. In the distance, a mournful howl echoed eerily though the damp air. A dog, he suspected. Or a coyote.

He peered into the darkness a moment longer, then reluctantly slid back into his truck.

To his relief, the engine roared to life with the first twist of his key. He had no idea his truck had been running on battery. He glanced at the digital clock on the dash. The numbers glowed that it was twenty-two minutes after one in the morning. Not that that meant much to him. He had no idea when they'd arrived here. His first thought once they'd parked had not been the time.

He glanced around once more, searching as far as his headlights would allow in the nearly black woods. Then he shifted the truck into reverse and back out the dirt road.

By the time he reached the main road and turned onto the

highway that led back to West Pines, he was starting to feel like the encounter had been nothing more than a figment of his imagination. A hallucination brought on by being back in his hometown, and all the memories the homecoming had evoked.

Hell, the idea made as much sense as anything else that had happened. The only flaw in his theory was the fact that if he was going to have sex with a figment of his imagination, wouldn't he have conjured Katie?

Katie.

Suddenly a wave of nausea flipped his stomach, but he managed to swallow back the sensation. He focused on the road rolling out in front of him.

The woman, figment or not, was the first woman he'd had sex with since Katie died. For three years, he'd had no interest in anyone. Hell, he'd gone into this evening *knowing* that his body was as dead as Katie's. It wasn't as if women hadn't approached him in the years since Katie passed. He just hadn't been interested, not in the least. He didn't believe he ever would. Then, there she was—the strange woman with the eerie eyes.

And he'd ended up on a deserted country road, banging her in the front seat of his truck like a crazed teen.

More nausea rose, twisting his stomach. He gritted his teeth. Somehow, this, tonight, that woman and what they'd done, felt like another betrayal to Katie. The final horrible injustice to her and her memory. His first sexual encounter since he'd lost her. With a nameless stranger.

As he pulled up to his grandfather's home, his childhood home, he still clung to the idea that the encounter was some kind of dream, the created fantasy of an overstressed mind. Then, when he opened the door, he spotted the tiny, lace panties. Panties he'd torn from the woman's body.

Disgust leapt through him again, pooling in his stomach. He had thought he'd felt all the disgust with himself that he possibly could when Katie died. He was wrong.

Chapter 5

As soon as he'd found her, he'd known something was different. Brody Devlin could sense these things. Of course, after what he'd just witnessed, there was no doubt she'd changed. In fact, he hadn't been prepared for just how different Lizzie was.

He'd been watching her for a while, running the perimeter of her house, watching, trying to decide what had changed. That was why he hadn't approached her yet. He liked to know what he was up against, and exactly who he was getting back once he took her. He wanted no surprises in front of the pack. None. He was counting on her.

She definitely wasn't the girl who'd left the pack in the dead of night all those years ago. Not even close.

He paced, his movements silent on the wet leaves. He had to admit he'd sort of liked watching her with that guy. Damn, that had been hot. Not that he wanted another male—especially a human male—screwing his woman. Or maybe he did. As long as he got to screw Lizzie, too.

He *had* missed that sexy body, which hadn't changed except to get more exciting. He'd always lusted after her, even though she was a cold fish. Or *had been* a cold fish. That woman in the truck had been on fire.

The Lizzie he knew had been as frozen as a witch's tit. She was far too high-and-mighty to allow herself to react to him.

She didn't seem to let anything touch her. She lived in a self-contained fortress, nothing affecting her.

Of course, that had been why he'd wanted her. She'd been so aristocratic, so well-bred, so damned beautiful. A lost little thing who had been tossed out of her pampered life and straight into a world she'd never known existed. She'd been his stolen bit of a world that he'd never been a part of, that had always been way beyond his reach.

Until he had her. Having Lizzie as his mate had elevated him. Made him someone. And he wasn't letting that go. She was coming back to the pack. She was fixing what she'd ruined when she'd left him. Humiliated him.

He knew she wasn't going to come back easily. He never had expected it to be willingly. But now, he could see he might have a spitfire on his hands. He'd enjoy that, too. He liked a good fight.

Again, he pictured her bobbing up and down on top of that mortal. Her lips parted, her heavy breathing. He liked a good screw, too. And combining the two—now, he'd really enjoy that. He growled low and hungry in his throat. Who knew she even had that in her?

Oh no, that woman was not the Lizzie he knew. But he planned to know her—well. After all, she was *his* mate. Of course, she'd never reacted to him like that. Irritation rose up in his chest. She rarely reacted to him, period.

He'd tried. He'd done things just to get her to respond. At first, kind things. But she didn't care for his kindness. So then he'd done hurtful things. Hateful things. He'd learned long ago that any attention was good attention, because her remoteness pissed him off. Her control, her tight rein on herself, drove him goddamned nuts.

He hated it.

His train of thought was interrupted as he caught sight of Lizzie. She remained stock-still behind a large oak, watching the mortal. She didn't react, didn't even twitch as the human called out to her. But she didn't leave, either; she just stayed silent, studying the human until he got back in his truck. As soon as the vehicle began to back slowly away, Lizzie fled, zigzagging easily through the trees and thick underbrush.

He glanced once more at the fading headlights. What a chump. Lizzie was obviously done with the loser. The fact it was just a hookup made Brody calmer. Watching had been fun. But he didn't share.

He'd overlook this, as long as the pack didn't find out. As long as she came back with him—and saved his hide. And since she didn't have a choice on that count, well, like he'd said, he'd overlook.

He started to follow Lizzie, his paws noiseless on the wet leaves. Then he paused. A scent wafted through the damp air, mingling with the smells of the woods. A sweet scent. An alluring scent. A scent that made his gut clench and his skin crawl.

He turned back to where the truck had been parked. The smell definitely came from that direction, although he hadn't noticed if it had been on Lizzie, too.

But if it was the scent of what he thought it was . . . Then he needed to stick around for just a little longer before heading back to the pack with his mate. This could be a situation that would ruin him. And he couldn't overlook that.

Elizabeth opened her eyes, blinking a few times as she tried to focus and get her bearings. Finally, recognition filled her sleep-fuzzed brain. She was in her bed nestled under the eaves, her thick pink-green-and-cream-checked quilt pulled up to her chin. Watery sunlight flickered and toyed with the idea of brightening the room. But so far, the room stayed dim.

She yawned and stretched her arms over her head, letting them drop heavily to the pillows. She didn't know what time it was, but she felt as if she'd slept for a long time. And she'd slept like a rock, a feat she hadn't managed in weeks.

She snuggled down into the mattress, soft down and warm

covers shifting to cuddle her whole body. Well, it certainly wasn't because the bed was uncomfortable. It felt absolutely delicious this morning.

She yawned again, stretching her legs, nearly moaning at the pleasurable release of pain from her limbs and back. Then she froze as a rather pleasant ache manifested between her legs as well.

Suddenly the previous night's events returned, unfolding in her brain like the slow stretch of her muscles. She sat upright, staring out at the room, yet seeing nothing but the flashing images of last night. *Oh God!*

"Oh God."

She'd picked up some mortal guy in her brother's bar, or rather, her sister-in-law's bar. Which meant both of them had witnessed her strange behavior.

"Oh God," she murmured again, dropping her face into her hands.

And the guy—Jensen—she groaned. What did that guy think of her? *Slut* seemed like a pretty apt word, and very likely option. Crap.

Letting out another groan, she fell back against the pillows. They didn't feel nearly as comfy as they just had.

Okay. Okay. She could make things right with Christian. After all, her brother didn't actually know that she'd gone off with some guy she'd essentially been stalking and jumped him in the front seat of his truck.

But he did know she assaulted one of his patrons. He had to have found her overreaction a little odd. Still, she could deal with explaining that better than explaining a random hookup. She didn't think she could even explain it to herself. She'd never done anything like that before. Her behavior had been bad—very, very bad.

"Christian could never know about that," she vowed to herself and the empty room.

Although . . . the act itself hadn't been bad. It had been really, really good.

She made another noise somewhere between a moan and a whimper. What was she thinking? She was reflecting fondly on the most embarrassing behavior of her entire life.

What had gotten into her since she arrived in Shady Fork? Was West Virginia like some kind of wolfbane to her kind? Making them act like lunatics at all times, instead of just on the full moon?

She hadn't had a "normal" day since shortly after she arrived here. At first she'd been fine, but about two weeks after she was settled, she began to feel strange. In fact, the most normal she'd acted *was* on the full moons.

Sure, she sprouted hair and morphed into the world's most deranged-looking *Canis lupus*—but she knew to expect that.

She hadn't expected last night. If she had, she would have locked herself up here. She hadn't expected the nagging restlessness and agitation to turn into . . . She didn't even know *what* it had turned into.

Yes, she did. Lust—pure, unbridled lust.

And she simply didn't feel like that. Not for a total stranger, whom she'd barely spoken to. Jensen.

She liked that name.

Good Lord! What was she doing? Now she was ruminating fondly over the man's name. A man who she was darned lucky she even knew his name, given the mission she'd been on. And he didn't know hers. Although that could be a good thing.

She'd actually asked him to fu . . .

She groaned again. She'd asked him to have sex with her. Not quite so tastefully, however. What was happening to her? The restlessness, the anxiety.

She didn't even remember how she got home. The last thing she recalled was thanking him, then stepping out into the night. Again she groaned. She'd actually thanked the man, like she'd done nothing more than gotten a ride from him. Which she had.

"Oh God," she moaned, dropping her head back into her hand.

This had to be related to the serum. It was the only thing that made sense. She needed to talk to Dr. Fowler. Now.

She scrambled out of bed and hurried to the cordless phone perched in its cradle on the dresser. From memory, she punched in the doctor's number. It rang several times, then went into voice mail.

She hesitated, but then simply said it was Elizabeth and she needed to talk to him as soon as possible.

She hit the disconnect button, but stood there with the phone in hand, debating what to do. What had happened last night was too strange. Her crazy behavior, paired with this endless anxiety, and now she couldn't even recall getting home. This was all so bad.

Except she didn't feel the restlessness, the agitation right now. With the . . . sex, that feeling had actually disappeared. In fact, it had disappeared as soon as she'd orgasmed. She could remember that.

But it wasn't the stunning, soul-stealing orgasm that replayed in her mind, or even the reprieve from the wearing agitation that had been plaguing her. It was the moments cuddled against Jens—the mortal's chest. Listening to the rhythm of his heart. That was what she could see in her mind, still feel in her body.

Don't go there, she told herself. Don't be sentimental about something that was so not about sentiment. Especially if her behavior was somehow created by the serum. Then none of her feelings were real.

The lust definitely had been real. Very real. That was pretty darned evident from her behavior, but it was probably manufactured lust, and it didn't deserve sentimentality. It deserved getting back to her lab and trying to figure out what was going on.

She set down the phone and opened her dresser, rummaging for clothes. What had happened to her physiologically? She'd acted like she was in heat. But that wasn't possible. With female werewolves, the need to breed . . .

Elizabeth smirked at her own wording. Catchy. But the need to breed was triggered by the male werewolf. His pheromones spurred on the female's, causing her own hormones to ready for mating. Human males couldn't do that.

She could be attracted—well, obviously she could. And she could have sex with one, again an obvious statement. But she couldn't go into heat over a human, and a mated werewolf always bred with its mate. Those were the rules.

Unless the last vaccination had altered her in some way.

For the briefest moment, Brody's roughly handsome face filled her mind. Brody. Her mate. The man she'd bound herself to because she was young and scared and alone. She'd realized her mistake quickly, but by then, she was a werewolf. And even more dependent on him. She'd needed him to help her understand her new life. She'd needed him—and he'd used her. Fair enough trade. Until she stopped needing him.

But that knowledge didn't stop a wave of nausea from coursing through her. No matter what her circumstances were with Brody, she didn't cheat. That had been his department. Not that she'd cared. She'd have to have cared about Brody for his infidelity to hurt. And she simply didn't.

Which was why she'd worked so, so hard on a cure. In her mind, if she was no longer a wolf, she was no longer mated. The cure was her only chance at a divorce, of sorts. Her only chance to find the real love and the family she'd craved for nearly two centuries.

Which was why she had to get to work. She pulled on a pair of sweatpants and a zip-front sweatshirt. The agitation was gone now. That was a positive out of all of this. Now she could focus.

Okay, there were the very distracting memories of last night to contend with, but she could control her recollections better than she'd been able to control that relentless restlessness in her body. She was wasting time thinking about the events of the previous night, anyway. It was one night of craziness—really, really crazy. But the side effect was calmness. At least in her body.

Now she had to get back to her work. She wanted her life back. Focus on that. The future.

But as she finished dressing, she couldn't say why a memory of Jensen's forest-green eyes appeared before her whenever she thought about her future.

"You got in a tad late, didn't you, son?"

Jensen looked up from the newspaper as his grandfather ambled into the room. Not for the first time since he'd been home, did Jensen notice that his grandfather looked frailer than he remembered. His tall frame stooped slightly, and his large hands were more gnarled.

"Later than I intended," Jensen agreed, taking a drink of his coffee. "I hope I didn't wake you when I came in."

"Nope, just happened to get up and see your truck was still gone."

"How was golf?" Jensen asked, feeling the need to change the subject. He'd thought about last night enough already.

His grandfather might look older, but he still stayed plenty active. Today being an example. He'd been out of the house before Jensen had even managed to crawl out of bed. Of course, sleep hadn't come easily last night.

"My putting was for shit," Granddad muttered. "And that Harold Wilks moves the ball, I swear he does."

Jensen chuckled. His grandfather had called his best friend "that Harold Wilks" for as long as Jensen could remember.

Granddad poured himself a mug of coffee, then joined Jensen at the ancient, scratched kitchen table. He sifted through the sections of the paper that Jensen had already set aside, finding the crossword. He pulled the ever-present mechanical pencil from his shirt pocket and began to study the puzzle. Moments later, the scratch of the pencil on paper filled the room.

Jensen returned to absently reading the sports page.

"Did you have fun?" Granddad asked, not looking up from his puzzle.

But Jensen glanced up, knowing the old man was more curious than his nonchalant inquiry suggested.

"When?" he asked, being just as cagey.

"Last night. Did you have a good time?" Granddad said, still penciling in the squares in front of him.

"Sure." Jensen fiddled with the handle of his mug.

Granddad nodded and he wrote in another word. Jensen returned to an article about the Mountaineers and their winning streak. Or at least he thought that was what the article was about. Maybe it was their losing streak.

"Did the good time have a name?"

Jensen's head snapped up. His grandfather had always been good at offhanded prying—and far too accurate.

"No," Jensen said, just as easily. "The good time didn't have a name." He didn't even have to lie about that.

His grandfather nodded again.

Jensen gave up on the paper and rose to refill his coffee cup. He was exhausted. Sleep had evaded him most of the night. He'd just lain in his childhood bed, remembering. Remembering Katie. Remembering his life here in West Pines.

And remembering the woman with pale eyes and no name. In fact, it was startling how much he'd thought about her. How many times he'd replayed what they had done.

Even now, he could feel her in his arms. He could taste her lips. Smell her heady scent. And feel the tightness of her body. So vivid, so exciting. His body nearly itched to touch her again. A nameless woman who'd hooked up with a stranger, then left. So unlike Katie. So unlike any woman he'd ever imagined himself with. But then, he'd only imagined being with Katie, hadn't he? Until now.

"You know," his grandfather said slowly, and Jensen blinked back to his grandfather. He braced himself for what was coming. They'd had this talk before. It always started this way. He didn't want to hear it again.

"You can't just hole yourself up here with an old man. You got to do a little living."

Jensen set his mug down, leaning against the counter, crossing his arms over his chest. "I have been living. And I'm not holing myself up. I'm here to take over the business you started. I want to do that."

"But that was never your plan."

"Well," Jensen said with a sigh, levering himself away from the counter, "it is now."

"Jensen, I just want you to be happy."

He smiled at his grandfather, trying to keep the gesture as genuine as possible. "I am happy."

His grandfather peered at him for a moment, studying him with eyes so much like Jensen's own. Then he turned back to his puzzle. The scratch of the pencil resumed.

"Don't think that I didn't notice that you didn't deny the old-man thing," his grandfather said after a few moments.

Jensen chuckled, that response not forced. He picked up his coffee and rejoined him at the table. Riffling through the paper, he found another section. The sports pages hadn't managed to hold his attention—maybe something else would. He perused the local news section, pausing on an article about a mysterious beast spotted near a farm a few townships over. This was the second article about this creature in the past week.

He shook his head as he read the newest sensationalized report. A giant beast. A wild wolf. Perhaps a mythical creature.

Try a coyote. A feral dog, at the most exciting.

"You got plans tonight?"

Jensen frowned up from the article. Was Granddad still fishing for more information?

Instead of answering, Jensen asked, "Have you heard all this nonsense about the 'wolf' sightings?"

Granddad looked up from his puzzle. "Gordon Banks said he's seen it out on Route 219, near Shady Fork. He says it's nothing like anything he's seen before."

Jensen stared at his grandfather for a moment, trying to

gauge if he was making light of Gordon Banks's claim. After all, the same man also maintained he'd seen a UFO out at the old fairgrounds.

But Jensen couldn't read his expression before the older man returned his attention to his crossword.

"So you didn't answer me? Are you going out tonight?"

Jensen sighed. "Nope. I'm planning to stay in tonight." Going out had proven to be too much. Much, much more than he'd ever imagined.

As if on cue, the phone rang, piercing the quiet.

Lord, he hoped it wasn't Brian or Jill. So far they hadn't called to reprimand him for slipping out on them when he'd excused himself to use the rest room. He wasn't in a frame of mind to hear their irritation with him—he was irritated enough with himself. Not for the same reasons, of course, but he still wasn't ready to talk to them.

Jensen answered the phone on the third ring, taking the maize-colored receiver from the cradle. His grandfather's phone was still the ancient rotary style mounted to the kitchen wall.

"Hello?"

"Jensen? Is that you, dear?"

"Yes, Mrs. Anderson. How are you?" Mrs. Anderson was the widow his granddad had been "dating" for years.

"Fine, dear. Fine. Your grandfather says you aren't getting out enough."

Jensen laughed slightly. Apparently Granddad was sharing that sentiment with everyone.

"I'm fine, Mrs. Anderson."

"Okay." She didn't sound like she believed him.

"Let me get Granddad for you."

Jensen handed the phone to his grandfather, and listened as the older man made plans for the evening. Jensen took a sip of his coffee. What was the woman from last night doing now? How could he find her again?

He set down his mug with more force than necessary.

What was he thinking? He'd had enough "good time." Despite what his body and wandering mind might think, staying holed up here seemed the best course of action.

Elizabeth fiddled with the magnification of her microscope, growing more frustrated by the second as she couldn't seem to fine-tune the sample into focus. The cells on the slide shrank and enlarged with each twist, but never came into sharp detail as they should.

She made a low noise in the back of her throat, then straightened from the apparatus. The muscles in her back protested, tight with tension, and she blamed it on leaning over her research for too long. But she knew that wasn't the cause. Just as she knew the inability to focus the slide wasn't the microscope's fault.

Just like she knew that the ache between her thighs wasn't still noticeable because of last night's activities.

No, the ache there had changed and morphed, going from a reminder of what she'd done to a nagging prompt to repeat the performance. The restlessness was growing inside her—again. And now she understood what her body was tense for. Sex. But not just any sex. Sex with him. Jensen.

Don't go there, she told herself. And not for the first time in the last few hours. But her mind didn't listen. Again she was reliving last night, the way Jensen—the mortal male—had felt buried deep inside her. Stretching her, filling her.

She closed her eyes. He'd taken her desperately, forcefully—their mating had been wild, uncontrolled.

It was just sex, she told herself, also not for the first time. But again, her body—and her mind, for that matter—didn't believe her claim.

Jensen had been different, although not in a way she could define exactly. There was a tenderness in his ferocity. His hands strong, his movements powerful, his eyes haunted.

She kept remembering his eyes. Beautiful eyes like a deep,

lush forest, varying shades of greens and browns. She'd seen something in those eyes.

"Yeah, lust," she muttered to the empty room. Well, the almost empty room. She crossed over to the opening in the plastic, peeking out at the barn. The owls still sat on the rafters, right where they had been last night. Only today, they weren't alone, either. She glanced over to see a black-and-white creature curled in a tight ball in a nest of hay.

A skunk. The little creature had been in the barn when she came in this morning. He'd waddled around, completely unconcerned with her presence. It had only peered at her, rooted for more bugs to chomp on, and then made itself a bed in the old hay. No scrambling away in fear. No spraying—thank God.

Something was definitely up with the animals in West Virginia. Including herself.

"No sense of self-preservation," she stated to the sleeping menagerie. One owl opened a golden eye, then they all continued to sleep.

She ducked back into her lab, shaking her head. Too strange. She couldn't believe any animal—with the exception of humans, who were notoriously unobservant—would sleep in her presence. She'd never seen that kind of behavior in all her years of lycanthropy.

She had to admit, she rather liked the company, no matter how unorthodox it was. It could be lonely here. Of course, she'd take loneliness any day, given her other choice. Briefly, she recalled the days with her pack. With Brody. No, loneliness was better.

Why was she thinking about Brody again? She could go months without ever thinking of her estranged mate.

Jensen appeared in her mind. Because of what she'd done with him. Guilt. Of course, her guilt didn't stop her from wondering what Jensen was doing right now. What was he thinking about her and about what happened?

Argh. She was truly getting a one-track mind here, but as she turned back to her lab table, she knew she wasn't going to get anything done. She needed a break.

She'd go in the house, have some dinner, and then maybe try to get more sleep. The fact that she'd slept was probably the reason she felt better this morning.

Okay, she could tell herself that. But she knew why she'd managed to get sleep, and that was all thanks to Jensen.

No. No. She would just stick with this idea. Food, then rest. And she'd see that she'd be fine. She'd be back out here working later.

"You'll see," she said up to the owls and the skunk as she exited her makeshift lab. The birds didn't react. Nor did that skunk. She suspected they didn't believe her any more than she believed herself.

Chapter 6

"Okay, I'm heading out."

Jensen stopped chopping onions to glance at his granddad. The old man sauntered into the kitchen, sporting a freshly pressed white shirt, khaki trousers, and what was left of his hair slicked into place.

Jensen gave him a low whistle, then grinned. "You look ready for more than just bingo."

"Maybe," Granddad agreed. "I sure ain't staying in and eating beef stew on a Saturday night."

"It's going to be some damned good stew," Jensen called after him as he headed out the back door.

Jensen turned back to his chopping, moving on to carrots. Cooking might not be the most exciting thing to do on a Saturday night, but it was a hell of a lot less upsetting than the events of last night.

He'd much rather chop veggies than be back with that woman.

Ha! Now if that wasn't the biggest lie ever told. He didn't feel proud of it, but he'd imagined himself back with her half of last night and most of the day today. Despite all his efforts to forget about it, to write the encounter off as a fluke—which it had been—he kept thinking about it. Which was why he stood here chopping carrots with more force than necessary as if they were the very cause of all his wayward thoughts and troubled feelings.

He finished the carrots, scooped them up, and added them to the simmering stew. Then he busied himself with cleaning the kitchen. Once that was done, he found himself alone with his thoughts, and nothing to do.

Maybe he should have joined his granddad for bingo, although he knew his grandfather would have had an even bigger issue with that. Bingo at the Congregational Church. Definitely not what his grandfather had in mind for him.

Glancing around the kitchen, he couldn't find anything else to keep him occupied. He moved to the living room and collapsed onto the sofa. Pressing the remote, he flipped through the TV channels, finding nothing to hold his interest.

"Who are you kidding, anyway?" he muttered, finally switching off the TV and tossing the remote onto the coffee table. Nothing seemed capable of keeping the mystery woman from his thoughts for long.

He paced over to the window. A breeze rustled the leaves of the huge oak on the front lawn. The sun had nearly disappeared behind the mountains. The crisp evening air was just the thing to cool the need in him.

Right, probably about as well as the cold shower had done.

But as soon as he stepped outside and the wind ruffled his hair and he smelled the earthiness of fallen leaves, he did feel his muscles relax. He strolled down the drive, focusing on the crunch of the gravel under his feet. The rustle of the leaves overhead calmed him. The bite of the cold slipped through the thin material of his shirt, and even that seemed to relax him.

This had been Katie's favorite time of year. She loved the colors, smells. She loved Halloween. She was the only adult he'd known who planned her costume for months in advance.

He pulled in a deep breath. Now, this felt right and normal. Thoughts of Katie. That's what he knew and understood. He didn't understand the wildness of the previous night.

In fact, he didn't want to understand. He wanted to enjoy his twilight stroll and lose himself in his memories of Katie. He walked for a while longer until the cold actually started to become uncomfortable rather than invigorating. Then he headed back to the house, feeling calmer. More normal.

"Hi, there."

Jensen stopped midstride as he heard the husky, purring voice that he'd finally gotten out of his mind. Or rather, the voice that he *thought* he had gotten out of his head—obviously he was fantasizing again. But slowly he pivoted in the direction of the fantasy voice.

He half-expected to see nothing, just the swaying of tree limbs, the shadows in the twilight. But there *she* stood, leaning against the porch railing of his childhood home.

"Hello," he managed, realizing he sounded as stunned as he felt.

They stared at each other for a moment, until she pushed away from the railing.

"So do you want to invite me in?"

This seemed to be the patented phrasing for her pickups. *So do you want to* . . . Fill in the blank. Of course he knew the real question she was asking. Just as he'd known last night, too.

"Are you having problems with your home?" he asked, stalling, also using the same approach of last night. He couldn't let her inside, even though his body was more than willing to invite her in. Hell, one part of his body was already pointing the way.

Damn, this was not good. Not good at all. But she did look so, so tempting. As tempting as he remembered. Although she looked different somehow, too. Then he realized the leather pants and jacket were gone, replaced by a long skirt, tiered with different-colored materials. She wore a faded jean jacket. The style was more chicly hippie than tough biker tonight. Even her hair appeared longer and thicker, framing her delicate features. He liked the look. A lot. Of course, he'd liked the other look, too.

She smiled widely. "No, my home is fine. I just want to see yours."

He nodded, then, almost against his will, he found himself stepping toward her. Once he reached her, he wedged past her and climbed onto the porch. Her scent enveloped him as he passed, spicy and delicious. The smell ignited him, making his body react. He pushed the front door open, then stood back to allow her to enter.

What the hell was he doing?

She didn't hurry, so obviously she couldn't see the war waging inside him. The part of him that was repeating, *send her away* as the other part blithely ignored it, urging her inside. Or maybe she did see, and she already knew which side would win.

She sauntered by him, her body not making contact with his, either. It didn't matter—his body reacted. Even more.

"So," he said, as he followed her into the living room, trying to stare at her narrow back, and not the sweet sway of her hips and bottom, "how did you find me?"

"Oh, I just sniffed you out," she said, tossing a smile over her shoulder.

He nearly groaned. God, this woman was sexy.

She paused in the living room, turning to face him, her pale eyes roaming down his body.

He shifted, praying that she didn't see the outline of his erection through his worn jeans. Good thing his shirt was untucked. Although her eyes did linger for a moment in that general vicinity.

He cleared his throat. "I was just making dinner. Would you like to join me?"

Her gaze came up to meet his eyes. "Sure."

Even though he knew he must look like a rattled teenage boy, he strode from the room as if he was afraid she'd attack. Or worse, that he wanted her to.

He busied himself with checking on the stew, wrestling with the lid of the old kettle, which hadn't had a handle for as long as he could remember.

He glanced at the woman. She smiled slightly, watching his struggle. He had the feeling that the small grin was about both his struggle with the lid and with her being there.

"My granddad really needs new cookware," he said, for no other reason than to fill the excited air between them.

She leaned against the kitchen table, idly fingering the back of one of the ladder-back chairs.

"Do you live with your granddad?"

Jensen nodded, his gaze locked on the gentle caresses of her long, elegant fingers over the smooth wood.

"Is he home?"

He shook his head. "Gone. Bingo."

The woman smiled—a wide, hungry, very predatory smile. Blood rushed through him at the sight, centering in one part of his body. A part that was already stealing its own fair share.

"Then we're all alone?"

"Yeah." At least he'd managed that one word without sounding like an overeager, yet scared shitless, teenager.

Her smile widened—she had an amazing smile. A smile he couldn't look away from. That is, until her hands slid down over her thighs, catching the loose fabric of her skirt.

Slowly she knotted the material, each bunching of the skirt drawing it higher and higher until her calves were exposed. Then her knees. Then the smooth, creamy skin of her thighs. Finally she stopped, the material billowing just high enough to glimpse the pouty curve of her sex and small thatch of tight curls hiding the moisture beneath.

His breathing stopped. His body hardened, ripcord tight. He stared, unable to look away from her sweet body.

"I thought . . ." Her words trailed off, and that finally brought him out of his dazed amazement—and trance.

When he met her eyes, he saw just a glimpse of apprehension there. Uncertainty. Somehow that, combined with the utter brazenness of hiking her skirt up, made his blood ignite. He wanted this woman. God, he did.

"I thought maybe we could have a repeat of last night."

For just the briefest moment, sanity held, and Jensen hesitated. They couldn't do this again. He couldn't. He couldn't have another day like today. The guilt, the regret, the longing for more.

Longing for more—that was what got him. The other two emotions hadn't tempered that one—not in the least. He still wanted this woman—as much as his next breath.

"Do you want me?" she asked, and again he thought he heard uncertainty in her voice.

He stared at her for a moment. Was she kidding? What man could turn down this invitation, offering herself to him as she was.

A man whose love of his life died in his arms, his lucid brain informed him.

But still, he took a step toward her. Then another and another, until he was standing directly in front of her, looking into her pale, pale eyes. Rather than down at her still-raised skirt, which brushed his thighs. He could feel it through the denim of his jeans.

Like last night, fingers traced the curve of lips, of cheeks, of jawline. Except tonight, it was his turn to explore her, tracing her features. Just as she'd done to him.

She remained perfectly still under his exploration, but her eyes seemed to touch him back. Pale moonlight caressed his skin.

"Why me?" he finally asked. This woman could have any man she wanted—why had she picked him? Why had she tracked him down? Why had she wanted him again? Had she spent the whole day remembering, just as he had?

"I . . ." She touched the tip of her tongue to the center of her lush top lip as she struggled for the words. "I don't know." The words were hardly satisfying, but they were enough. It was fair that she, too, didn't understand this all-encompassing need between them.

He caught her chin between his fingers and captured her mouth. Just as the night before, the meeting of their lips erupted into a blazing, wild fire.

Lust just wasn't a strong enough word to describe what coursed through him. It was as if, from the moment he saw her, he had to possess her. He had to drive himself into her tight body repeatedly until there was no doubt as to why she'd come back to him.

He wanted to make her his—in the most elemental way possible.

His hands left her face, moving to her waist. He lifted her onto the scratched oak of the table. Then he positioned himself between her spread thighs. She gasped as his pelvis ground into hers.

He paused. "Did I hurt you?"

She shook her head. "No, you feel good."

He smiled at that, immediately thinking of things he'd like to do that would make her feel much, much better.

But again he caressed her face, tracing the delicate point of her chin, then the fullness of her lips.

"You know," he said, moving in closer so their mouths were nearly touching. "I'd begun to believe that last night was nothing more than a figment of my imagination."

"Is it real now?" she asked.

"Yes. Between you being here now, and the torn panties in the front seat of my truck, I do believe it is."

She pulled back and blinked up at him. He could see she hadn't expected that response. Then she laughed, the sound full and rich and making more desire curl through him. He smiled, too. Then he kissed her again, catching the warm, rich sound into his mouth, into his body.

The laugh immediately transformed into a moan, a sound no less appealing and even more arousing.

Knowing it showed zero-to-no finesse, he couldn't stop his fingers from drifting to the part of her body she had so daringly and deliciously offered to him.

The damp curls tickled his fingertips. Fiery heat burned them. Instantly, he was overwhelmed by the scent he'd experienced back in the bar. A scent that made his head spin, his body tighten with barely restrained need, his mouth water.

He pushed her backward on the table. He barely registered the flutter of newspaper scattering to the floor. He was too focused on the sight of her bared to the waist, the scent of her enveloping him, luring him to her.

A scent he wanted to taste on her skin. He leaned forward, kissing her, taking small tastes with little flicks of his tongue. She did taste every bit as good as she smelled, as she looked. And he wanted to taste more of her.

His mouth left her lips, moving to her jaw, to her throat. Encountering the barrier of her T-shirt and her jean jacket, he moved farther down, positioning himself between her thighs.

He pressed a kiss to her bare knee, trailing open-mouth kisses up her inner thigh. As he edged closer to the place he most wanted to taste, he felt her tense, her legs not moving, but the muscles under her smooth skin growing tight.

He lifted his head, really enjoying the position they were in. Him practically kneeling between her spread thighs, she lounging back amongst the remaining sections of newspaper, looking down her body at him with intense moonstone eyes.

"Are you okay?" he asked, purposely leaning closer so his lips were lined up with the moist curls between her thighs. God, she smelled delicious. Like hot spices, like pure sex.

Again, he noted that her muscles tightened, barely contracting, not noticeable to the eye, but there nonetheless.

"I'm . . ." She nodded.

He wondered at her sudden hesitation. Shyness certainly

didn't correlate with the woman who'd just bared herself to him. The woman who came here with this exact intent.

And it was going to happen. Most definitely. Just like last night, it was impossible to stop it. Even as small scraps of his mind told him he shouldn't. For his own sanity.

What was sanity? Who needed it?

He shifted forward a little more, his lips just grazing her. The tickle of her curls, the searing moisture, the scent. Damn.

This time, she sat up. Her knees pushed against his shoulders.

He moved back, looking up at her. Her pale eyes held easily readable uncertainty now. Her full lips pulled down at the corners.

"You don't have to do that. I'm ready for you."

He blinked at her words. Businesslike and informative. Not at all what he was feeling. He was on fire; he was out of his mind to get his tongue on her.

"I'm glad you're ready. But I'm not."

She frowned at that, her gaze flicking down toward his crotch, which she couldn't see from her angle on the tabletop.

He chuckled ruefully. "Okay, I'm ready. But I'm not ready to stop touching you."

He slid his palms up her thighs, nudging her back into a reclining position. He moved back toward the apex of her thighs.

"Or to stop tasting you," he murmured as he ran his tongue up the pink fold of her sex.

Elizabeth cried out as Jensen's tongue parted her, tasted her. She had to brace her arms to keep from falling back on the table and writhing under his amazing mouth. What was he doing?

She wasn't so naïve that she hadn't heard of a male pleasuring a female with his tongue and lips. But she'd never experienced it. It wasn't something she'd wanted from . . . anyone other than this man.

He swirled his tongue, focusing his attention on her clitoris, his tongue hot and raspy against her. Then the velvety brush of his lips, then followed by the occasional fleeting hard edge of his teeth. Then that amazing tongue again.

"Jensen," she murmured, knowing his name sounded like a religious word on her lips. But she'd never known. Never believed that she could want this so badly. That she could enjoy the want so much.

Then his lips closed around the straining bud, the center of all her sensations. He pulled on her, suckling the hypersensitive flesh to the point of near pain.

She moaned, bucking her hips. He licked her, more swirling, more long rasps.

She collapsed back against the table, unable to hold herself any longer. And still he continued, each sweep of his tongue more intense than the last. Until she could barely catch her breath—she could barely even remember to breathe. Then he suckled her again.

Lights, brilliant starbursts of color, exploded behind her closed eyelids. Through her body. Wave after wave of lights, of pure sensation, of ecstasy.

Then Jensen was levered over her, entering her in one thrust. Her body clenched him, as if seizing onto him in desperation. In an attempt to keep some hold on her sanity. But the thickness of him, the stretch of her body to accommodate his size, only heightened the other sensations radiating through her. A kaleidoscope of release.

She cried out again, her voice sounding hoarse, as if she'd been crying out over and over. Maybe she had. She couldn't recall. She couldn't remember anything beyond Jensen, and his body moving inside hers. Powerful strokes, rocking her toward something that was life-changing.

You should be scared, she thought, even as she anchored her legs around his hips, pulling him deeper inside her.

You should stop. She'd have laughed at the ludicrous impossibility of that thought if she'd been able, but only another gasp, another moan, another strangled repeat of his name escaped her lips.

She opened her eyes to find Jensen watching her, his eyes hooded but his expression intense, as if he was memorizing her every reaction. And that look, that intensity, was the trigger that threw her over the edge again, headlong into the abyss of release.

"Jensen," she breathed, then locked him tight to her, keeping him buried fully inside her as she shuddered around him. And he pulsed in response, his body tensing as his wet heat filled her.

Chapter 7

Slowly reality seeped in, the lovely blur of her release fading, focus returning from the edges toward the middle, until she realized she was flat on her back, staring up at a ceiling light. Copper with scrolling flowers, the metal tinged brown with age.

Jensen's weight pinned her to the wooden table, the sensation pleasing rather than confining. His head was nestled between her breasts, and when she tilted her head to the right, she could see his features—his eyes were closed, his lips parted, his breathing gradually slowing to an even rhythm.

He was a beautiful, beautiful man. Far more beautiful than any mortal man she could remember seeing. For a moment, her heart soared at the idea that this man was hers.

Then reality hit again—this time, not the mellow fade-in. This time, a stark, unforgiving truth.

What had she done? She'd come here with the intent of seeing him, just seeing him again. To tell herself that her behavior from last night was a fluke. A strange anomaly.

Then she'd pulled up her skirt, like a street-corner hooker. Hell, hookers were probably more subtle. But that's what she had come here for—there was no point denying it. The lack of panties sort of stated that, although she didn't recall dressing to come here. She didn't even recall how she got here.

She'd been in her house, resting on her sofa; then, her next memory was greeting Jensen. Something was really wrong with her.

Panic filled her, and she made a strangled noise in her throat. Immediately, Jensen lifted his head, his gaze searching her face.

"Am I too heavy?" He levered himself off of her before she could answer. Again, his eyes roamed her body as if looking for obvious signs of discomfort. Her hands flew to her skirt, now bunched up under her bottom and back.

Seeing her struggle with the uncooperative clothing, Jensen caught her frantic fingers and tugged her into a sitting position. Then his hands gently caught her waist, and he lifted her to a standing position. He brushed down the material, and then his long, masculine fingers moved to arrange his own clothes. She watched, unable to do otherwise. When he finished, it took her a moment to realize he was aware of her staring.

"I've got to say," he said with a crooked grin, "you know how to get a man's attention."

Elizabeth stared at that lopsided smile, her heart tugging, even as she told herself that it couldn't be her heart that was making her chest so tight. Then heat burned her cheeks. What must this man think of her? What did she think of herself? Nothing good, that was for sure.

But instead of showing her shame, she offered him a cocky smile. "Well, that was the plan."

It had been the plan—it just wasn't a plan she realized she had until she'd done it. Actually, that wasn't exactly true.

Hadn't she just spent most of today thinking about doing just this? But hadn't she also told herself it wouldn't happen again? Yet, it had—without her even realizing what she was doing.

That scared her—and that was also dangerous. What if she'd arrived here in her wolf form? What if she'd hurt him? Although she knew she hadn't shifted to get here, there were side effects to her shifting. An aftermath. And she didn't feel any of those sensations. But it could have happened. God, she had to get out of here and never see this guy again.

A sharp pain stabbed again at the area of her heart. Ignore it, damn it. The feeling had to be her imagination.

She took a deep breath, trying to dispel the painful tightness. Then she forced another carefree smile in Jensen's direction, and she waved her fingers, trying to make the action as light and negligent as possible.

"Thanks." The same ending as last night, only this time she wouldn't be back. She couldn't see this man again.

She stared toward the living room, remembering the front door was that way. But Jensen caught her hand.

"Wait."

His fingers were strong and warm and made her want to turn back and curl against him. But he couldn't help her. He couldn't explain what was happening to her. And all she could offer him was far more strangeness than anyone could handle.

She glanced up at his green eyes, concern making them a shade darker. Even a nice guy like this wouldn't understand the truth.

"What's your name?"

More shame filled her. Twice she'd been with this man, and he still had no idea what her name was. She hesitated, thinking maybe that was for the best.

No, she couldn't bear having him remember her as the sleaze whom he'd met and shagged and never saw again.

Oh yeah, and the sleaze named Elizabeth whom he'd met and shagged and never saw again was just so, so much better.

Still, she found herself answering him. "Li—Elizabeth."

Now, she really couldn't say why she gave him the name she hadn't used much in years. Surely she wanted all of this bad behavior to be Lizzie's, not Elizabeth's.

"Hey, Elizabeth," he said with another of those crooked, yet a little cocky, smiles. "Do you have a last name, too?"

She hesitated again, then nodded. "Young. Elizabeth Young." Now she'd outright lied. Lizzie Devlin. That's who she was. But damn, she wanted to go back and be the person she'd once been. For this man.

"Well, Elizabeth Young, why don't you join me for dinner?" For the first time, Elizabeth realized the kitchen smelled of something delicious. Something more than the musky sweetness of sex. Her stomach growled. For the first time she realized she was starving for something other than carnal pleasures.

She supposed that was a pretty good sign that she was back to normal. Elizabeth had an enormous appetite.

But she shook her head, even as she breathed in the tempting smells again. This time, Jensen's masculine scent, woodsy and clean, mingled with the food. That, as much as anything, made her say no. She would not have a repeat of what had just happened. She had to leave.

"Come on, you can't go yet. I'm pretty sure social decorum demands that once you've had sex on the kitchen table, you at least have to stay long enough to eat at said table."

Again Jensen smiled in a way that made her chest flutter, and she could almost ignore her embarrassment. Almost.

"I don't think—"

Jensen tugged her back toward the table, pulling out a chair with his free hand. Then he positioned her in front of it.

"Please. Sit." Another winsome smile.

Against her better judgment, she did sit, perching on the edge of the wooden seat, as if not getting comfortable would make staying okay. Except she knew staying was a very bad idea. She couldn't afford to actually like this guy. What she'd done with him thus far was unforgivable, as unforgivable as it was unexplainable. And as it was, she felt inexplicably fond of him. And very, very drawn to him.

"I've got beef stew simmering," he said, moving to the stove where he'd originally been fiddling with the pot with the lid that was missing the handle. Again, he struggled with the top, finally reaching for a fork to lever it off.

Steam billowed out of the kettle, the smell filling Elizabeth's nose and making her stomach rumble again.

"I also have fresh bread. And butter." He gave her a look that was designed to tempt her. "Now, how can you pass that up?"

"I can't," she finally said. After all, given what they had done, could one meal really hurt? In truth, sitting with this man and not jumping his bones would actually make her feel better, make her feel as if what they'd done wasn't so strange, so random.

Or, rather what *she'd* done.

Jensen hadn't pursued her either night. The pursuit had been all hers.

She watched Jensen as he moved around the kitchen. The stretch of his t-shirt across the muscles of his arms and back as he reached into the cupboard to get bowls. The graceful stride of his legs as he walked to the refrigerator and got out a dish of butter. The masculine shape of his hands and wrists as he ladled stew from the pot.

Oh, she definitely understood why she found him attractive. She just didn't understand why she'd acted the way she had. That had been abnormal to the extreme.

"Do you live around here?" he asked as he leaned over her to set a bowl and spoon in front of her. Elizabeth wasn't sure which was more appealing—the smell of the thick soup or the scent of Jensen. He returned to the counter, getting a knife out to slice the bread.

"I live pretty close to here," she said vaguely, scooping up a bit of the stew on the tip of her spoon. She sniffed it, then took a taste. Delicious. She spooned up more.

"Pretty close, huh?" he said, glancing toward her as he filled a bowl for himself. "So you can have sex with me, but you can't tell me where you live?"

Elizabeth paused, a full scoop of stew nearly to her lips. She gave him a sheepish look. "Well, you could be a crazy person."

He chuckled at that. "True enough. I guess a girl can never be too careful. Avoid going off with strangers in their trucks. Avoid being alone in a stranger's house. That sort of thing."

Elizabeth knew she should have been embarrassed by his words, but he said them with such an endearing grin on his face, she couldn't help but smile back.

"Exactly."

She took a couple more bites of stew before offering, "I live in Shady Fork."

"Near that bar?" He finished cutting the bread and arranging the pieces on a plate. "What was the place called?"

"Leo's," she said automatically, and almost added that the bar belonged to her sister-in-law, but she caught herself. It wouldn't do for him to track her down. After all, this would be the last time they'd see each other.

She glanced at him as he settled on the chair to the left of her. He offered her a piece of bread.

For a second, her heart constricted. By wolf rules, Jensen was acting as a mate should. A male made sure his female ate before he did.

Unless, of course, you were mated to a rogue wolf like she was. Then none of the laws, human or animal, applied.

She didn't want to think about that. And she certainly didn't want to think about how much she'd rather be mated to Jensen. That train of thought was pointless. She wasn't. He was human. And after they shared this meal, she wouldn't see him again. It was dangerous, both mentally and physically. To both of them. She was out of control and that made her *very* dangerous.

"Do you want more?"

She frowned up at him, not understanding the question at first. Then she noticed he was looking at her nearly empty bowl. Heat crept across her cheeks and down her neck. God, like she needed to add her enormous appetite to the list of objectionable things he knew about her. A slut with the appetite of a large land animal. It was a wonder he'd even thought about asking her where she lived—unless he was planning to avoid that location.

"I'm—I'm fine," she said, even though her rumbling belly told her it could easily handle another bowl. And some bread.

"Well, let me get you a little more." He took her bowl and returned to the stove. Again a pang of longing filled her, longing that wasn't sexual. This was more about the novelty of being with him. About enjoying security and kindness.

Don't go there, she told herself. It was a fruitless line of thought. In fact, she should just leave now. It was too hard being here. And not because of the embarrassment of her earlier behavior, but because she liked being with Jensen too much.

She liked watching him. She liked the timbre of his voice, deep and smooth. She really liked his smile—cocky, but not conceited. Dashing, charming . . . beautiful.

"You know, I really should pass on the second helping."

Jensen paused, ladle in hand, his forest eyes roaming her face, trying to understand her.

He might as well not try. She didn't even understand herself at the moment.

"Don't leave. I haven't eaten yet. And I don't want to eat alone."

Jensen had no idea why he was practically begging this woman to stay—when earlier he'd been hesitant even to allow her in the house. He just knew he wasn't ready for her to leave. She fascinated him—and it wasn't just the unorthodox nature of their relationship thus far, although that did merit a lot of contemplation. He just liked her being here. He liked it a lot.

"Come on. Stay."

She glanced in the direction of the back door, looking a bit like a wild animal desperate for escape. But instead of bolting as he thought she would, she gave him just the slightest nod.

He finished filling her bowl and set it in front of her as he retook his seat. Again, she reminded him of a nervous animal as she regarded the second helping of stew, then reached for her spoon.

They ate in silence for a few moments, until she finally said, "This is delicious. You're a good cook."

"I think it's a little too salty," he said, frowning down at his bowl. "I tend to be heavy-handed with salt."

When he stopped considering his culinary faux pas, he realized Elizabeth was studying him.

She tilted her head, giving him a speculative look. "You don't look like the kind of guy who would be staying in on a Saturday night, cooking."

Jensen chuckled. "What does that guy look like?"

Elizabeth shrugged, a smile pulling at her lush lips. "I don't know. Not you."

He nodded, then leaned forward and said quietly, "Do I look like the kind of guy who stays in on a Saturday night and has sex on the kitchen table?"

He regretted the question as soon as Elizabeth broke eye contact and pink stained her high cheekbones. She fiddled with a piece of the bread, pulling off bits to create a small mound of crumbs.

He didn't know why that question would embarrass her. The woman who walked in here tonight and raised her skirt didn't seem like the type to be embarrassed by anything. That woman had been a go-for-what-you-want-and-don't-take-no-for-an-answer kind of gal. The Elizabeth here with him now seemed almost shy. But he had seen shades of that uncertainty before, hadn't he?

And maybe a smarter man would have been a little frightened by the two extremes, but Jensen always managed to remain woefully below his potential. He found her fascinating.

"I—I just want you to know that I've never acted this way before," she announced suddenly. Her cheeks grew pinker.

"I never have, either," he told her, hoping the admission would make her feel better. Instead her brows drew together in an adorable look of consternation.

"I . . ." She looked around again, her eyes landing again on the back door. "I really think I should go. Thank you for dinner, and . . . everything."

"Well, I think I know one thing about you," he said, hoping his announcement would stop her. It did.

She paused at that, giving him a confused look.

"You are always in a rush."

Before he thought better of it, he shifted his chair closer to hers and leaned over the table to catch her chin between his finger and thumb. Then he kissed her. A slow, unhurried kiss. So unlike anything they had shared so far.

She remained still for a moment, then her mouth moved against his, tasting him back. They remained that way, leaning over the table, kissing gently, leisurely. A first kiss. A shy kiss.

Jensen pulled back, blinking at her. An earthshaking kiss.

"I don't suppose you'd consider going out with me. You know, on an actual date. Not that I haven't really enjoyed our encounters so far."

She straightened away from him, her retreat pretty telling as to what she thought of that suggestion.

"I don't think that's a good idea."

"It seems like a pretty natural idea to me," he pointed out. Why was he even pressing for this? He didn't want a relationship with anyone outside of Katie. And Katie was gone. Why was he pursuing this woman? The strange woman with the possible morals of an alley cat. A woman who was nothing like Katie.

"Um," she glanced around, looking decidedly trapped. Despite his own train of thought, he was rather offended. He didn't like the idea of being used for sex. Many men might, he suspected, but he wasn't one of them, apparently.

But instead of voicing his irritation, he simply let it go, deciding to retreat to safer topics. "So what do you do for work?"

She shifted again. Apparently work wasn't one of her safer subjects. But she did answer.

"I'm a research scientist."

Okay, he didn't see that one coming. "Really? What kind of research?"

She shifted again, then added to the mound of crumbs she'd created with her uneaten bread. "Cellular science. Cell mutation and regeneration."

Wow—again, he was surprised. "Is it cancer research or something like that?"

She nodded, brushing the crumbs off her fingers. "Something like that. And what do you do?"

"I'm a veterinarian."

Elizabeth's eyes widened slightly, then she laughed. "Of course you are."

He frowned, not understanding her reaction.

She seemed to realize that he wasn't getting the joke, and she sobered—after a few more giggles.

"Do you live here? Or are you just visiting?" she finally asked, keeping her expression impassive.

"Yeah, I live here. This was my childhood home. I just came back. About a month ago—August 15, actually." He only remembered the exact date because it was his grandfather's birthday. Jensen started to add that, when he realized something was wrong with Elizabeth.

All the pinkness drained from her face and she sat perfectly straight as if she was frozen.

"Are you okay?"

She nodded, staring at him as if she'd suddenly seen a ghost.

"Can I get you a drink or something?" She looked awful—as if she might pass out.

"I . . . I have a headache," she said. "Do you have any aspirin?"

"Sure. In the bathroom." He stood. "Just a second."

She nodded, her complexion looking more gray than white now, and that shade didn't make him feel any better.

He hurried out of the room, heading up the stairs to the bathroom. The ancient medicine cabinet squeaked as he pulled it open and rummaged through his grandfather's brown medication bottles to find any sort of over-the-counter painkiller.

What had brought on that reaction? Maybe she had problems with migraines, although even migraines didn't come on that quickly. Still, something had been very, very wrong with her, and physical ailment seemed to make sense.

He found a bottle of ibuprofen and rushed downstairs, taking the steps two at a time.

"Here you go," he said, holding up the bottle as he entered the kitchen.

Except the look of relief he'd expected wasn't there. The kitchen was empty. Her chair pushed in, her bowl placed in the sink, and even the mountain of crumbled bread wiped up. But Elizabeth was gone. Only the heady scent of spiced vanilla lingered. The only distinct proof she'd ever been here, and they'd done what they'd done.

He stood there for a moment, uncertain what to do. Then he wandered to the table and set down the bottle.

He glanced at the table, then at the newspapers, which were still scattered on the floor. The headline about the unexplained wolf-like creature jumped out at him, seeming oddly apropos. Some residents had seen mystery wolves, while he had his mystery woman.

It was best that she'd gone, he told himself. After all, what had they really had to talk about?

Oh, they'd had a lot to talk about. He'd had questions galore. Why him? What was she getting out of their meetings? What made her seem so brazen one minute and so timid the next? What did she want from him? But he hadn't asked many of them, and now he may not get any answers.

Chapter 8

Brody loped behind Elizabeth, keeping a safe distance between them. Not that she'd have noticed him. She was too intent on racing away from the scene of her latest indiscretion. And, he had to admit, he no longer found this behavior of hers entertaining or a novelty.

He hadn't thought much about Lizzie's behavior since she left the pack. In fact, he hadn't cared. But he did now, because he needed that proper, prudish girl back. He was counting on her to give him credibility, and if she continued to act like this, well, the pack wouldn't believe he'd changed. They'd only see that Lizzie had changed. That wouldn't work. He needed that regal, icy princess—proper and refined.

But something else still bothered him even more than her changed behavior. That scent. The scent that wafted through the forest air like a noxious, stifling stench. A very dangerous scent.

He'd wanted to believe that he'd been mistaken about what he'd smelled the other night. But now, there was no doing that. And she'd returned to that same man. She wanted something from that man, even if she didn't know it.

No, there was no mistaking what was going on here.

He leapt over a fallen tree, his paws silent as he moved a little closer to Lizzie. She raced over the uneven terrain, not as graceful in her human form as he was as his wolf self.

Maybe he should just kill her now. He could kill her out here, and who would even know who'd done it? Who would even find her for weeks?

He picked up speed, kicking up leaves as he gained on her. It would be so easy to bring her down. Go for the legs. Humans were clumsy, moving on just two long appendages.

She didn't even sense him. That alone told him the state she was in. He could just kill her. Cheating bitch.

He got closer still, close enough to smell that strong scent. The nauseatingly spicy odor fired his anger. He snapped his jaws, his teeth clacking. Just bring her down. But just as he would have lunged, his jaws locking on her fragile calf, he veered away.

He came to a halt beside a large pine, watching Lizzie dash off toward her place.

The wolf in him still hungered for the attack, but he couldn't kill her. Not before he got what he wanted from her. She was his access back into the pack. The pack wouldn't turn him away if he came back with her. She was above all of them, and they knew it.

He hated to admit it, but he needed her. And once he got what he wanted, then he'd make her pay.

No one double-crossed him. Not his pack. And especially not his female.

Elizabeth collapsed on her sofa, pulling in deep breaths, her tired lungs and her pounding heart unhappy with her breakneck sprint home. A werewolf could run faster than a mortal in their human form—but ten miles at top speed through the forest was a bit much, even for her.

But she hadn't been thinking about the effect on her body when she'd run out of Jensen's. Not thinking about her body—that was novel as of late. But then, her body was satisfied. Just as it had been the last time she'd been with Jensen.

Of course, now her mind was racing. And she couldn't stop thinking about what he said. He'd moved here about a month ago. August 15. And maybe she wasn't remembering her own dates correctly. Heaven knew, she wasn't herself. She was forgetting huge chunks of time. She could easily mix up a few dates.

But she didn't think she had. She took a couple more calming breaths, then struggled off the sofa and headed to the kitchen. Hanging on the wall, near the phone, was a calendar. A calendar with puppies and kittens on it. An innocuous enough calendar, until you saw the days of the full moon highlighted in bright orange. High-alert days.

She flipped back a month and looked at August 15. Then her eyes skipped ahead. August 20 was highlighted in yellow, the color she used to mark the days when she gave herself an inoculation of the serum. She'd also made a small notation on August 18—something that hadn't meant much to her at the time. Just a reminder that she had taken something to help her sleep. Valerian root. That's why she'd waited until the 20th to give herself the serum. She didn't want anything to interfere with her serum, so she'd made sure the herb was out of her system before she inoculated herself.

But that proved that her restlessness had started before the vaccination. In fact, she was certain it had started on the 15th. The day Jensen returned to town.

So it couldn't be the serum making her act like a crazy woman—well, at least not in this case. Although it could be exacerbating what was happening inside her.

Still, what was happening? It made no sense. None.

So was it Jensen? Was he the trigger to all these feelings? Could she really become physically aware of him even before they met? That wasn't possible.

A werewolf could be aware of other werewolves. Especially their mate. But she'd never heard of one of her kind being so in tune to a human.

She turned away from the calendar and dropped into a kitchen chair. Okay, she couldn't keep obsessing about this and she couldn't let it happen again. She needed to concentrate on her research. Maybe she had really been suffering from insomnia and stress because of her research, and somehow when she gave herself the serum, it had done . . . something that made her aware of Jensen.

"That makes no sense," she stated aloud. But then, none of the things that happened in the past month had. She got up and checked the answering machine on the counter. No messages.

"Damn," she muttered. Dr. Fowler had to call soon. She really needed his input on all of this.

She glanced over at the calendar—she still had several days before the next full moon, so she had to focus on her research. It was obviously her only hope. Maybe she could detect what in the cells' mutation would cause this—it had to be the serum. Nothing else made sense.

She got up and walked to the door, then paused with her hand on the knob. Maybe she should put on some underwear before she went to work.

"I cannot believe you cut out on us like that," Brian said, leaning on the counter of Jensen's grandfather's veterinary office.

Jensen paused at that thought. No, *his* office. This was his office now. One would think he'd remember that, since he'd lost so much to make this a reality.

Jensen managed the good grace to look embarrassed. "I just wasn't feeling well and decided I needed to head home to bed." With a little detour.

"Well, you should have let us know where you were going," Brian said, then his usual easy smile returned. "Plus, you missed all the excitement. This woman and this man got into it, while you were in the bathroom. Or maybe you'd snuck out by then."

"Really?" Jensen said, trying to sound interested as he went over the very few calls he'd received. Very few. Turns out that people were as unwilling to accept new vets as they were doctors.

"Yeah, this tall, thin woman hit this huge guy. Some of the people in the bar said it looked like she actually picked the guy right up and threw him. I didn't see that, but I heard her growl. Just like a wild animal."

Jensen's head snapped up. Could that have been Elizabeth? And the hulk she'd been talking to?

He started to ask more, then stopped himself. He just had Elizabeth on the brain. Which was understandable, given their two encounters. She did tend to make quite an impact. Still, the odds of her assaulting a man . . . and growling . . . seemed low.

Yeah, like he knew enough about her to make any judgment.

And worse than that was the fact that she hadn't returned on Sunday. He'd hated to admit it, but he'd waited for her to show up at his door. Even his grandfather had mentioned that he'd seemed distracted. He'd claimed that he was just overtired. Which was true enough—sleep had remained a distant aspiration since meeting Elizabeth.

It was best just not to think about her. Given her past behavior, the likelihood was that he'd never see her again. She'd probably moved on to another man who'd caught her fancy in another bar.

He paused. No, she'd said that she didn't do that sort of thing. And even though he couldn't imagine why, he believed her.

No, he did know why. He wanted to believe her.

But it didn't much matter what he believed, because the fact was, he probably wouldn't see her again.

And that was a good thing.

". . . really enjoyed meeting you," Brian was still talking, but Jensen realized he'd missed what was being said.

"What? I'm sorry."

Brian gave him a look as if he thought Jensen was pretty much gone. Jensen had to admit he was feeling a little nutty.

"Melanie. She really enjoyed talking with you the other night. Before you pulled your little disappearing act."

Jensen nodded, not sure exactly what to say. He didn't want to give his friend the idea that he'd want to see Melanie again. He wasn't interested in dating.

But hadn't he asked Elizabeth out? Hadn't he been disappointed when she wasn't in the kitchen, and she'd never given him an answer? Although her disappearing act had pretty much said it all.

Apparently his own hadn't made the same point to Melanie.

Unfortunately, his lack of reply hadn't been the right one for Brian, either.

"She'd love to go out on a date with you," he said, wiggling his eyebrows.

Jensen shook his head and straightened away from the counter, wanting to stop this conversation now.

"I'm not interested, Brian."

Brian straightened, too, and Jensen realized he hadn't stopped it. Damn.

"You do know that you can't stop living just because Katie died."

Jensen ground his back teeth. Here we go again. The talk he'd received from dozens of people since Katie died. For the first time, however, he did feel maybe people were right. Even as he thought that, guilt tightened his chest. After all, this wasn't just about Katie dying. This was about his role in her death. This was about his selfishness and what it had cost Katie.

"Melanie is a nice woman," Brian was saying, and Jensen held up a hand to stop him.

"Brian, I know that. But I'm just not interested."

Brian stared at him for a moment, obviously trying to decide if he should try to press his point. But finally he just nodded. "I know you've had a hard time of it."

Jensen nodded, too. Brian had no idea. And frankly, his time wasn't getting any easier. Thanks to a beautiful woman, a pair of peculiar pale eyes, and possible multiple personalities.

"So, have you heard there've been more sightings of a large wolf-like creature over near the Steadbetter Farm?"

Jensen knew that was Brian's way of dropping the uncomfortable subject, and he appreciated it. "Really?"

Brian nodded. "I read in the *Journal* that old Mr. Steadbetter said the thing was huge. He said he'd never seen anything like it." He widened his eyes and made a little howl, his very poor imitation of a wolf.

Jensen smiled, shaking his head. "I think the locals are desperate for news."

Brian nodded. "It's always pretty quiet here."

Jensen would have liked to agree, but things had been pretty crazy for him recently.

"So tell me more about the woman shoving the guy in the bar," he heard himself asking his friend.

"I didn't really see it," Brian said. "But I did see the aftermath. The huge guy was pissed."

"What did the woman look like?" He tried to sound casual, asking himself why he was even going there. He needed to stop thinking about Elizabeth. For his own sanity. But his mouth kept on going. "I mean, you said she was pretty small?"

Brian smiled, seeming to warm up to the change of topic. "Tall, but thin. Definitely not the type you'd peg as being tough enough to take down a guy this size."

Tall and thin could be Elizabeth, and she had been talking to a huge guy, but she'd hardly looked disheveled when he'd seen her in the parking lot. Nor had she looked shaken. She'd been pretty damn calm and determined.

"The only thing I recall about her was her eyes. I've never seen eyes like that. The lightest blue I think I've ever seen. They looked eerie, really."

Jensen paused. That could be Elizabeth—not that he'd describe her eyes as *eerie*, but rather *mesmerizing*.

"Actually, that's not true," Brian said. "I noticed the bartender had the same eyes—eerily pale. He also came over to the woman after the scuffle. I wonder if they are related or something."

Jensen considered that for a moment, then promptly told himself it wasn't likely. So the bartender had light blue eyes. What were the chances he was Elizabeth's relative?

Jensen paced back and forth, watching the building as if gun-toting gang members were going to burst outside and shoot him down.

Getting shot down? Maybe that was what he was worried about—figuratively, rather than literally. And it wasn't by the bartender, who likely wouldn't have any idea who Elizabeth was, anyway. It was definitely the possibility of Elizabeth shooting him down.

"Just go home," he muttered to himself, but then, instead of heading back to his truck, he paced again, watching the bar.

The neon lights were a beacon, just not the beacon they were designed to be, luring revelers in for a cold beer or a drink. He stared at the Miller Lite sign.

No, what lured him was the far-fetched idea that the bartender was somehow related to Elizabeth, all based on Brian's offhanded comment that the bartender also had light blue eyes. It wasn't as if Brian was the most observant person. In high school, Jill was forever getting annoyed with him for not noticing a new hairstyle or a brand-new outfit.

Okay, this argument was actually backing up his far-fetched theory. If Brian noticed, then the guy *must* have the same unusually pale eyes.

Jensen hesitated a moment longer, then breathed a deep sigh. What could it hurt just to walk in and see if the bartender reminded him of Elizabeth? And even if he didn't, it wouldn't hurt to ask the guy if he knew her. Maybe Elizabeth was a regular here.

A wave of anticipation curled up his spine at the idea. Even if no one knew her, he could just hang out for a while and see if she showed.

Okay, he was apparently an official stalker. His determined march paused for just a second, then he continued on through the parking lot. He wasn't stalking her, he was just looking for her. Because he wanted an explanation of her behavior. That was it.

He pushed open the bar door. Well, that and he did want to see her again.

The bar was relatively empty. A group of young men—obviously construction workers or laborers just off from work, given their rumpled t-shirts and dirt-layered jeans—played pool. Three other guys, clad in leather and jeans, sat at one of the round tables, not speaking, just sullenly drinking and watching the room as if they were waiting for something to happen. And at the bar was an old man, a cigarette dangling from his beard-surrounded lips.

A redhead puttered around behind the bar, wiping down glasses and occasionally saying something to the old man.

Jensen didn't see this bartender with the pale eyes. Maybe it was the guy's night off. Jensen considered just turning around, when a figure came out of the back room. The man was wearing an expensive gray shirt, obviously tailored to fit him, with an equally expensive pair of black pants. He didn't look like he belonged here. Jensen could see that much, but from his angle by the door, he couldn't see what his eyes looked like.

Slowly, as if he was casing the joint, Jensen walked around a few of the tables littering the floor, trying to get a look at the man's eyes.

Okay, I'm now officially stalking a guy, too. This was pathetic.

But Jensen's thoughts of pitiful behavior disappeared as

the man turned to face the old man, also facing Jensen directly.

Jensen stopped. There was no doubt about it. This guy had to be related to Elizabeth. Same eyes. Their coloring, aside from that, wasn't the same. Elizabeth had dark hair, while this guy was lighter. But there was still no denying they did look alike.

And it was his best shot at finding her. His only shot.

He started toward the bar, only to pause again. But how did he ask about Elizabeth without sounding like . . . well, a stalker?

He always came back to that, didn't he?

Screw it. He had to find her. He was desperate. He still couldn't say why she'd had this effect on him, except for maybe the fact that Elizabeth had made him think about something other than Katie. Even for a little while.

"Hi," he said, taking a seat beside the old man.

The old man glanced at him and grunted a greeting around his nearly burnt-out cigarette.

"Hey," the man with Elizabeth's eyes said, placing a drink napkin in front of him. "What can I get you?"

"A club soda," Jensen said, even though he realized that if he wanted information, he should probably buy an actual alcoholic beverage. Wasn't that how these exchanges went down?

But the bartender didn't seem fazed by his drink request.

The old man to his left, however, did seem to take exception.

"Who comes to a place like this to have a club soda?"

The redhead, who seemed to be taking inventory of the beer coolers, shot the old man a disapproving look.

"Ignore Jed," she said, offering Jensen a wide, warm smile.

Jensen couldn't help but smile back. "Well, I guess it is a little strange to come to a bar on a Monday night to drink club soda alone."

The pale-eyed man returned, and Jensen noticed he stood

close to the redhead. Very close. And there was a possessive glint in his unusual eyes.

"That is an interesting question," he agreed. "What does bring you here tonight?"

Well, that was an open segue, if he'd ever heard one.

He reached for the drink, taking a sip, and trying to think of how to ask his question—in the least stalker-ish way possible.

"I'm actually looking for someone," he finally said. "A woman I met here over the weekend."

The pale-eyed guy studied Jensen for a moment, then his gaze seemed to flick past him, over his shoulder. Jensen realized he'd glanced to the men seated at the round table.

Jensen wondered if they were about to cause trouble— they seemed to be the type. But before he could look, the pale-eyed man looked back to him. His eyes held the same unnerving intensity as Elizabeth's. Although it was definitely more pleasant to be studied by Elizabeth.

"Do you have a name?" the redhead asked, and Jensen noticed that the man at her side didn't seem pleased that she was willing to help. Definitely the possessive type.

But then, his woman did work in a bar. He probably had to be pretty careful of the men. The redhead was a knockout. Not as striking to Jensen as Elizabeth, but then, no one ever had been.

He paused at that idea. No. Katie had been. She'd been perfect. She'd been his soul mate, and all he'd ever wanted. While Elizabeth was . . . an enigma. A strange obsession.

"I'm actually looking for a woman named Elizabeth."

The pale-eyed man's gaze sharpened. "Elizabeth?"

"Yes. Do you know her?"

He tilted his head, and for the first time, Jensen noticed something odd about his appearance. It was almost as if his face was too symmetrical, too perfect. His features didn't look fake, but they were almost distractingly flawless.

Jensen blinked. He'd never really taken into account a

guy's looks before, but this guy was oddly disconcerting. He glanced at the redhead and realized she had the same look about her. Absolute perfection.

He blinked again, wondering why he was considering their appearance when he just wanted information about Elizabeth.

"Yeah. I do know Elizabeth. She's my sister. I can tell her you stopped by."

Jensen wasn't surprised by the admission that he was her sibling, or by the fact that he wasn't willing to give some random guy her address.

Jensen probably wasn't the first guy to come in here looking for her. That idea really, really bothered him.

Jensen nodded. "I'd appreciate that." It wasn't as if he was going to get this guy to say anything that he didn't want to. Coming here had been a long shot, anyway.

He took another swallow of his club soda, trying to act like he wasn't dying to grill her brother for more information.

Elizabeth's brother seemed satisfied that his few questions would be the end of it. The redhead gave Jensen a small, regretful smile, as if she'd like to help him more, but then she left to go tend the music.

Jensen sat there for a few moments, halfheartedly sipping his soda, and also half hoping Elizabeth would show up.

Pathetic.

He downed the remainder of his drink and rummaged in his jeans pocket for some cash.

"You know," the old man next to him leaned forward and said in a hushed voice, "I heard there was a place for rent out on the Boyd Road."

Jensen frowned at the man. "Is that so?"

The old man gave him a significant look, raising his bushy eyebrows until they nearly met his hairline.

"Oh," Jensen said, understanding dawning on him. "Is that right?"

The old man nodded, his eyes twinkling. "Only house out on that road."

Jensen paused at that. Was it really wise for this old guy to be cluing him in to where Elizabeth lived? After all, he could be a psycho-killer. At the very least, he could be the guy who had random booty calls with her. Of course, she had been the one to initiate those. But still.

Jensen eyed the old man. "Why are you telling me this?"

"I saw her watching you the other night." He nodded his head like that was enough to clarify all, but then he added, "She likes you."

Jensen mulled that over. He wasn't sure Elizabeth liked him for more than an easy lay. But somehow the old man's observation made him feel better, maybe a little less pathetic. Still, like and lust were often hard to tell apart.

Jensen's doubt must have showed on his face, because the old man leaned a little closer, nudging him with his bony elbow.

"Trust me. I'm good with these types," he said, his eyes twinkling wickedly. "They are actually easier to read than our kind."

Jensen frowned at the old man. *These types? Our kind?* What the hell was he talking about? Okay, maybe the old man was just a crazy old drunk.

"They'd still be edging around their feelings if it weren't for me." The old man jerked his head in the direction of Elizabeth's brother and the redhead.

The couple was locked in a brief embrace, but Jensen could easily see the adoration in their expressions.

Jensen took a deep sigh. Crazy old man seemed his only option here. Jensen tossed a few bills on the bar, and nodded to the old man, who nodded back in a way that said, *Go get her.*

Jensen left the bar, just hoping she wanted to be gotten. No, he just wanted her to answer a few questions. A relationship still seemed way too out of his reach.

Chapter 9

Well, for whatever other craziness, the old man had been right about the Boyd Road. It did lead right to an old farmhouse. The only house on the road.

He felt like an intruder, pulling into the drive, but the temptation to see Elizabeth was too much.

Lights glowed in several of the windows, but otherwise the place appeared quiet. He stepped up the stairs onto a large wraparound porch much like his granddad's and knocked on the front door.

Waiting, he peeked in the windows into a kitchen, which was very tidy. He knocked again, and he listened.

Maybe she could see him out there and she was avoiding him. He raised his hand to knock again, but stopped himself. He could hardly force himself on her. If she didn't want to see him, she didn't want to see him.

From behind him, a noise sounded, like something being knocked over. Something hard and heavy. He spun, peering into the darkness, not seeing where the noise could have come from. He stood stock-still, listening.

He heard another sound, not the same as the first. This time a low growl rumbled from across the yard. The sound of an animal rather than a human.

"Hello?" he called anyway, stepping down off the porch.

Silence greeted him. He walked slowly across the lawn, trying to peer into the dark.

As he approached the barn he noticed light seeping around the hinges of the old double doors. Another sound like something falling over echoed out of the large structure.

He picked up his speed.

He hurried over to the barn and tugged the large door open. The old hinges squeaked, and he heard a scurrying sound that he wrote off to mice running for cover.

The interior of the barn was relatively empty. Remnants of hay, cobwebs, and other signs of lack of use, all exactly what he would picture in an old, unused building like this. Except, on the far end, heavy plastic sectioned a makeshift room away from the rest of the barn. It glowed like a cocoon lit from within.

He frowned, taking a cautious step forward. Which was a good thing, because as he stepped down, he nearly trod on a small, bleary-eyed skunk. The animal peered up at him with unconcerned black eyes. Jensen fought the urge to recoil. A sudden movement could startle the creature and lead to a bad and very smelly outcome.

The skunk disregarded him and trundled off to disappear into one of the old horse stalls.

Jensen let out a pent-up breath. That had been close, in fact, he couldn't believe that the little animal hadn't sprayed. Definitely not the usual behavior of a surprised skunk, but he was thankful he'd been spared.

He cast another quick look around, looking for more wandering animals—and for what could be making all the noise. When he saw nothing, he took another step into the shadowy barn, illuminated only by the strange plastic room. The floorboards creaked, and he heard a responding shuffle that seemed to emanate from within the plastic room. For the first time, Jensen noticed a shadow in the plastic cocoon—what appeared to be the silhouette of a figure.

Or at least he thought it was a figure, even though the object didn't move. It gave the impression of large shoulders and a head, almost like a figure of something crouched, poised to attack.

"Elizabeth?" he called, keeping his voice low, his eyes trained on that shadow. Something wasn't right here. The air actually felt thick, and his skin prickled like he was in the presence of something far more dangerous than a skunk. Although wandering skunks, strange noises, and an eerie glowing plastic room all seemed like valid reasons to be a little cautious.

"Elizabeth," he said again, a little louder. He had the feeling she was here, and she was in danger.

He took another step, when a strange noise overhead caused him to freeze. What the hell was that?

He glanced up and saw several owls lined up on one of the exposed beams. They blinked down at him, then one spread its wings—the whispery whoosh of the long appendages was the sound he had heard.

Jensen frowned again. A skunk undisturbed by a human. Several barn owls. That was all a little strange, not to mention that thing in the plastic. He looked back to the makeshift room, only to see that the dark shape was now gone. The plastic glowed, pale and oddly alienlike in the dim barn.

No, something was really wrong here.

"Elizabeth?" he called again, this time louder, more concerned. He didn't understand why, but he knew she was in trouble.

He strode toward the makeshift room and peeled back the heavy plastic. Before his eyes could adjust to the change in light, something lunged at him, barreling into him so hard that his feet left the ground. He and his attacker flew through the air and landed in a heap against one of the wooden stalls.

Jensen remained sprawled there, half-lying/half-upright, struggling to pull air into his stunned lungs. The thing scrambled off him and backed away, crouching in the dark corner, regarding him with pale eyes. Jensen tried to make out what the thing was, but between the shifts of light, the speed of its movement and his own winded state, all he could make out was a dark, curled ball. What the hell?

He carefully struggled into a sitting position, his eyes locked on the thing, trying to keep his movements slow and nonthreatening. If this was a wild animal, his best strategy was to remain as still as possible.

The shadow in the corner remained just as still. Then, as Jensen watched, the form changed, shifting like a darkness disappearing with the movement of the sun. Stretching and shrinking, until he realized he was staring at a human. Not an animal at all.

He blinked, certain he couldn't possibly be seeing what he thought he was. The form went from appearing large and black and threatening to a slight, curled body.

"Elizabeth?"

The form lifted its head, and for the first time, he could make out actual features. Long, dark hair, a pointed chin, and wide, frightened pale eyes.

"J—Jensen?" Elizabeth's voice sounded dazed. As dazed as he felt.

Jensen immediately overcame his own confusion, scrambling over to her, touching her. Brushing her tangled hair away from her face to reassure himself she was real. That he'd imagined the hulking shadow. That he'd imagined her brutal strength.

That strength . . . His hand paused on her cheek. Good God, her skin was on fire.

"Elizabeth, you're burning up." He brushed back her bangs, testing the temperature of her forehead. Her cheeks. She had a raging fever. Sweat dampened her hair.

"Jensen, you—you should go." She tried to push up to her feet, but she lost her balance, falling onto her bottom, her legs curled awkwardly under her. For the first time, Jensen realized she was naked.

He reached for her, trying to help, but she jerked away.

"Don't touch me," she said, the words more a plea than an order.

"Elizabeth, you're sick." God, he hoped she was just sick, but again that feeling that something was terribly wrong assaulted him. Had she been attacked? And what had he just seen?

Elizabeth's hoarse, humorless laugh drew his attention back to her. "You have no idea."

Jensen frowned, not understanding her words. But then, her fever had to be high enough that she was likely delusional. That could explain why she was here, undressed. But that didn't explain what he saw.

She made a small, whimpering sound, and again his thoughts were back to her. He needed to get her fever down. Even though she attempted to push him away again, he managed to lift her, holding her tight against his chest. She still strained against him, her slight frame surprisingly strong. But he held her, hushing her with soothing noises and words. Eventually she calmed against him, her body burning hot and her limbs becoming boneless.

For a brief moment, Jensen worried that she'd fallen unconscious.

"How did you find me?" she murmured.

He didn't want to get that old man—what was his name? Jed. He didn't want to get Jed into trouble, so he opted for her answering strategy.

"I just sniffed you out."

Elizabeth cracked one eye. "But you can't do that. You're only human."

Jensen stared down at her for a moment, remembering Jed's odd words and how hers somehow seemed to tie in with them. But then she let out a reedy breath, and he realized she probably had no idea what she was saying. From the feel of her skin, he'd guess her temperature was close to 104, if not higher. She needed a doctor.

He strode toward his truck, trying to recall the fastest route to a hospital from this location. Probably east on 219.

He held her more securely as he reached for the door handle of his truck.

"What are we doing?" Elizabeth asked, the words a little slurred.

"We have to get you to a hospital. I'm really worried about this fever."

Elizabeth actually managed to stiffen in his grasp. He would have thought it impossible, given how weak she had seemed just moments before. She wriggled in his arms, determined to break free. He nearly dropped her, before hooking her tightly around the waist.

"Stop, Elizabeth," he ordered, hoping his sharp words would pierce her fever-hazed mind. "Stop it."

She didn't immediately, although eventually she stopped squirming. Still, her body remained coiled, as if she planned to struggle again at any moment.

"I don't need to go to the doctor," she told him, her voice low and reedy, her pale eyes determined.

Jensen attempted to open the truck door, but he shook his head. "Elizabeth, you are very sick."

She shook her head, her eyes still holding his. "No. It will pass. Plus, you're here."

Jensen laughed. "Elizabeth, I'm a vet."

She smiled, just the briefest quirk of her lips. "I know. It's so appropriate, isn't it?"

He had no idea what she meant, and he knew he shouldn't be looking for logic in her words—she was sick. Yet, he couldn't quite disregard them. They meant something.

Even though he still believed the decision was wrong, he felt himself moving around the truck toward her house.

As soon as she realized where they were going, Elizabeth relaxed against him. Her eyes drifted shut, and her fingers curled into his shirt front as if she wanted to hold him close.

Much better than fighting to be freed, but Jensen still wasn't sure he was making the right choice.

He managed to turn the knob to the front door without jarring her too much. Then he kicked it shut behind him. He scanned the rooms, considered laying her down on the sofa in her living room, but then he decided against it. The first thing he had to do was get her fever down.

"Elizabeth, is the bathroom upstairs?" he asked, in part to rouse her—her stillness concerned him. She didn't reply. Not good.

He headed toward the stairs, assuming that was where he would find the bathroom with a shower or a bathtub. Elizabeth's head lolled against his shoulder. He doubled his steps, taking the remainder two at a time.

Sure enough, he spotted the bathroom at the end of the hallway. He carried her straight to the small, tidy room.

He looked around, debating where he should set her. She couldn't sit by herself, so he gently placed her on the floor, trying to get as much of her body as possible on the blue-and-green bath mat. He searched for a towel to cover her. Despite their past interactions, it somehow felt wrong for her to be naked now.

Hell, he hadn't even had the opportunity to see her fully nude, and seeing her that way now just felt wrong. As he draped a large sea-green towel over her, he did assess her systematically for injuries. He didn't think she'd been attacked, but he wanted to be sure. Her creamy skin was flawless—no signs of struggle.

He tucked the towel around her, feeling slightly better. Slightly.

Then he turned to assess the bathing situation. A shower/tub combo. That was good. He turned the knobs, testing the water until it was tepid—not so cold that it would shock her system, but cool enough, he hoped, to bring her fever down.

While the tub filled, he turned to the medicine cabinet. She needed to get some ibuprofen or aspirin or something into her to help lower her temperature.

He opened the mirrored door to discover the shelves neatly lined with toiletries. He shifted a few around, searching for any type of fever reducer. There were none—the only thing she seemed to have in abundance were hair-removal products. Waxes, depilatories, tweezers, razors. He stared at them for a moment, then heard Elizabeth moan.

He turned back to her to see she was struggling to sit up.

"Shh, darling," he said, kneeling down to catch her around the back, cradling her against him. "You've got to just rest." He was glad to see she was conscious.

She frowned at him. "Why are you calling me *darling*? I'm not your darling. Am I?"

He smiled at that, realizing she never would have asked that question if she was fully lucid.

And he took advantage of the fact that she probably wouldn't recall much in the morning. "I'd like you to be my darling."

He smoothed back her hair, noticing again how soft and thick it was against his fingers. Her eyes drifted shut and she sighed, seeming to like the touch.

"No, you wouldn't," she murmured, the soft words filled with conviction. And again, he wondered why one minute she seemed to want him and the next, not so much. But right now she was far too sick to provide any answers.

"Do you have any ibuprofen? Or acetaminophen?"

Elizabeth shook her head, her eyes already drifting shut. "Makes me sick."

Jensen paused at that, glad she was lucid enough to tell him that bit of information. All he needed was to make her condition worse. He brushed her damp hair away from her forehead, studying her pasty complexion. Katie flashed through his mind. Helpless. Pale and hurting.

He blinked away the image, focusing his attention on the tub nearly filled with water. He reached over to test the temperature. Not too hot, not too cold.

"Elizabeth? Let's get you in the tub."

He glanced down at her to see she was again motionless, her eyes closed. He eased her off his lap and back onto the bath mat. She didn't stir. He shut off the water, then tried to decide what he should do.

Her skin still burned his fingers—her temperature hadn't gone down. Hesitating only a second more, he scooped her up. She didn't rouse, which worried him more. The fever was raging.

Slowly, he slipped her down into the water. Her body seized up immediately, her arms tightening around his neck until she was nearly strangling him. Water sloshed over the edge of the tub, soaking him and the floor.

"Shh, darling. I'm sorry. I'm sorry," he soothed. "We have to get this fever down."

She gaped at him, her eyes wide but not focused. She shivered violently, but she allowed him to settle her in the tub.

"I—I'm o-o—kay," she insisted. "W—will pass."

"I know," he assured her. "But this will make it pass quicker. I know it doesn't feel good."

She shivered, but closed her eyes and let her head fall back against the edge of the tub.

He looked around, spotting a washcloth hanging on the towel rack near the sink. He reached over, grabbed it, and dunked the cloth in the water. Gently, he brushed the wrung-out towel over her forehead and cheeks.

She moaned. "I like that."

He watched her, her eyes remaining shut, her full lips parted. He forced his gaze away. He shouldn't be noticing how lovely she was—not when she was so sick she had no idea what was going on.

"I like when you call me darling, too," she murmured, her eyes still closed.

And if that wasn't proof that she didn't know what was going on, nothing was.

But he smiled. "Just rest, darling."

She smiled slightly, then did as he asked.

He continued to dampen her face and head, keeping all his thoughts on getting her temperature down. He had no idea how much time passed, but eventually her skin grew cooler, the pastiness lessening until her coloring grew a bit pinker. Much better than the awful white/gray she had been.

He rolled up his already wet sleeves and dipped his hands under her slight frame. She curled into him, water seeping through his shirt. He ignored the oddly arousing combination of the cool water and her now normal body heat against him.

Wrangling a towel off the hook on the way out of the bathroom, he carried her down the hall, peeking into the rooms, trying to decide which one was her bedroom, which wasn't too hard.

One room was totally empty, while another was piled with boxes; the third was very feminine with a white wrought-iron bed and floral quilt.

Not at all what he would have expected Elizabeth's bedroom to look like—somehow he'd pictured dark colors and thick satin sheets. Not that he'd thought about her bedroom, of course. But this dainty room was the only option, so it had to be hers.

"Where are we going?" she asked, barely lifting her head from his shoulder, her voice thick with exhaustion.

"To put you to bed."

"I can't. I need to work."

Jensen laughed dryly. "Darling, I don't think you could work right now even if I tied you up at your lab table."

She harrumphed, which got another smile from him. But she didn't argue further as he set her on her feet just briefly, anchoring her to his side while he pulled back the covers. She tottered slightly, but did manage to stay on her feet.

"Darling, I don't want to put you to bed still wet."

"Okay," she agreed willingly, and held out her arms to signal he could dry her. He nearly groaned again. Did she have any idea what a temptation she was?

Knowing the Elizabeth he knew, probably.

Then she began to weave again, and he had to tug her tight to his chest to keep her from falling. Or maybe not. Maybe she was just too out of it to know what she was doing.

Quickly, he patted the towel over her skin and lifted her onto the cushy mattress, pulling the covers over her nakedness before he could be even more of a pervert.

He tucked the quilt around her, then debated what to do next. He didn't want to leave her, when she was obviously too weak to get something if she needed it. He spotted a chair in the corner and started toward it, when her low voice reached him.

"Even though you shouldn't, please lie down with me, Jensen."

He paused, looking back at her. Those peculiar eyes of hers watched him, drowsy yet so inviting.

His first thought was to deny her—he didn't trust himself to be close to her, knowing she lay naked under the covers. Then he admonished himself. He certainly had enough control to lie with her until he was sure she was all right.

"Sure," he agreed, not really sounding as confident as he should.

He crossed to the opposite side of the bed and sat down on the edge. He considered pulling back the covers and joining her underneath, but he knew that was too much temptation. The last thing this tired, ill woman needed was a man with a raging hard-on rubbing up against her.

He stretched out on top of the covers. Elizabeth immediately rolled over to curl against him.

"You're all wet," she complained, shivering.

That was true—and the cold, damp clothes were doing nothing for his growing arousal.

"You'd better take that shirt off, or you'll get sick." Her finger plucked at the button just above his navel. Altogether too close to the erection pressing against his jeans.

He sat up and undid the buttons, then shrugged out of the shirt, tossing it onto the floor beside the bed.

He started to fall back against the pillows, when she murmured, "Your pants are wet, too."

He chuckled at that. "Even sick, you're a seductress."

She smiled, the curve of her lips far more sleepy and sweet than seductive. "Only with you."

A pang of something like hope zinged through him, mingling with the longing in his body. Was that true? Was all this something rare and strange for them both?

"So why shouldn't I lie with you, then?" he couldn't help asking.

Silence greeted his question and for a moment he thought she'd dozed off. But finally she murmured, "Because I'm not good enough for you."

Then Elizabeth shifted against him, her fingers splaying over his bare chest, her face nuzzling on the pillow against his. His body reacted, even as he warned it not to. Then she sighed, the soft sound followed by a very distinct snore.

He lay there for a moment, not sure how to react. This woman really had a way of surprising him, fascinating him and leaving him with lots of unanswered questions. And it didn't appear there would be any answer for a little while longer.

He closed his eyes, prepared to wait.

Chapter 10

Once more, Elizabeth was surprised by the comfort of her bed. Soft, warm, scented like woods, and . . . male? She opened her eyes to see Jensen's profile illuminated by the lamp on her dresser. Mellow light accented the cut of his jawline, the wonderful shape of his lips, the smudge of his thick, dark lashes against his cheeks.

What was he doing here? She reached out to touch him, as if she couldn't quite believe he was here. Her fingers grazed over his lips, velvet soft, to the hint of rough stubble surrounding their fullness.

She sighed as her fingers strayed down to his chest. The skin there was smooth and velvety, too, but underneath was hard steel. Her fingers continued to stroke him, the desire that she'd been trying to keep at bay for two days roaring to life. God, she loved touching this man.

Her hands shaped over the curved muscles of his chest, trailing slowly downward over the ripples of his hard stomach. The hair around his bellybutton, and beneath, tickled her fingers, making her insides feel the same teasing tickle.

She rose up, watching her hands against his skin, the way she looked touching him. She loved all the textures of his body. Her gaze flicked to the fly of his jeans. Of course, there were some she hadn't gotten enough chance to explore.

Without pause, her fingers honed in on the button and the

zipper. Although she did stop, just for a second, confused as to why the worn material was a little damp. But she quickly dismissed it, more intent on what lay underneath.

He started as she slipped her hand inside and touched him, the tickle of more hair, the rise and hardening of his arousal.

"Elizabeth?" His voice was low and rough with sleep. She loved that sound.

Her fingers curled around him, moving over the length. He let out a slow, hissing breath and his hips rose into her touch.

"Darling," he managed, his voice raspy, sliding over her, "you are sick."

She felt that hoarseness deep inside her, his voice making her womb feel heavy and ready. His use of that husky endearment making her sex moist. She wanted him, had to have him.

She didn't know what he was talking about, though. Sick? She felt great. Now that he was here.

"I'm fine. More than fine."

She crawled out from under the covers, prowling on her hands and knees like the animal she was. For the first time, that idea didn't repulse her. She wasn't thinking about her past, about what she was. She was thinking about what she wanted. Jensen. Her only thought was Jensen—being with him, feeling his skin against hers, feeling him deep inside her, filling her, stretching her. But first, she wanted to taste him. To please him, as he'd pleased her.

She tugged at his jeans, pulling at them until he lifted his hips and helped her work them off. His boxers, which she liked very much, joined the abandoned pants. Then she positioned herself between his legs, running her hands up his inner thighs, more tickling of hair. She smiled at the sensation, loving it.

Reaching the thick thatch of hair surrounding his penis, she lingered. The dark curls were coarse yet oddly soft, too. She explored him, feeling such possession over him, over what she was doing to him. Her mate.

For just a second, the part of her mind that wasn't wolf corrected her. Her man—maybe. Not mate.

Then all thoughts were gone as his thick length pulsed under her fingertips. Mmm. She liked that. She liked feeling all his power.

She leaned over and pressed her lips to the broad underside, deeply breathing his musky, aroused scent. Her tongue flicked out, wanting to taste that arousal. Hot and tangy and more delicious than she could have imagined. She licked him again and again, until his fingers knotted in her hair. She heard his hitched breathing. Then she took him fully between her lips, swirling him with her tongue.

"Elizabeth," he breathed, raising his hips as she took him deep. She hummed a response and that elicited a low groan. She smiled and repeated the sound. Jensen repeated his own.

She continued the game until he caught her under the arms and dragged her length up his body. The thrilling friction of skin across skin. Then his mouth caught hers, taking control of their touch. He rolled her, until he had her pinned onto the soft mattress, his hard body heavy and wonderful on hers.

His legs nudged hers apart, his erection hard and hot against the moist folds of her sex. She parted her legs wider, begging him silently to enter her. To bury himself so deep they were one.

He obeyed, angling back to penetrate her with one stroke. Deep, hard, and so, so right. Her aroused body reacted instantly, her vagina clenching him, pulsing and vibrating, her release a violent thing that she couldn't contain. She cried out, her voice breaking at the height of her ecstasy. And still he moved inside her, his movements forceful, demanding. Rocking her toward another powerful release. And another until she couldn't tell where one orgasm ended and another began.

Finally, he joined her, his own release spurting hot and deep inside, his penis pulsing in response to her body's rhythm.

He collapsed on top of her, his breathing quick, his heart pounding. Matching her own. In the same way her body always perfectly matched his.

After a few moments, he rolled off of her, only to tuck her tightly to his side.

"Elizabeth, I don't understand what you do to me."

She didn't understand, either. She just knew she had to have him. She closed her eyes, her last thought before she drifted off was that she finally felt sane. Calm. At peace.

The next time Elizabeth woke, gray light had appeared outside the windows. And with that pale light came the clarity of what she'd done. Again.

She could feel Jensen beside her, his heat, his strength. She could smell him and taste him on her lips, although she couldn't say how he'd ended up here. But she did remember making love.

Which wasn't supposed to happen. She'd avoided him for this very reason, hard as it had been.

"Did you know you chew on your bottom lip when you are worrying?"

She started, turning her head to see that Jensen rested on his side, his head on his arm, watching her. He smiled, and her heart fluttered almost painfully in her chest.

"No," she managed, still staring at his mouth. How was it that his smile could affect her so? It was just the curve of lips, just like everyone else's. Except nothing like anyone else's.

"Well, you do." He reached over and brushed her hair away from her cheek. His fingers lingered. "You still feel a little warm, but nothing like last night."

She pulled away, not sure what he meant. She couldn't recall.

"I feel fine." How did she explain that her temperature was always a few degrees higher than a human's? Of course, he was a vet so he knew—say, a dog—had a higher temperature than a person.

"Okay," he said easily, although she got the feeling her response didn't please him. "So what are you worrying about?"

You. Me. Everything. The fact that I can't remember how I ended up with you.

But she could hardly say that without encouraging more questions. But she couldn't say nothing, either. He was too astute for that.

"My research." She should be worried about that, but she hadn't been thinking about it. Even though she'd been trying to concentrate on it for the past two days. With very, very little success. If anything, she was going backward. She tried to focus, to do the work that needed to be done, but mostly she'd obsessed about Jensen—and this strange, uncontrollable need to be with him.

And now that she was, it was as if the fierce, almost crippling ache that she'd fought for the past two days was gone. Not even real any longer.

She still felt attracted to Jensen—that never seemed to go away. But that feeling that she had to make love with him or die wasn't there. She felt calmer, her attraction more rational, not driven by something she didn't understand.

Okay, her need for him still wasn't rational, and she didn't understand it. At all. But . . . well, she felt normal. She felt content.

Jensen touched her, his large hand shaping the indentation of her waist. And she totally wanted him to keep touching her, and she wanted to touch him in return, but this was *her* wanting him—not the wolf.

And oddly, this felt just as dangerous, only in a different way.

"Is that what you'd been doing? Trying to work while you were sick?" he said, stroking his hand up and down her side. His fingers were long, strong, the skin slightly rough from calluses. She tried not to arch up against the wonderful caress like a cat. But mmm, it did feel so good.

"I still think you should go to the doctor," he said. "That was a really high fever and you were obviously hallucinating—to be out there in the nude."

She froze under his touch. She'd been nude? Is that how she approached him this time? Then his words clicked, falling into place in her mind. A high fever. Nude.

Dear God, she'd shifted. She'd shifted with him here. She could have injured him, made him like she was—or worse, killed him.

She fought the urge to jump out of bed. To put space between herself and him. To keep him safe.

"I'm fine," she managed to mumble. "Just pushing myself too hard." Of course, she wasn't fine. She started to shift without the full moon. She never did that. And she'd done it with Jensen here! That was *not* fine.

"With your research?"

She blinked, not immediately understanding his question. Then she nodded. Busy trying to do her research. Busy trying to stay away from him. And failing miserably at both.

"I . . . I don't really recall a lot of last night," she finally said, needing to know what he saw. How they ended up here.

"Like I said, you were very ill." Again he stroked the skin of her side, of her hip. And God help her, she let him, even as she told herself to pull away. "I found you in the barn. You were . . ."

She studied him, holding her breath. She was what? Hairy? Scary? A wild animal?

"You were in a state."

Well, that was putting it nicely. But she should have realized he didn't see her wolf form, or he wouldn't be here.

She suspected the reason she'd shifted was because she'd fought so hard to stay away from him.

She'd been on the edge, and if he'd startled her—not an easy thing to do to a werewolf—then she must have just acted on instinct. Her wolf instinct.

And she could so easily have attacked him.

She glanced down at their bodies, touching from chest to knee. Suddenly she felt the need to separate herself from him. That just by being near him, she was tainting him.

She started to pull away, but he tightened his arm around her, holding her fast.

"Where are you going?"

"I—I need to use the bathroom."

He smiled at her, the curve of his mouth indulgent. "Do you really? Or are you running again?"

She tried to look offended, but she knew she failed. He really was too good at this. Too aware of her.

"Tell you what—you answer a few questions for me, and I'll let you go."

Despite herself, she felt herself giving in to his gorgeous smile. "You are holding me hostage from the bathroom?"

"Hey, whatever works."

She smiled, but then sobered. She wasn't sure she could answer the questions she suspected he was going to ask. Not truthfully—and she didn't need to add any more to her sins, which had been piling up since they'd met.

"Okay," she said slowly, "but just remember you do this at your own risk."

He glanced down between their close bodies, then raised an eyebrow. It was probably for the best that he thought she was talking about urination.

"What is it about your research that is so important that it's worth trying to do when you were so obviously sick?"

That was a relatively easy question—and one she didn't really have to lie about. "I've been working on this particular problem for a long time, and time is running out. I need to figure it out soon."

"Is your research for a company or a particular lab?"

She hesitated at that one—apparently the questions were just going to get harder. Which was what she was worried about.

"I work independently—but if I did find this cure it would help a lot of people."

"A cure? Is it a vaccination? Or a medication? For what illness?"

She took a deep breath. How strange to talk of this with a human. She'd never thought she would, but she found herself continuing.

"It's a vaccination to cure a very rare illness. One that I doubt you've heard of." Oh, he'd heard of it—he just didn't believe it existed. Werewolves, vampires, fairies—mortals never believed in those creatures. Until they met them. Then they usually wished they could go back to being nonbelievers.

Jensen levered himself up on his elbow, his gaze more intent. "Try me. I've heard of a lot of illnesses."

"Not this one," she assured him again.

"But you have this disease, don't you? That was what happened last night. You had a bout of this—illness?" His eyes had darkened to a deep green, a color that she now realized showed his concern.

She thought to tell him no. There was no point in him knowing that she needed the cure—in some ways, worse than anyone. But she found the truth tumbling over her lips.

"Yes."

The one hand, still holding her waist, slipped upward, out from under the covers. He caressed her cheek, the touch heartbreakingly sweet, the look in his eyes just tragic.

"The fever is part of it?"

For her it was. Her fever usually spiked to around 106 degrees, which always happened after her shift. She'd spent many a day after the full moon nursing a terrible werewolf hangover. Some werewolves could shift without any repercussions. She wasn't one of them.

She nodded. "But that always passes. I won't die from this . . . disease—I just won't have a normal life. I—I'd really rather not talk about it."

He looked like he wanted to argue, but then he nodded.

They were silent for a moment, but then he seemed to remember he had more questions to ask.

"So if this isn't your normal way of approaching men—"

She frowned, at first surprised by the change of topic. Then she rose up on her elbow, catching the sheet to her chest. "It isn't. Honestly."

Why it was important to her that he know she wasn't a hussy made little to no sense when the truth was, she was practically a husky. Which was worse?

"Since this isn't your normal way of approaching a man, how did you pick me?"

She stared at him for a moment, taking in his mussed short hair, his gorgeous eyes, his mouth. She managed to keep her eyes from drifting lower, but she knew what an awesome body he had. Instead, her eyes returned to his.

She could see intelligence, kindness, humor there. His looks definitely drew her—but it was what she saw in his forest eyes that made her feel like she could easily get in too deep. Those eyes were what made her pick him. But she couldn't say that. It revealed too much.

Instead she said airily, "I saw you and wanted you." Not a lie, but not the whole truth. Not by a long shot.

He smiled slightly at that, then nodded. "I guess that's fair enough. Because I felt the same way."

"You did?"

His smile turned to that lopsided curl she loved. "You haven't noticed?"

She hesitated as she felt heat creep up her cheeks. "I sort of thought you found yourself attacked." She tried not to think about the potentially real attack of last night.

"Oh, you made your intentions very clear, but I think I've done my fair share of attacking back."

He leaned in and kissed her. Soft and sweet and lingering. A very different sort of attack but just as effective. Even as she told herself to pull away, to let him go, she sank into his arms. The sheet slid down so her bare breasts were pressed firmly to his hard chest. Their arms and legs tangled until there was no space between them.

Jensen pressed several small kisses to her lips before he angled his head back to look at her. "I have one more question. Although this one is a bit late in coming—and my only excuse is that when I'm with you I really do forget everything else."

"What?"

"Are you on birth control? Because we have been woefully negligent in that area."

Birth control. She paused. She'd never even considered it as she'd never used it. Never needed it. Female werewolves could only conceive when they were in heat. And she couldn't conceive with Jensen at all.

"Yes. I am." That was her first outright lie to his questions. Although she wasn't going to get pregnant, so was it really a lie?

"Good," he said, and leaned in to kiss her again. But she couldn't respond as she had before. The weight of what they'd been doing, what she was, and her past were too heavy for her to ignore.

"I think I do have to use the bathroom."

He smiled. "I guess you held out for a pretty long time."

She nodded, not really knowing what to say. She didn't feel quippy at the moment, just guilty and miserable. She started to slide out of the bed, then realized she was naked. She looked around for something to put on.

Jensen guessed what she was doing and rolled over to retrieve something from the floor. He held out a mass of wrinkled blue material.

"It's still damp, but it will work to get you to the bathroom."

"Thanks." She reached for it, but he pulled it back at the last minute, leaning forward to steal another kiss. Another of his sweet, heady kisses that she knew she'd never get tired of.

She forced herself to pull away. "Bathroom."

He nodded and handed her the shirt. The material was chilly and a little difficult to pull on, the moisture making it stick to her skin. But she managed and scrambled out of bed. She didn't look back at Jensen as she fled the room.

Jensen watched Elizabeth go, feeling overwhelmed by her. Physically, emotionally, even mentally. She had answered his questions, but with each question he had more. Not the least of which being, what was wrong with her? What disease did she have?

There were many illnesses that could cause fever. And was she lying when she said that it wouldn't be fatal? Certainly she'd been working like she was running out of time, if she'd somehow staggered out there in the buff. He could tell she was stressed and she seemed a little scared, and that worried him.

No—*worried* wasn't the right word. It scared the hell out of him.

Suddenly he had to see her. He had to know that she was all right. The need swirled in him, growing more and more until it was all he could do to remain on the bed and wait for her to return.

As if barging into the bathroom would help her in any way. Still, he felt anxious, like something dangerous lurked just outside the perimeter of their fragile world. A place where it was just the two of them.

The two of them. Hell, he didn't even know if that was what she wanted. He had no more answers about their relationship than when he'd arrived here. In fact, he had more. For every answer she'd given him, another question popped into his brain.

Hell, he hadn't even gotten the one answer he'd wanted most. He didn't know what she wanted from him. Did they even have a relationship? She hadn't said one way or the other. Why had she chosen him? He wanted to believe it was for a reason.

Again, the idea that she was sick jumped back into his mind. Then he was reminded of what he'd thought he'd seen. How she'd appeared almost—inhuman when he'd first found her in the barn. How strong her impact had been when she'd barreled against him.

He sat up, another wave of agitation flooding him. His eyes must have been playing tricks on him. He must have imagined what he thought he saw. There was no other valid explanation. After all, there wasn't a disease that transformed you into some sort of . . .

He shook his head. He'd imagined it. Tricks of light. And she'd caught him off balance. That was it.

His eyes locked on the half-closed bedroom door. He listened for some noise to indicate she was okay. But the house was quiet.

He couldn't wait any longer. He crawled out of bed and tugged on his damp jeans. He wanted to ask her more. But he paused with his hand on the door, realizing he could hardly grill this woman for more answers while she was using the bathroom. He didn't know much about the state of their relationship, but he did know they weren't there yet.

He paced the room instead. Looking around, trying to know more about her. Everything was very tidy. Everything in its proper place. She had a wooden box on her dresser, carved with leaves and flowers. The box looked old, and he suspected it was an antique. A jewelry box, he guessed.

There was also a bottle of perfume. This, too, looked old, the liquid inside a golden color. He lifted the bottle to his nose. He grimaced at the scent—cloying and slightly off. Definitely not the scent that always seemed to surround her. That wonderful spicy scent. Strong yet somehow not overwhelming.

He put the bottle back, careful to place it in the exact spot where it had been. He turned and wandered across the floor again. On the walls were several needlepoint pictures. He walked up to them, studying the precise stitches, the intricacy involved. The person who did these had to be very patient, very focused. Then he noticed tiny initials along the bottom of the picture on the right. EY.

Could Elizabeth have done these? He moved to the next. The initials appeared on all of them. EY. Some of them seemed to be quite old, the cloth yellowed in the frames. He supposed that could be caused by sun damage or other factors. Still, he couldn't take his eyes off the one over her bed. It looked very old. Fragile, almost.

A sound caused him to look away. A thump that seemed far away. Downstairs, maybe. He frowned, then glanced at the door. How long had she been gone? A long time.

Again, a feeling that something wasn't right snaked through him. A cold feeling. An unnerving feeling.

He decided it wouldn't hurt to just go to the bathroom and knock. She might find it a little invasive, but he was driven by the need to be sure she was okay.

As soon as he stepped into the hallway, he knew something wasn't right. The bathroom door was wide open, and the light was off. He walked down to peer into the darkened room. Empty, as expected.

"Elizabeth?" he called as he started back down the hall, stopping at each room, hoping she was there.

The upstairs was empty. He hurried back to her bedroom to finish dressing, only to realize she'd taken his shirt when she left. He hoped that was a good thing. He then bounded down the stairs, hoping she'd just gone to get something to drink or eat. But he had a feeling that wasn't the case.

The living room was empty, as was the dining room. He strode into the kitchen hoping he'd find her, even as he told himself he wouldn't.

He didn't. The light was on over the large, round kitchen

table, but otherwise there was no sign anyone had been there. He walked farther into the room, anyway.

"Elizabeth?"

As he got to the center of the kitchen, he spotted a yellow sticky note, stuck to the middle of the table. He hesitated, not sure he wanted to look at it. Even though he knew it was a note for him.

The yellow paper was indeed marked with small, precise, very feminine writing.

> *Jensen,*
> *I'm sorry I'm saying this the way I am.*
> *But this isn't going to work out.*
> *I cannot see you again. I'm sorry.*
> > *E.*

Jensen stared at the yellow paper, the adhesive sticking to the pads of his fingers. She'd done it again—her usual disappearing act. Only this time, he did have an answer.

They didn't have a relationship. That much he finally got, loud and clear. And he wasn't getting his shirt back.

Chapter 11

Elizabeth stood in the woods, watching her house. After what seemed like ages, Jensen stepped out onto her porch. The first thing she noticed was that he wasn't wearing a shirt.

Then she recalled that was because she wore his shirt, and she felt even worse about her actions. Even though they had been the right ones. She couldn't see him anymore. Not when she was what she was.

Last night, she could have really hurt him. It was sheer luck she hadn't. It certainly hadn't been something she'd controlled. She didn't even know why it happened, and she couldn't risk it happening again. Lycanthropy was easy to transmit, and she couldn't risk passing it on to him. Then he would really hate her.

She watched as he cast a glance around, still looking for her, even after the cold and impersonal note. Given the repeated impressions she must have made on this man, she couldn't begin to understand why he kept looking for her. She certainly hadn't done anything to make him think she was worth his time. Still, the idea that even now he wanted her made it nearly impossible to remain there, hiding, watching.

But she did, keeping her muscles absolutely still, barely even pulling in a breath. She wasn't sure if that was because she didn't want him to detect her, or if it was because she was too busy trying to commit Jensen to memory.

His skin looked more golden in the early morning light, his muscles undulating easily with his strides down the steps. He glanced at the barn, then, to her surprise, he headed in that direction. He entered, but only stayed inside a few moments. Long enough to see she wasn't there. Then he strode to his truck.

She opened her mouth, the urge to stop him almost making her cry out. But instead, she snapped her lips shut, biting the inside of her cheek until the pain of the squeezed flesh almost overshadowed the pain of watching Jensen leave.

Almost.

She *was* doing the right thing. Even if he could get over dating a woman who turned a little hairy and toothy once a month, she still had the equally monumental problem of being mated. The two problems together were insurmountable.

You are doing the right thing. Until you are free of this curse, you have to let him go.

She knew it was true. But that didn't make the pain any less crippling.

Brody watched the scene, feeling a smug sense of satisfaction. That was his Lizzie. His good girl. The one who always did what was right.

He'd seen her pain, the nearly crushing yearning that had burned deep inside her for the past two days. She'd been half-insane with her desire for that pathetic mortal. But she would have stayed away. His Lizzie was nothing if not strong. She was nothing if not moral.

He paced back and forth, watching her. Wanting her. Not with the same unbridled lust she'd felt for the mortal loser. No, he wanted her like he always did, with a selfish need to taint her. To dirty what she was. He knew he was little more than scum. He was okay with that. He just wanted to make sure he took others down with him. Scum or not, that made him powerful. That made him the one in control. That's why the pack cast him out. He was a threat. And with Lizzie back at his side, he was a threat with real power.

He considered going to her now. But he'd wait. He didn't want her with that weak mortal's scent still clinging to her skin. But he was relieved that this time the scent—the smell that could have ruined all of his plans—was gone. Not even a hint of the spicy odor drifted through the air.

Maybe he'd imagined it. It wasn't as if it was possible. A werewolf and a human? No, it wasn't possible.

The truck rolled down the dirt road, but Elizabeth didn't move from her hiding spot. Brody watched her. Trying to read her.

Maybe now was the time to approach her. He'd only waited because of what he thought that scent meant. He couldn't take her back to the pack if she was just going to run again. Back to the mortal. But now, he could sense this was the end. There was a hopelessness radiating from her.

But Brody still didn't approach her as she finally stepped out of the woods and crossed her lawn to the house. He'd give her a little time—to mourn her loss. A loss he did not understand.

But never let it be said that he didn't do a nice thing for Lizzie. Of course, he was just giving the situation time, to make sure she didn't crack and go to the human. He wouldn't have the pack seeing that his woman had left, again, and this time for a weak human.

And if she did give in and go back, he'd handle that. He couldn't kill her. But the human—yeah, he could die.

Jensen nodded at his granddad, trying not to look like a teenager busted after curfew as he entered the kitchen and headed straight for the back hall and the stairs. A damned hard thing to do when he was walking into the house at nine A.M. with no shirt on.

"Wait! Where the hell have you been?" his grandfather asked.

"Out." Jensen did not want to explain this.

"I know that. Where's your shirt?"

"Gone."

His grandfather frowned, his brows coming together in a nearly straight, if somewhat bushy, line. "You need to be more forthcoming here, Jensen."

"Nothing to tell, Granddad. I need to get in to work."

His grandfather gave him a look that was somewhere between dubious and disappointed.

"When a fella stays out all night and returns home without his shirt, and there's no story in that, then that is one dull man."

Jensen nodded. "That's me. Dull to the core."

His grandfather crossed his arms over his chest, looking for all the world as if he planned to pout.

Jensen glanced at his watch. "Gotta get ready. I don't want to be late."

He left his grandfather indeed pouting, but that was too bad. Jensen had no intention of telling him about his complete failure with the first woman who'd captured his attention since Katie. He couldn't do it. As it was, he just wanted to forget himself.

As luck would have it, Granddad was gone when Jensen had come down from his shower. And although his grandfather's disappearance wasn't unusual, he was probably out on the links griping about his weird grandson to that damned Harold Wilks. Jensen couldn't help feeling a little deserted again.

"Ridiculous," he muttered to himself as he filled his metal travel mug to the brim with black coffee. He hadn't wanted to continue his conversation with his granddad, anyway. Plus, he'd wanted the time to consider what he'd noticed in Elizabeth's barn. Thick chains and heavy manacles anchored to the rafters. He'd seen them when he'd gone in that last time to look for her. What were they? Did she put them up there? And for what purpose?

He had no answers. None that made any sense. But he wasn't making sense, anyway. He was offended that his grandfather disappeared, even though when that's what he'd wanted. But then, disappearing people were a sore spot today.

He grabbed the newspaper, stuffed it under his arm, then picked up his coffee and his laptop and left for the office.

Pulling up to the small building that housed his office, he told himself he needed to concentrate on the vet hospital. He was trying to get the place online, the records put into the computer as well as the appointments. His grandfather had resisted all that, but Jensen knew it would make things easier and more efficient. That was what he needed to focus on— not some woman who had as many issues as he did, and clearly didn't want him.

He walked into the office and was greeted by Molly George, the receptionist who'd been working for his grandfather for nearly twenty years. Molly had a habit of trying to mother him. Jensen supposed that was the risk he'd run being a motherless kid, raised by his granddad. Everyone felt the need to mother him.

"You are late," Molly said, peering at him over the top of her bifocals. "I almost called the hospital."

Jensen smiled, shaking his head. "Always try my cell phone before the hospital."

He pulled his phone out to show her he had it with him. And also to show her what it was. Molly was as resistant to technology as Granddad.

She raised an eyebrow to that, then looked down at the appointment book. "Luckily your first appointment is late."

As if cued by Molly's comment, the bell on the front door

rang as the patient and owner entered. Jensen turned to see Melanie, holding a very fat, very satisfied-looking tabby.

"Hi, Jensen," she said, offering him a warm smile. A smile that he couldn't help noticing still held that hint of interest.

His battered ego perked up at the look.

"Hi there, Melanie." He approached her, reaching out to the cat, scratching his neck and ears. "Who is this?"

"Mort," she said with a fond smile at the animal. "He's in for his shots. And maybe a diet, too."

"He is a big boy," Jensen agreed.

"Well, as I told you, while I do love it here, I tend to be a little lonely. So I think I may dote on him a bit too much."

Jensen nodded at that, picking up on the mention of her being lonely. He didn't comment, however. Instead, he turned to Molly.

"My first patient is in."

"I see that," she said, eyeing Melanie rather than the cat.

Jensen gestured for Melanie to go ahead into the exam room. She did, saying hello to Molly on the way.

"I'll make sure you are not interrupted," Molly called after him as he followed the blonde and her obese cat.

He didn't miss Molly's pointed look as he closed the door.

Was everyone in this town a damned matchmaker?

Melanie set Mort on the table and smiled at Jensen.

He smiled back, noticing her blond ponytail and fresh-faced beauty. In truth, it was hard to imagine she was finding West Pines lonely. She should have lots of dates.

He turned to the counter where all his supplies were stored, as well as a sink and other necessities for a veterinarian's exam room. He got his stethoscope and otoscope, and crossed over to Mort. And Melanie.

She cooed to the cat, helping hold the beast while he checked the cat's ears and eyes. He noticed that Melanie had a nice voice, a little high. Higher than Elizabeth's huskier tone.

He frowned as he continued to examine the cat. He'd told

himself he was just going to let Elizabeth go. There was no point thinking about her. The yellow Post-it note said it all. She didn't want to see him again. There was nowhere to go with that. Nowhere. So what was the point of thinking about her? He hardly knew her, anyway.

And in truth, she wasn't his type. He glanced at Melanie, who continued to murmur at her cat. Brian and Jill had been right when they'd asked her to join them that night at the karaoke bar. She was his type.

And now that he was back on the horse, so to speak, then maybe he should consider asking her out.

"Looks good," he told her as he left to go prepare the feline's inoculations, and by the time he'd returned to the room, he'd decided a date with Melanie held a lot of merit.

As he injected the cat with the first of three shots, and the large animal laid back his ears and shot him a look designed to kill, he asked Melanie offhandedly, "I don't suppose you'd be interested in going out this Friday night?"

Elizabeth stood in the middle of her kitchen, trying to remember why she'd come into the room. She kept doing this—headed somewhere with something in mind, but when she got there, she had no idea what she'd been after. It was frustrating—and it was unnerving.

She wandered back to the living room and sat down on the couch. She reached for the TV remote and flipped the set on. Conversation filled the room, followed by an irritating laugh track. She turned the television off.

God, why couldn't she focus? Why couldn't she seem to think straight at all? She got up and paced the room. She was surprised the wood floor didn't have a path worn into it. She couldn't concentrate on anything. Anything but Jensen.

She hadn't seen him for three days. Every day it grew harder to stay away. But she knew she had to—she couldn't risk shifting around him again.

She knew she had to work on her research, too, but she

hadn't gotten much of anything done. She was clumsy and distracted, and all she managed to do was make a mess of any of her still-viable cell samples. Now she'd have to wait to draw more blood right before the full moon. That was when the cell definition was most apparent. That was the blood she needed.

So all she did was pace and fixate, but this agitation wasn't like it had been. Her body, while it did miss Jensen, didn't feel like it had a life of its own. Now, she just felt like she . . . missed him. She wanted to see him and talk to him. And yes, touch him, too. But . . .

Suddenly the phone rang, the loud jingle in the quiet house actually causing her to jump.

"Hello?" she said breathily into the receiver, once she'd managed to calm herself enough to answer it.

"Hey, sis." It was Sebastian.

Elizabeth tamped down the disappointment at hearing her brother's voice. She didn't want it to be Jensen. She didn't. What good would it do if it was?

"Hi, Sebastian. How are you?"

There was silence on the other end. "Elizabeth, are you all right?"

She probably sounded as frazzled as she felt.

"Sure. I'm fine."

"Okay." He sounded unconvinced. "Well, I was calling to tell you that Mina and I are planning to visit on Friday. We'd like to see you."

Elizabeth tried to feel excited, but instead she felt dread. She was in no shape to see her brothers.

"Is Rhys coming, too?" God, she really couldn't see her oldest brother, the one who'd been her brother, her father, her champion. She'd failed him the most, and with what had happened over the past two weeks, she had totally failed him. Rhys would never know about Jensen, of course. But she knew. She knew her whole sordid past.

"No. Rhys and Jane are all wrapped up in the adoption."

That statement actually dragged Elizabeth out of her miserable thoughts.

"Adoption?"

"Yes. Can you believe that Jane convinced Rhys that he'd make a great dad?"

"He would be a great dad." He'd been a great dad to her.

"Oh, I agree," Sebastian said readily. "I just didn't think Jane would ever get him to let go of the whole 'undead with razor-sharp fangs and insatiable blood lust' thing. She's a serious miracle-worker. I just hope he doesn't take to wearing cardigans and smoking a pipe."

That image of her handsome older brother did manage to make her smile. A rusty laugh even escaped her lips.

"You laugh, but I caught him watching *Mister Rogers* the other day. He actually TiVoed it."

She laughed again, realizing talking to Sebastian was helping. Maybe being alone with her thoughts wasn't the best idea. Of course, if she left her house she'd been afraid of where she'd end up. She knew where she'd end up.

"So what's bringing you here this weekend?" she asked, stopping her repeated pacing of the kitchen floor. She actually sat down—and didn't feel the immediate need to stand and move again.

"Mina and I are groupies."

Okay, whatever she'd expected Sebastian to say, that wasn't it.

"What?"

"Groupies. Mina and I are really into this band called The Impalers, and we've been going to most of their shows on the East Coast. I convinced Christian and Jolee to book them at the karaoke bar."

"Really?" She didn't know why she was surprised. It wasn't as if Sebastian hadn't done the same thing back in the 1800s. He'd loved music then, too. He'd always pushed Rhys to hire this one quartet for their house parties—the first musicians to break their violins at the end of a particularly rousing waltz.

"Mina is totally into these guys. I'm actually more than a little jealous. But she's a wild woman in bed after a show, so I suffer through them."

Another burst of laughter escaped Elizabeth. "Okay, I don't even want to know about that."

"TMI?" Sebastian asked with a laugh of his own.

Elizabeth frowned for a minute, unsure what the letters stood for—then she pieced it together.

"Yes, definitely too much information."

But even with that info, Elizabeth realized she would like to see her old friend. Mina—or Wilhelmina, as Elizabeth had known her—had been her roommate, neither of them realizing that while they shared an apartment in Manhattan, Mina was falling for her long-lost brother.

She suddenly wanted to see Mina very badly. She didn't think she'd tell her about the weirdness with Jensen, but it would just be nice to see her friend and maybe feel like she had when they'd lived together. Not obsessed with a man she had to let go.

"Sure," she said, her voice already sounding less scattered to her. "I'd love to see you guys."

"Good. See you Friday."

By Friday, Jensen was seriously wondering why he'd decided to ask Melanie out. Jill had called three times. Her calls were guised as vet questions about her two-year-old golden retriever, who apparently kept eating miscellaneous plants and articles of clothing.

But concern for the gluttonous dog always veered toward Melanie's favorite things, whether it be food, flowers, or wine. Brian had stopped by the office to see how he was—feeling around for info about why he'd asked Melanie out. And even his granddad had gotten wind of the date, and not so subtly left condoms on the back of the upstairs toilet.

He'd done the same thing the night before Jensen had taken Katie to the senior prom. Jensen had thought the gesture was cool that time. He'd also had the opportunity to use two. This time, he left the prophylactics where he'd found them. He wasn't going to be having sex with Melanie.

Although as he got ready for the date, showering, shaving, finding the appropriate clothes, his gaze kept going back to the box of condoms. He should have had those for his times with Elizabeth.

She said she was on something, but he'd noted a distinct look of discomfort on her part. He wanted to trust her, but something didn't seem right. Part of him wanted to go back to her house and ask her again, watching her reaction closely. But then another part, the part with the wounded ego, remembered the cold little sticky note. Short and to the point.

He glanced at his reflection in the mirror, making sure his plain blue button-down shirt looked wrinkle-free and appropriate. Then he headed into his bedroom to get his shoes.

As he sat on the bed and untied his plain black oxfords, he glanced at the picture still on his nightstand. A picture of himself and Katie, right before they headed to New York for him to enter college. He used to look at the photo every day, stopping to consider all that his stupidity and ineptness had cost him. He realized he'd barely noticed the picture in over a week.

He stared at Katie's cheery smile, her pale blond hair cascading over her shoulders like a halo of pure sunlight. She looked like the girl next door, the wholesome beauty, a woman who was beautiful both inside and out. And she had been, but she'd also hidden a lot of pain behind her sweet smile.

What would she think of what had happened over the past two weeks? Not even two weeks, although oddly he felt like Elizabeth had been part of his life for much longer.

"What would you think, Katie-did?" he asked the smiling image. Then he picked up the frame, staring into her gray-blue eyes as if he would find an answer there.

He stared for a moment longer, then carefully placed it back on his nightstand. He returned to tying his shoes.

Going out with Melanie was the right thing to do. He realized that. She was the type Katie would have picked for him. The type of woman who would want the same things he did. A house, a family, contentment.

Immediately his mind returned to Elizabeth. Wild Elizabeth. She wouldn't want those things. Even if she was interested in him, theirs was a relationship that was eventually doomed to fail. Then he remembered the hominess of her house. The embroidered wall hangings. The things he wouldn't have expected to see in her place. But then, there was no saying any of that was Elizabeth's. And there was no point even speculating on the future. He had none with Elizabeth.

"You're right," he said to the picture, as if Katie had answered him. "Melanie is the right choice."

The smart choice. The safe choice.

Chapter 12

"Aren't they awesome?" Mina said, leaning in toward Elizabeth so she could be heard over the loud Journey cover.

Elizabeth glanced up at the band, all the members obviously immortals of some kind. They were good. But she wasn't quite sure why Mina and her brother were obsessed with them. Then Sebastian gave Elizabeth an anticipatory smile, and she remembered what the appeal was.

Apparently her friend had gone from uptight Wilhelmina to wild, rock-and-roll Mina. And apparently the classic rock had a particularly aphrodisiacal effect on her.

Again, that was a bit too much information, but that was okay. She had to admit it was nice to see her friend so happy. And so in love.

And Sebastian was so damned smitten, a sight Elizabeth couldn't have imagined seeing all those years ago. He had been too much of a flirt, and too fickle to settle down with one woman. Now Elizabeth couldn't see him with anyone but Mina, proof that there *were* soul mates out there. In fact, all three of her brothers were proof of that.

Jensen appeared in her mind, but she shoved his memory aside, focusing again on the band on stage. The band was sort of southern rockers meet the undead, and there was no denying the effect they had on the crowd. Everyone was into it. She tried to be, but soon the music faded and she was remembering Jensen.

Maybe because she'd met him here. Or maybe just because she rarely thought of anything else for more than a few minutes at a time. Even though she had noticed that her body didn't seem to be having that same uncontrollable need for him it had even just two days ago.

Maybe staying away was working. Maybe she'd gotten her crazy lust under control. Finally. Again, his beautiful features filled her mind. No, she still wanted him. Very much, but she didn't feel almost insane with that need. She just wanted him because . . . she just did.

The band finished the Journey song, and the crowded bar erupted into applause. Elizabeth joined in automatically, and that reminded her of Jensen, too—the way he'd seemed to react to his friend's singing only because he was expected to.

What had he been thinking about that night? It hadn't been her—she had committed the moment when he'd noticed her to memory.

Okay, she was doing it again. *Stop*. Don't think about him. There was no point.

"Sebastian, would you get me another drink?" Mina asked, smiling sweetly at him.

"I've created a rock-and-roll obsessed lush," he grumbled as he stood, even as his twinkling golden eyes showed that he loved everything about his woman.

"So what's going on?" Mina asked as soon as Sebastian left the table.

"What?"

"You have been a million miles away all night. And you look exhausted."

Elizabeth was surprised Mina had noticed anything aside from the music and Sebastian.

"I've been working a lot." That was a lie. She hadn't done

anything with her research for the last few days. She'd just pined for Jensen like a pathetic, heartbroken fool. Which just didn't make sense. Why did she feel so much for this man?

"You always work too much," Mina said. "This is different."

It was true—when she and Mina had been roommates in New York, she'd always been working, too. Her research was her primary focus. Her obsession. Now there was only Jensen.

"I guess I'm just getting discouraged." That much was true. Elizabeth had been very discouraged, since this last formulation of the serum. Since nothing had improved. In fact, the full moon was only a couple days away, and she could feel it coming, just as she had for the last hundred and eighty-eight years.

"Moving here hasn't helped? I'd hoped it would. I know you like the quiet."

Normally she did. But now? Nothing felt right. Part of her wanted to tell Mina that. To share what had happened. But she couldn't. She didn't even know how to explain what had happened, especially without it sounding hideously sordid. But maybe if she said her thoughts aloud, it would help her sort them out.

"Wine," Sebastian said from behind them, stopping her train of thought in its tracks. He reached between them to place glasses of white wine in front of them.

No. There was no way she was going to talk about Jensen now. Her brothers would never know about that. She couldn't bear adding that information to the bit she'd already told them of her past.

"I didn't ask for this," Elizabeth said, forcing a smile.

"But you look like you could use it," Sebastian answered.

Great. She must look bad if Sebastian could see she was a mess, too. And Sebastian could grill with the best of them. He'd been the one who'd gotten her to crack about every misdeed she'd done as a child. Sebastian had a way of lulling a person into revealing secrets.

But she wasn't letting him go there. "So are you friends with the band?" Changing the subject was the best defense.

"You don't recognize the lead singer?" Sebastian said, giving her an incredulous look.

Elizabeth peered up at the stage. She looked at first one musician, then another, finally taking in all of them. Nope, none of them looked familiar.

"No," she finally said.

"That's Renauldo D'Antoni. He played pianoforte at your sixteenth birthday."

Elizabeth stared at the men again—none of the faces seemed familiar to her.

"Wait until their break, and I'll introduce you again," Sebastian said.

Elizabeth nodded, feeling oddly dazed. Only in the world of the undead and immortal could you run into someone who played for your birthday in 1898. Even though she, too, had lived that long, moments like this still had the ability to seem surreal. And also remind her that she couldn't possibly have a normal relationship with Jensen. She could picture it now.

"Jensen, this is So and So. He played for my sixteenth birthday at the turn of the last century."

Yeah. That relationship was so doomed.

She lifted the glass of wine, suddenly feeling a strong need to drown her sorrows. But as soon as the wine hit her tongue, she felt a wave of nausea. She wasn't normally a wine drinker, but she knew Sebastian had chosen good wine. She supposed it was just another side effect of her stressed body.

She sighed, glad that at least Mina and Sebastian were again listening to the band. They played "Summer Of '69" now. God only knew what that would do to Mina.

She was studying the men again, trying to remember her

sixteenth birthday, and which one of the musicians had been there, when the hair on the back of her neck rose. Every nerve-ending in her body snapped to life, every cell aware of the change in the room.

She fought the urge to jerk around in her chair and see who'd come into the bar. There wasn't much point to, really. She knew who'd come in.

Jensen.

She remained still for a moment longer, then slowly glanced over her shoulder. He strode into the room, a woman walking beside him. The blonde from the first night they'd met.

Jensen had his hand on the small of her back. Elizabeth's hackles rose, and her teeth ground, but she forced herself to turn away. He wasn't hers. She'd told him she didn't want to see him again. He had every right to date. He had every right to move on. She couldn't be hurt by that.

But she was. She ached at the sight of him touching another woman. She ached as if she was seeing the love of her life, a man she trusted and adored, with someone else.

But he's not the love of your life. You don't adore him, you don't know him enough to have any trust in him. He's a mortal. You are a werewolf. That's like a bird and a fish falling in love. Or a human and an animal.

She had to let this go. She had to pretend that the sight of him and that woman wasn't ripping her apart inside. Pretend, then maybe it will be true.

On the drive to Leo's, Jensen told himself that he was only going there because the waiter at the West Pine Inn had told them that a great band was playing there tonight.

"Killer classic rock, man." The kid had been seemingly too young to appreciate classic rock, but then the classics never died, right?

And the kid hadn't lied. Jensen had heard the good, hard rock blasting as soon as he'd pulled into the parking lot.

So right until he pushed open the door of the bar, he'd almost believed the band was why he was here.

Even as he found a seat and sat down across from his date, he'd had himself pretty much convinced. They were going to see a band. That was a fun thing to do on a date, spend some time listening to good music and chatting. Those were the only reasons. Then he realized he was scanning the bar, looking for long, dark hair and pale blue eyes.

He forced himself to stop what he hoped was a subtle perusal, and focused on Melanie. She was asking what Brian and Jill were like in high school. He did manage to hear her, to follow her words, as everything inside him told him to look around. Find Elizabeth.

He ignored the urge, and frowned at Melanie, realizing that he hadn't heard what she'd asked after all. He gave her a sheepish smile.

"I'm sorry. I missed that." He gestured toward the stage. "The music." At least he had that to blame.

She nodded with understanding and leaned closer. "They're good, though."

He nodded, glancing toward the stage again. But this time, he didn't see the musicians. He saw exactly what he'd hoped he would. Elizabeth.

Deny it all you will, buddy. You were praying she would be here. Damn, he was an ass.

He glanced at Melanie, afraid she would see he was staring at the beautiful brunette with the delicate features and hypnotic eyes.

Of course, Melanie wouldn't know about her eyes. Elizabeth was in profile to him, her eyes gazing down at her drink. She hadn't seen him. Yet. He could just tell Melanie that he didn't feel well. That the music was giving him a headache. And they could leave before Elizabeth even realized he was there.

He glanced at Elizabeth again, wanting to go to her. Then he realized this was a mistake. Frankly, it was pathetic.

Elizabeth had made it abundantly clear she didn't want to see him. She'd not come to him since the last night in her house, and frankly, he doubted if he would have seen her again, if he hadn't gone to her. She didn't want him, and he couldn't pine for her like a lost puppy. He also couldn't stalk her. He was on a date with another woman, who really didn't deserve to be in the middle of this.

What the hell had he been thinking? He turned to Melanie to tell her this was a mistake. But when he faced her again, Elizabeth's brother stood beside the table, his pale gaze, so like his sister's, burrowing into him. From his expression it was clear there was no chance that he didn't remember Jensen. And he didn't look too impressed that the guy who'd come looking for his sister a few days ago was now on a date with another woman.

Not that Elizabeth's brother had any idea why Jensen had been looking for her. They could just be friends. They could have been acquaintances. He could have been returning something she lost.

But from the unfriendly look on the brother's face, he got the feeling that her brother was very aware of why Jensen had wanted to see Elizabeth. And Jensen also knew that her brother was the protective type.

"Can I get you a drink?" he asked, his gaze not leaving him.

"I'd like a vodka tonic," Melanie said.

"And you?"

Jensen could definitely see the animosity in the man's gaze. Which really seemed unjustified. After all, if Jensen could, he'd be with Elizabeth.

He glanced at Melanie, who waited for him to order. Guilt made it hard to speak, but he managed to say, "Club soda, please."

Elizabeth's brother nodded, his wintry eyes frosty.

"You never drink?" Melanie asked, no judgment in her tone, just curiosity.

"No. I guess I'm a bit of a stick-in-the-mud." Not to mention a total ass for bringing her here. So he could look for another woman. A woman who told him she didn't want him.

"Well, not drinking is definitely more appealing than drinking too much." She smiled as if she was ticking that off as a check in his favor. She shouldn't.

He forced himself not to look at Elizabeth, even though every fiber of his being told him to just glance at her. To see if she saw him.

If she did, she likely didn't care except to think he was truly pathetic.

"Oh, I like this song," Melanie said, drawing his attention back to her. He registered the song, then tried desperately to listen to Melanie, the whole time his eyes practically twitching to watch Elizabeth.

Elizabeth nodded at something Mina said. Possibly about her honeymoon. But she just couldn't follow her friend's words. She was too upset. Too near tears. And she knew she wasn't doing well at masking what she was feeling. Her distress must have been like thick perfume all around her.

"Elizabeth? What's wrong?"

Yep, Mina had sensed her emotions. And from Sebastian's deep frown, so had he. Even though she was trying her damnedest to temper them.

"It's . . ." What did she say? "It's nothing."

That wasn't going to dissuade them, but she couldn't think of what else to say. She swallowed back the ache, trying not to look at Jensen. But he was like a flashing lighthouse to her right, and if she looked at him, she'd end up smashed on the rocks. Okay, maybe that was overdramatic, but at the moment, it seemed apropos.

God, she wanted him. And she couldn't watch that woman touching him. Her man.

She vaguely recalled watching them in this bar that first night. She also remembered wondering if they were a couple, and then not caring. She'd only wanted one thing from Jensen that night. Or so she'd thought. Now that night seemed like years ago. She felt so much for that man sitting across the room, not looking at her. It made no sense. But there it was. She did, and she felt like she was dying, watching him with another woman.

"I—I need to get a breath of fresh air," she said, realizing she wasn't going to be able to hold her emotions together.

She stood, the chair nearly toppling with her need to escape.

"Elizabeth," Sebastian said, standing, too, although far more elegantly than she had.

Elizabeth raised her hand to stop him. "Just give me a minute. I'll be fine." She forced a smile, even as she doubted she'd ever be fine again.

She rushed through the tables, trying to weave as far away from Jensen and that woman as she could. As she passed the bar, she saw Christian watching her, a frown marring his perfect features. He looked as if he was going to call out to her, but she again raised her hand. She picked up her steps, until she was running. She didn't care. She had to get away.

Once outside, she ran around to the side of the bar where no one leaving would see her. She collapsed against the building, shrouding herself in the shadows. She covered her face with trembling hands and let the strangled cry escape her clenched throat.

This was what it was like to want so desperately the one thing she couldn't have. It felt like she was dying, the ache was so strong. And maybe the ache was worse, was stronger and more painful, because she could have had him, but she'd let him go.

She dropped her hands. No, she couldn't have had him. Maybe if her cure had worked. Maybe if she wasn't mated to a werewolf. Maybe if she were even marginally normal. But none of those things had been rectified, and she had to let him go. But she didn't have to watch him move on. She could do the right thing, but watching him, she couldn't do.

She rested her head on the side of the bar, staring up at the pale moon overhead. The orb looked like a lopsided circle. Only a couple more days until the full moon.

She had to focus on her research. She had to make that her priority again. She couldn't pine for a "what if." She had to let him go. She had to.

The pain would stop eventually, and the level of pain made no sense, anyway. She had to acknowledge he was better off without her. And she was better off without him.

She remained where she was, absolutely still, except for the hot tears rolling down her cheeks.

Chapter 13

"**D**o you know her?"

Jensen frowned, looking away from the door where Elizabeth had rushed outside, staring at Melanie as if he'd just remembered she was here.

"Sorry."

"That woman? Do you know her?"

He didn't know how to answer. Did he know her? Not really. Yet, in some ways, she seemed to have overtaken his life to the point that he couldn't remember a time when she wasn't on his mind. But he couldn't very well tell Melanie that.

"Yeah. I know her."

Melanie nodded, and he could see the wheels turning behind her sky-blue eyes. Melanie was a smart woman, and she could tell his vague answer said plenty.

She looked down at the table, tracing a white ring from a drink staining the wooden tabletop. Jensen knew she was considering what that meant. He glanced back to the door, which remained closed. Where had she gone? Disappeared like she always did.

Again, when he looked back to the table, Melanie was watching him, and it was clear that she'd made up her mind about his vague words.

"Did you bring me here to make her jealous?"

He pulled in a deep breath. He hoped not. He didn't think his plan had been that clear. He'd just seen the opportunity to possibly see her, and he'd taken it. Without considering what it would do to Melanie.

"No. I just . . ." What the hell could he say?

Apparently that wasn't the right thing.

She turned in her seat to gather her purse and her jacket. "Maybe we should call it a night."

He started to stop her, but there wasn't much point in dragging this on. He'd done something terrible to this woman who was truly a nice person.

He nodded. "Let me just go up and see if the drinks are done."

When he approached the bar, he saw that Elizabeth's brother was talking to another man, and while the other man had different coloring, he could see similarities in their features. Great—another brother.

Both men turned to look at him as he approached, and from their hard expressions, there was no doubt they were brothers and thus both related to Elizabeth. And they were not happy.

"Hi," he greeted them with a stiff smile. "I just wanted to settle my bill."

"Are you leaving?" asked the brother Jensen hadn't seen before.

"Yes," Jensen said.

"That's good," the pale-eyed brother said. "Because you are upsetting our sister."

Jensen nodded. "That isn't my intent."

Both brothers looked as if they didn't believe him.

"So what do I owe?"

"Nothing," said the pale-eyed brother. "Just leave Elizabeth alone."

Jensen nodded again. "I plan to."

Again, neither man looked convinced.

"Thanks," Jensen said and returned to the table where

Melanie sat perched on the edge of the seat, her coat on, her purse in hand. She rose as he approached and didn't say anything as she headed to the exit.

Jensen didn't speak, either. He didn't know what to say. He could think of nothing that she would want to hear.

Once out in the parking lot, he resisted the urge to look for Elizabeth or her bike. He focused on getting Melanie home, hopefully without too much more upset. He felt terrible—he'd never done anything like this to a woman. Although since meeting Elizabeth, he'd done a lot of things he'd never done.

The ride back to Melanie's house was also a silent affair. Not until he pulled up to her small house, did she speak.

"Jill said that you had been very much in love with your fiancée."

Jensen stared out the windshield. He didn't know what to say—he didn't know where this was going.

"Yes. I was."

"Jill also said that you never noticed another woman from the moment you met Katie. That she was the only one for you."

He nodded again. Yes. Katie had been his whole world.

"She also said that you hadn't seemed to notice anyone since she passed away."

Jensen swallowed. Was she implying that what Jill had told her couldn't be true? Given how he'd watched Elizabeth tonight, he was sure Melanie was finding Jill's assertions hard to believe.

"Yes. I've had a hard time moving on."

Melanie nodded, too. "But I could see how much you wanted to go after that woman. Is she the only one you want?"

He pulled in another deep breath. "I—I don't know." But he did know. He wanted Elizabeth so desperately it had totally overshadowed what he'd felt for Katie, although that fact only made him feel worse. Made him feel like more of an ass.

"Well, I can tell you," Melanie said. "It was written all over your face when she left the bar. You should go to her. Tell her how you feel."

He'd done that. Or tried. Elizabeth didn't want him. Except that wasn't what he'd seen on her face, either. She'd looked hurt by him being there with Melanie. She'd looked more than hurt. She'd looked devastated.

Melanie reached over and touched his arm. "You need to go to her." She gave him an encouraging smile. "You do."

He stared at her for a moment, then gave her a regretful smile. "I'm very sorry you got dragged into this. It wasn't my intention when I asked you out."

She smiled back, although the curve of her lips appeared more saddened than happy. "I know. Jill also said that you are a really kind person."

"All behaviors to the contrary."

Melanie shrugged. "We don't get to pick out who we love. It just happens."

Jensen wouldn't have believed that once. But now, he wondered.

Elizabeth forced herself to go back into the bar. When she stepped inside, she knew Jensen was gone. The air felt totally different. Instead of making her feel better, as she thought it would, she felt worse. Had he taken the blonde back to his house? Had he gone to spend the night at her place?

"Lizzie?" Mina said, coming toward her. "Are you okay?"

She paused for a second at the use of her nickname. She hadn't heard it for a while. It was amazing how quickly she'd let it go. But somehow it seemed appropriate tonight. She needed to remember who she really was, and why she couldn't be with a mortal. She was Lizzie Devlin. Werewolf, mate of Brody Devlin, and no longer Elizabeth, the gentlewoman who would have married well, had children, and lived a normal life.

She had to remember that. And she had to remember that

Jensen would have all those things she lost. If she left him alone.

"I'm a little tired." She didn't know why she bothered to lie. Mina could feel every emotion radiating from her as if it were her own. But she still couldn't voice the truth.

But Mina wasn't going to accept her avoidance. "Who is he?"

Elizabeth didn't pretend that she didn't know what Mina was asking. She shrugged.

"He's just some man."

Mina shook her head. "He's much more than that."

Elizabeth felt tears welling in her eyes again. Mina gently took her elbow and led her to a table in the corner away from her brothers, who watched from the bar like worried mothers.

"He's more than that. We can all feel it."

Damn vampires and their ability to read emotions.

Still, Elizabeth considered denying it. Then she couldn't. Her emotions were simply too high to keep them bottled in.

"Yes. He is. I don't know what, exactly. I just know that I . . ." She couldn't find the right words. Her feelings made no sense to her, so how could she explain them to Mina?

"You are in love."

Elizabeth's gaze snapped to Mina, who just shrugged and offered her an almost sympathetic smile.

Opening her mouth, Elizabeth thought to argue the claim. But she couldn't.

"You love him," Mina stated. "And he loves you, too. It's clear in the air."

"No. No!" Elizabeth shook her head.

"Okay, but I know what I'm sensing."

Elizabeth stared at her friend. That couldn't be the case. She couldn't be in love with Jensen. And worse than that, he couldn't love her in return. No.

Her eyes brimmed with tears. "No."

Mina reached across the table and caught her hand. "This is a good thing."

Elizabeth shook her head. No. It was a terrible thing.

"I can't be with him."

"Why not?"

Elizabeth gaped at her friend. "Because I'm a werewolf!"

Mina glanced around to be sure no one heard her. Then she said calmly, "So? He can learn to accept that. Look at Jane and Jolee. They learned to accept your brothers."

Elizabeth shook her head. "It isn't the same."

"Vampires are probably harder to deal with than werewolves. After all, you can go out in the day. The sun isn't a threat. You can eat. You are normal except on the full moon."

Elizabeth shook her head. "You don't understand. I can't be with Jensen."

"I know it's scary, but—"

"I can't be with Jensen because even if he could accept me, I'm mated."

Mina stared at her. "Oh."

Elizabeth still didn't want to tell Mina all of it, of why and how she was mated. Or what her pack was like. But now that she'd admitted this much, she couldn't seem to stop.

"My mate's name is Brody Devlin. And frankly, he isn't a good or kind man or wolf. He found me, because he was a resurrectionist."

Mina frowned.

"He dug up dead bodies. Fresh bodies. He'd robbed the graves and then sold the cadavers to medical schools or doctors for experimentation. When he dug up my grave, he just happened to find me alive. He took me back to his pack, and there they nursed me back to health, but by the time I was well enough to go back to my home, everything was gone. My brothers had disappeared. I believed them dead. So I agreed to stay with the pack. I agreed to become one of them. And to mate with Brody."

Mina stared at her. "Do your brothers know any of this?"
Elizabeth shook her head. "Not much."

"But why? They would understand. Surely if anyone could understand, it would be them."

Elizabeth glanced over to Christian and Sebastian who still watched, concern clear on their faces. "Maybe. But I can't forgive myself. The pack I was with, they were the scum of the London underworld. Thieves, drunks, prostitutes. And when I was left on my own, I went with them rather than flee. I was too scared to walk away. I stopped being Elizabeth, the gentle-born lady, and became what they were. I stole. I lied. I helped with the grave-robbing."

"You did what you had to do to survive," Mina stated.

"I can't even bear to think of the things I saw, the things I just let go on around me."

Mina squeezed her hand and repeated, "But you did it to survive. And you did leave. You left when you were strong enough."

Yes, she had. But it was after years of turning a blind eye. Years of falling farther and farther away from the person she'd been raised to be.

"You have nothing to be ashamed of," Mina stated, her voice stern rather than sympathetic. "You know I can testify to the fact that you do whatever it takes to keep going."

Elizabeth's gaze roamed her friend's face. That was true. Mina had suffered a lot—she'd seen a lot, too, and never had Elizabeth considered her weak or a failure.

"But I am still mated. So how can I be with Jensen?"

Mina considered that. "I don't know. But the truth is, from what I feel in the air between you two, I just don't see how you can stay apart."

Elizabeth sighed. Mina was right. She'd been naïve to think she could just send him away. Hell, it hadn't worked thus far.

* * *

Jensen stopped at the end of Boyd Road. What was he doing? Hadn't he told himself that there was no point going to Elizabeth? Only several dozen times as he drove around West Pines and Shady Fork for over two hours. But Melanie's words kept replaying in his head. *You need to go to her.*

Except Elizabeth had told him distinctly that she didn't want to see him again. But then the look on her face as she'd passed him tonight also repeated in his head. She'd looked like a woman who was truly hurt and upset. And that expression, that kind of devastated emotion—especially from her—was killing him. He had to know she was okay.

He stared down the dark dirt road. Who was he kidding? He wasn't going to leave now. He pulled onto the rutted lane. Although he hesitated for a moment before he put the truck into Park. What could he say? Because all of her blow-offs weren't enough for him? He needed yet another one?

The house was dark except for the outside light, glowing on the porch. Then he noticed the halo of light around her barn door. Maybe she was working. As he got out of the car, he noticed her motorcycle parked near the house. She had to be here. And the best bet was the barn.

He headed in that direction. He didn't know exactly what he was going to say, but he had to talk to her.

He just reached the door, his hand on the wooden handle, when he caught a flash of movement out of the corner of his eye. Then he was hit with the force of a battering ram to his side. The impact was so hard it knocked the breath from him as he flew through the air and landed hard against the cold ground.

He rolled over, trying to pull in a breath and get his bearings, but before he could do either, something grabbed him, fingers knotting into the front of his shirt. Then he was bodily lifted from the ground and slammed into the side of the barn. Weathered clapboards dug into his back and shoulder blades.

Still completely unsure what the hell had just happened and who was attacking him, he tried to remain calm. He had to figure out what was going on.

He squinted, trying to see the features of the dark, very strong form that held him. Literally held him off the ground. He dangled in the air like an insect held by a long, steel pin.

Jensen wasn't a small guy. Six feet tall, a good 180 pounds. Yet, whoever held him didn't even seem to be straining. Again, he told himself not to panic.

"You said you were going to stay away."

The voice sounded familiar, but it took a moment to register where he'd heard it before.

It was Elizabeth's brother. The pale-eyed one. For the first time, he was also aware of another black silhouette a few feet away, pacing as if he was anxiously awaiting his turn.

But before Jensen could reason with the guy, he was lifted away from the wall and pounded against it again, hard.

A groan escaped him. Damn, this guy was strong.

"You—" the brother started again, but his words were halted by a light flicking on behind them, then the front door banging shut.

The brother holding him turned in the direction of the sound. Jensen remained still. His head and back throbbed from where he'd made repeated contact with the side of the barn. Yet he did manage to focus past the pain to see Elizabeth. She stood on the porch, stock-still, as if she couldn't figure out what she was seeing; then it suddenly seemed to register, and she dashed down the steps.

"Put him down!"

His captor didn't let go. Jensen struggled again, but he was held fast.

"Christian, what are you doing?"

"We told him to stay away from you." Christian glared at him, then turned back to his sister. "He didn't listen."

"Oh my God," Elizabeth said. "Am I still fifteen years old and need you two to watch out for me?"

"This guy upset you," the other brother said. "We aren't going to let him bother you again." He stepped toward Jensen, and he tried to steel himself for whatever the other brother intended to do. Not easy when he was winded and hanging in the air.

Elizabeth made a disgusted noise. "Sebastian, don't. Christian, let him down."

Christian stared at Jensen, fury clear in his eyes. Then Jensen dropped, barely managing to get his balance as his feet hit the ground. But thankfully, he did manage to keep his footing. It was embarrassing enough that a guy who was about the same size as he was had managed to restrain him so easily. Not just restrain—he'd seriously manhandled him.

Trying not to show his pain, he stepped away from the brother, which put him farther away from Elizabeth. He peered at her in the shadowy light. He couldn't see her face clearly.

"I want you two to go," she said, her voice sounding huskier than normal.

"No way," the brother named Sebastian said. He crossed his arms over his chest and shot Jensen a look that matched Christian's.

"Elizabeth, just let us make him leave."

Jensen found his voice. "If she wants me to leave, I will." He peered at her, willing himself to see her expression. "But Elizabeth, *you* have to tell me to go. Not these guys."

Christian made a noise low in his throat, and took a step toward Jensen. Jensen didn't move, but he did brace his body to take another hard hit to the barn wall.

But before Christian could make contact, Elizabeth grabbed his arm, pulling him to a stop.

"No! Don't touch him."

Christian looked as if he wanted to shake his sister's hand off and attack.

"Jensen, I do want you to stay."

"Eliza—" Sebastian started, but Elizabeth turned and glared at him.

"You two need to go. And I need to talk to Jensen by my-self."

Christian and Sebastian looked at each other, then reluctantly stepped away from Jensen. They didn't leave, but they moved from between their sister and the man that they obviously thought was the spawn of Satan.

"Go on," she said, like she was shooing away a bother-some pair of vermin.

"Elizabeth," Sebastian started again, but Elizabeth's raised hand stopped him.

"I'm a big girl. I can handle this."

Again the brothers looked at each other, the need to argue clear even on their partially shadowed faces.

"Please," she added. "Leave us alone."

Jensen had the feeling that she knew what she was doing. "I can handle myself," she told them.

"It isn't you that we're worried about," Sebastian stated, and even with the lack of lighting, Jensen could see that he was looking at him like he thought he was a degenerate.

Their reaction seemed a little over the top, given that they knew virtually nothing about him other than that he'd been interested in Elizabeth, and then he'd showed up with another woman. While that had been stupid, it hardly merited being smashed, repeatedly, against the side of a barn.

He fought the urge to rotate his aching shoulder.

"You don't have to worry about me or him," she said. Then she added in a flat tone, "Both of you should know, if anyone can handle a situation, it's me."

Jensen studied her, trying to decipher what her words and tone meant. She sounded ashamed. Was she ashamed of what had happened between them? Was she ashamed of her be-havior? Because he'd be the first to remind her that he'd gone along with everything very, very willingly. In fact, he'd en-couraged it.

Of course, saying anything like that in front of her irate brothers was akin to a death wish.

"Go!" she said again, the one word just a fraction of a decibel from a full-fledged yell.

"Elizabeth," Sebastian said, his tone almost coaxing.

"Don't. Don't do that," she warned him. Apparently that was a tone he'd used with her before. "I can handle this."

The brothers hesitated, but then Christian finally nodded. "You call me if you need anything."

She nodded, not moving, still watching them as if she knew if she turned her back, they might not leave.

They both gave pointed looks at Jensen. Looks that clearly stated he was a dead man if Elizabeth ended up hurt.

He didn't intend to hurt her.

As soon as they left, speeding away in a silver Porsche that easily cost as much as the bar Christian owned, Jensen took a step toward Elizabeth.

She held up her hand to stop him, just as she'd done with her brothers. Again, he wished that the lights from the porch weren't behind her. He really wanted to see her face, to see her eyes.

"Jensen, why are you here?"

Chapter 14

"I had to see you."

"Why? That blond woman seemed like she was nice. She—she suited you."

"She is nice," he agreed. He didn't agree that she suited him, however. Once he would have agreed that she was his type. Now he realized his type had changed.

He waited for Elizabeth to say something more, but she only stared at him, remaining still in a way that was unnerving.

"Then I think you should go back to her. She would be good for you. A nice woman is what you need and deserve."

"Well," Jensen took a step closer, keeping his movements slow and steady as if he were approaching a skittish animal, "I know another nice woman. And I'd really rather be with her."

Again she stared at him, but this time he didn't need to see her features to know what her expression was—disbelieving.

She spun and headed toward the house, her long legs moving her in a near trot across the grass.

"Just go, too, Jensen," she called over her shoulder, not slowing her pace to see what he was doing. "You shouldn't have come."

He hurried after her, not catching up until she was on the steps to the porch. He snagged her arm, tugged her to a halt. Still she didn't turn to look at him.

"Elizabeth," he said softly. "You know as well as I do, we seem powerless to stay apart."

She stared down at the worn boards making up the porch stairs.

"Please," her voice sounded huskier than usual. Tired. "I asked you to go away."

"I can't," he said simply. "I just—can't."

She remained still, not struggling against his hold, but not turning to him. Not letting him in.

"Elizabeth. Just tell me why you don't want to give us a chance."

She lifted her head then, and pulled in a deep breath. Slowly, she turned toward him. The light was still behind her, casting her features in shadow, but he could see her. He could see her beautiful moonstone eyes, her lush lips. And he could see she'd been crying. Redness rimmed her eyes, making her thick lashes more pronounced. The sight made him feel like more of a cad. More selfish.

"Elizabeth," he said softly, stroking his thumb up and down the soft skin of her wrist. "I didn't mean to hurt you tonight."

Her eyes held his, and he could see emotions warring there.

"You should just go," she said again.

He didn't release her, he just continued to stroke her skin as if she were an agitated animal. She didn't pull away.

"I'm not that nice girl," she told him.

"I think you are."

"How can you possibly think that after the way I've acted around you? The ways I—I pursued you."

He smiled at that. "I found your pursuit particularly nice."

Her gaze left his, dropping to the ground, and he knew she was blushing, even though the damned light wouldn't allow him to see it.

He still held her wrist, but with his other hand he touched her hair, brushing back the short tendrils that clung to her temple.

"Elizabeth, I realize we don't know much about each other, aside from this strong attraction. But I do know I want the opportunity to find out more about you. Everything, if you let me."

She started to shake her head, but he cut off her motion by stating sharply, "If you decide that I'm not a person you could be interested in, then the next time you tell me to go away, I will. I will leave you alone forever. But I really think we have something here that we should check out."

She didn't respond immediately, and he could tell she was weighing the idea.

"Jensen, I'm not the right kind of girl for you."

She'd said that more than once, and for a moment, he wondered if she somehow knew about Katie. Except she didn't know anyone he knew. She couldn't know about his deceased fiancée.

"I'd like to be the one who makes that decision," he informed her, then gave her a little smile.

Her gaze dropped to his lips just briefly, then snapped back to his eyes.

"I think you should just trust me on this. It will save you a lot of time."

His smile widened at her glum tone, but more than that, he smiled because he realized he was wearing her down. She wasn't saying, no, outright.

"Come on. We can date."

She lifted an eyebrow at that suggestion. "Can you go to dating after the things we've already done?"

"Absolutely. And we won't do those particular things again until we decide we actually do like each other."

Elizabeth glanced down, staring at the ground but not really seeing it. She had a hard time looking at Jensen, both because of her own embarrassment, and the fact that she found his smile so appealing.

"You have to admit it's a rather backward way to start a relationship."

He shrugged. "Well, I don't think there's any right or wrong way. I just want the opportunity to get to know you."

She wanted that, too. She wanted to know him. But she wasn't sure he could ever know everything about her. Mina's words rang in her head. She couldn't control this. It was too powerful. And maybe he would understand.

She looked up at him, and again she was so tempted to just say, yes, she would date him. She'd do anything just to spend more time with him. And not have to see him with that other woman ever again.

But reality held her back. She could have him for a while. But she couldn't ever offer him anything long-term or permanent. Hiding the fact that she turned into a wolf once a month was feasible with a casual relationship, but she'd never be able to be with him as a wife or even live with him.

Not that she could be his wife, anyway. She was mated to another—that was the fact, even if she wished it wasn't so. And that wasn't fair to Jensen, either.

Still she gazed at him, seeing the hope in his green eyes. Seeing that adorable tilt to his lips, and she felt her own lips moving before she even realized what she intended to say.

"Okay."

Jensen's smile faded, and he narrowed a probing look at her. "Okay?"

What was she doing? She couldn't tell him that she would date him. The whole idea was ludicrous.

"Yes. Okay." Who the heck had control of her mouth and her brain?

Jensen rocked back on his heels and looked for all the world like he'd won the lottery. Which he had, if the lottery winnings were a female werewolf with a mate. That was more like a booby prize, really.

Still he grinned at her, and she was lost. Lost and suddenly excited that she'd agreed to see him. Even though she knew it was doomed. What was wrong with her?

"So I think we should start tonight."

His words managed to pull her out of her confused thoughts. "Tonight?"

"Yes, I want to go back to your brother's bar."

"I don't think that is a good idea. My brothers aren't exactly fond of you at the moment."

Jensen rotated his shoulders slowly and stretched his back. "Yes, I noted that."

She frowned, immediately moving to his side, placing her hands on his shoulders to shift him around. He allowed her to, and stood still as she untucked his shirt, peeling it upward.

She gasped as she saw his back. The skin was already mottled with red and purplish bruises.

"Oh my God, Jensen," she whispered, heartbroken that he'd been hurt. Hurt over her at the hands of her brothers.

"I'm so sorry." She trailed her fingers lightly over the marks as if her touch could erase them.

After a few moments, Jensen stepped away from her, then cleared his throat. "I think maybe you should stop that, if we plan to have our first official date."

She frowned, confused at first by his meaning. Had her touch caused him enough pain that he'd have to leave? Did he need medical attention?

Then she saw the way his eyes had darkened to a deep pine green, hooded and intense.

"Oh," she managed to say, even as a surge of reaction coursed through her.

"Let's go to the bar."

She tried to push away the longing growing inside her and focus on his words. Words that made no more sense.

"The bar? Leo's? I don't think that's a good idea. You really are hurt—maybe you should just go home and rest."

When he looked unimpressed with that idea, she added, "I will see you tomorrow."

He smiled, her promise seeming to appease him a little.

"No. I want to go to the bar. I feel fine."

She raised a dubious eyebrow.

"Okay, I'm a little sore," he admitted. "But I don't want to leave you yet. I think I definitely earned some time with you." He rolled his eyes to the side to indicate the beating his back had taken for her.

"Then come inside." She walked up the steps and waited on the porch proper for him to follow. He glanced at the house, a definite expression of longing on his face, then he shook his head.

"Nope. Come to the bar."

She frowned. "Why? Why would you want to go anywhere near my brothers? I know I don't want to see them for a long while."

"Because the bar is where we first met. And I want it to be where we meet again—this time on a real date."

She paused, touched by what he was saying.

"Plus, I should have been with you there tonight. So I want to start the night again."

God, he was sweet.

But instead of telling him that, she glanced at her watch. "It's nearly midnight. Isn't that rather late for a date, anyway?"

"The bar stays open until three. Not a long date, but it's a start."

She shook her head at his persistence. Then she laughed. "I guess it's time we did something slow."

"Oh, we'll do plenty of stuff slow." Then he grimaced. "That probably wasn't an appropriate comment for a first date, was it?"

"That's okay." Elizabeth had to admit, it was hard to take things slow. Not when she already knew what he felt like against her and inside her.

"Come on, let's go back to the bar and start this all over again."

Damn, he was so appealing—and damn, didn't she want to say yes?

She nodded, then touched her face, running her fingers underneath her eyes. "I hardly look ready for a first date." She gestured to her black yoga pants and gray sweatshirt.

He stepped forward, touching her cheek. "I think you look beautiful."

She laughed. "Hardly."

He studied her for a moment, then gestured to his truck. "We'd better get going. I hear there is a great band playing at Leo's tonight."

His response caught her off guard, and she laughed. "Yes, I've heard the same thing."

He held out his hand and she accepted, loving the feeling of his broad palm against her smaller one and the way his fingers curled around hers.

He led her to the passenger side of his truck and opened the door for her. She remembered him doing that the first night. He'd been a gentleman then, while she'd been more like a wild animal. The memory caused her to hesitate, a blush burning her cheeks. That behavior now seemed so over the top, so not like her.

"Are you okay?" he asked when she just stared into the cab of the truck, not making a move to get inside.

She nodded and untangled her fingers from his to brace her hand on the door and lift herself in. Jensen's hand moved to her elbow, helping her. He hadn't done that the first night. In fact, she'd been the one who first touched him. His lips.

She cast a sidelong glance at him. His mouth was still the most beautiful she'd ever seen.

He hesitated as if he was going to say something, then he closed the door.

He rounded the front of the vehicle and opened his door. He didn't speak as he got inside and turned the ignition.

Elizabeth tried to focus on the road, on the sound of the engine, on her own breathing, but all she could remember was what they had done in this truck. On this very seat. The steam on the windows, the hitched sounds of their breathing, the way he smelled, like woods and sex. The way he'd felt deep inside her, her legs straddling him as he pulled her down against him, groin to groin.

She realized that he'd pulled out of her road onto the one leading to the bar, before he spoke.

"This is harder than I thought."

"What?"

"Pretending this is our first date."

"Yes," she agreed.

"I really kind of liked our first date," he said, slanting her that adorable, cocky grin.

Elizabeth felt herself blush. "I don't think that constituted a date."

"Oh, I do," Jensen said adamantly.

"I'm really not like that," she felt the need to reiterate.

"I do know that. Frankly, I choose to be flattered."

She paused at that, then cast him a small smile. "Well, I guess you should be."

He smiled back. "Well, I am."

They both still sported a smile as they turned into the gravel parking lot of Leo's Karaoke Tavern and Saloon.

Then Elizabeth's smile faded. "I really don't know if this is a good idea. My brothers are a little bit protective."

"I hadn't noticed," Jensen said, then gave her a wink.

She frowned. "You have to be in pain. You really should be resting."

"Remind me to tell you about the time that I got kicked in the head by a mare in labor."

Elizabeth turned on the bench seat, gaping at him. "That really happened?"

He nodded.

"Wow."

"But I've got to say, your brothers are pretty damned protective."

"And you haven't even met Rhys."

Jensen cringed. "He isn't going to be here now, is he?"

"No."

"Then I'm good to go. I can handle your brothers. They just got the jump on me."

It was on the tip of her tongue to mention that they were, in fact, vampires, and it had been an unfair fight from the get-go, but she caught herself. That would be damned hard to explain, wouldn't it?

As hard as explaining what she was.

"Hey, they are playing 'Here I Go Again.' That seems rather appropriate, doesn't it?"

Elizabeth listened to a few of the lyrics, then laughed. "You're funny."

"I am," he agreed, and they stared at each other for a moment.

"I really want to kiss you. Can you start a date with a kiss?"

She nodded. She actually knew nothing of dating. She'd flirted a bit at balls. She'd even stolen a kiss at one of the soirees, from a man, a lord who she'd dreamed of marrying and now who she barely remembered. She didn't know anything about how real dates worked.

"I think we can," she said, her eyes drifting down to that luscious mouth. She did know one thing for sure. No one on earth kissed like Jensen Adler.

He leaned across the seat, his mouth brushing very gently against hers. A faint touch, a mere hint at what his lips could feel like possessing hers. Then he pulled away. The fleeting touch was so entrancing, so erotic, she remained still, swaying toward him, until he touched her face.

"If we kiss any more, our new first date is going to end up pretty much like the original."

Elizabeth blinked. For a moment she really couldn't find a problem with that. Then she realized she'd degraded to pretty much what she'd been just a few days ago. Acting totally on sensation, on need.

Except this was more dangerous, because with this kiss she also felt emotions that she knew she shouldn't. Emotions that she was liking far too much.

Still, she didn't suggest they stop. She didn't demand they just let things end here. Like she knew she should. She simply wanted him too much.

"Okay, are you ready to go inside?"

She noticed that he was casting a rather wary look at the bar's entrance.

"We really don't have to do this. I appreciate your thought of going back to where we met, but I do realize my brothers are a bit—intimidating."

Jensen frowned at her comment, then straightened, his broad shoulders straining against his button-down dress shirt. Oh, if he were undead or immortal in any way, her brothers would be in big trouble. Jensen had a fine, fine physique—he just didn't have anything paranormal on his side.

For a moment, guilt hit her again. Then she cast it aside. She wanted this man so, so badly. And she'd never wanted anyone like this. She'd never believed it possible, really. She just couldn't let it go. Call her selfish. She *was* selfish. But she just couldn't turn him away. Not while he wanted her, too.

"Let's go in," he said, opening his door.

She started to reach for the handle, too, then she saw that he was coming around. She waited as he opened the door for her. Again she was struck by what a gentleman he was, reminding her of her life so long ago. When she'd been a real lady—and he would have been the type of man she'd had a right to marry.

It was too appealing, too wonderful to let go of now.

She accepted his hand as he helped her down from the cab of the truck.

"My brothers really are very nice," she suddenly felt the need to say, knowing that if they knew Jensen, they would agree that he was the type of man she'd expected to be with. For a moment, Brody flashed through her mind. Huge, unkempt, coarse. He wasn't even close to what anyone would have thought she'd be with.

She pushed that thought aside. She didn't want to go there. Too much guilt was involved, too much regret.

Not about Jensen, she realized. But about why she'd made the choices she had earlier in her life. She wished she'd been stronger. But as Mina said, she had made her choices to survive.

"So you have three brothers?"

She nodded. "Three too many, huh?"

Jensen grinned. "Well, you are loved, that's for sure. Are you the baby?"

The question gave her pause. How did she answer? She had been the baby, but now she was actually older than Sebastian. Sebastian was eternally twenty-five, and she was about twenty-seven now. Werewolves did age, just very slowly. But given birth order . . .

"Yes, I'm the baby."

"Well, it's good to have family that cares about you."

She noticed he struggled not to wince as he pulled open the door to the bar.

"Jensen, we really don't need to go here."

"I want to," he assured her, the slight set of his jaw stating that he wasn't going to leave, no matter how many times she asked. He was determined to do this, and she realized his decision was based on him showing her brothers that he was not intimidated by them.

She smiled slightly. That realization was oddly appealing. And oddly sweet.

"It is good to have family," she said, deciding if he wasn't going to be dissuaded, they might as well go back to what they were discussing. And she did love her brothers—having them back was one of the most important things in her life. She wanted Jensen to know that. "But they did act like bullies, which I intend to inform them of, repeatedly."

Jensen shrugged—again, the movement was done gingerly. "They were looking out for you. I'd be a bully for you, too."

She smiled at that. "Hopefully you won't have to be."

She slipped past him into the loud bar.

"Hopefully not tonight," he agreed wryly.

Chapter 15

The bar was still crowded, despite the hour, and the band still played on the small stage usually allotted for the karaoke singers.

Elizabeth saw both Christian and Sebastian look in their direction as soon as they walked into the room. Christian started to move as if he was going to leave the back of the bar and approach them, but Jolee laid a hand on his arm and stopped him.

Sebastian continued to watch, but didn't move from the stool he sat on beside Mina.

"So far, so good," Elizabeth said as they found a table and sat down.

"Well, they sort of look like they want to kill me."

Elizabeth glanced at them, slanting them a warning look of her own. Christian had the good grace to look away. Sebastian, however, watched, a curious glint in his eyes, until Mina caught his chin and leaned forward to whisper something to him, then kiss him soundly.

"Well, at least they seem to listen to their women."

Elizabeth turned back to Jensen, smiling. "Yes. They are putty when it comes to Jolee and Mina."

"Are they married?"

Elizabeth nodded. "Yes. Sebastian and Mina just mat— married about six months ago."

"They are newlyweds, then."

She nodded. "It's funny, because Mina, that's Sebastian's ma—" she caught herself, "wife. She was my roommate and I didn't even realize that she was dating my brother."

Jensen leaned closer. "Really?"

"Yes, I . . ." Again she stopped.

How did she explain why she hadn't seen her brothers for years, literally for decades and decades. Again, Brody popped into her mind, and with that image, more guilt. How could she do this? Even attempt a normal thing like dating this man, when she could tell him so very little about herself.

Yet she heard herself continuing her story. "I actually got separated from my brothers when I was about seventeen, and I believed they were dead. I didn't find them again until I happened to find them with Mina."

Jensen stared at her for a moment as if he couldn't quite believe her tale. It was pretty unbelievable, and that was the most believable part of the story.

"That's like a fairy tale. That sort of fantasy that a kid has when you lose someone, that somehow they will come back."

Elizabeth saw the wistful look on his face, and she started to ask him about it, when Jolee appeared at the table.

"Hi, Elizabeth. Can I get you two anything?"

Elizabeth smiled at her sister-in-law, appreciating that she was attempting to keep things normal.

"I'd like a soda." She looked to Jensen.

"I'd like a club soda."

Jolee nodded, giving Elizabeth a small, encouraging smile.

"I guess your sister-in-law isn't so convinced I'm Satan," Jensen said, obviously pleased that someone in her family thought he was okay.

"Well, from what I hear, Jolee has some experience with really evil people. Her own family, for example."

Jensen cast a look at Jolee, who had returned to the bar to give Christian their drink order. Christian appeared reluctant to fill it, but finally did reach for two glasses.

"Well, I guess it's good she has someone like your brother," he said.

Elizabeth agreed.

"Hi, Elizabeth."

They both turned to see Mina. She studied Jensen, not even disguising her curiosity.

"Mina." Elizabeth smiled, the gesture easy because she knew her friend understood what she was feeling.

"I just wanted to meet your friend." Mina smiled at Jensen.

Jensen responded in kind, obviously sucked in by the naively sweet quality so inherent in Mina. It was probably that same quality that brought Sebastian over to the table. He stood close to his mate.

Elizabeth cast her worries aside and answered Mina's question.

"This is Jensen Adler. Jensen, this is Mina."

Jensen stood and offered his hand to Mina. She accepted it, shaking it very briefly before Sebastian offered his hand.

"I'm Sebastian." He gave a pointed look to Jensen and Mina's clasped hands.

Jensen followed her brother's train of thought easily and released Mina. He took Sebastian's hand, shaking it firmly.

"Yes," Jensen said. "I believe we met earlier."

Sebastian's lip quirked in amusement, which made Elizabeth immediately feel more comfortable. But, of course, she'd known Sebastian would be the easier of her two brothers. Christian was another story.

Still, she leaned toward Sebastian and murmured, "When did you get so damned alpha?"

Sebastian puffed out his chest. "I always was." Then he looked at Mina. "Well, since I found someone I want to keep forever."

Mina smiled adoringly at her mate.

Elizabeth glanced at Jensen, fully expecting him to find the whole scene a tad nauseating. Instead, he watched her.

For some reason, she felt her cheeks burn.

Jensen studied her for a moment longer, then smiled at Sebastian and Mina. "Why don't you join us?"

Mina hesitated, but Sebastian readily grabbed the back of one of the chairs. "That would be great."

Mina gave Elizabeth an *I'm so sorry* look, but she also sat down.

"So Jensen, what are your intentions with my baby sister?"

"Sebastian!"

Even though that was exactly what Elizabeth was thinking, it was Mina who cried her brother's name.

Elizabeth threw Jensen a mortified look, but to her surprise, Jensen just laughed.

"Well, I have to admit they aren't all pure. But mostly, I just want to be with her."

Sebastian laughed, the answer obviously good enough for him.

As soon as the words truly registered with her, Elizabeth stared at Jensen. But before she could say anything, one of the band members, the lead singer, came over to speak with Sebastian.

Elizabeth glanced at Jensen as Sebastian introduced the musician, whose name was Ren, to the others at the table. Jensen shook the singer's hand, and Elizabeth was again overwhelmed with the surrealism of what was going on.

A werewolf, several vampires, and a completely unaware human.

Elizabeth stopped fixating on the weirdness of the situation, only to realize that the singer was speaking to Sebastian about her.

"Yeah, I remember Elizabeth," the singer said, giving her a wide smile.

And for the first time, she noticed his eye. Or rather the lash of his left eye. It was totally white—all pigmentation gone. She didn't remember that, but she did recall him playing in her parents' parlor. Then she remembered who he was . . .

Renauldo D'Antoni, a composer who'd gained some attention in the 1800s.

"I played at your birthday," he said.

"Yes," Elizabeth said, hoping he would say nothing more. She didn't want him to elaborate, and reveal things that would be hard to explain.

Renauldo must have sensed her uneasiness, because he announced that he needed to go sing some Journey and headed back to the stage.

"He played your birthday?" Jensen asked. "When?"

"When she was a teenager," Sebastian answered, before Elizabeth could speak. Then his mouth snapped shut as he realized that might seem strange to Jensen.

And it did. Jensen looked up at Ren, assessing him. "He must have been young. He can't be much older than we are now. Was he sixteen or so when he played your birthday?"

Elizabeth shot a glare at her big-mouthed brother.

"He's a lot older than he looks," Sebastian supplied, feebly.

Jensen seemed to accept that, and thankfully he dropped the subject, and for a moment, Elizabeth hoped their "date" could go back to being a tad more normal. She glanced at Sebastian and Mina. Okay, not normal, but . . .

Just then, Jolee and Christian walked up to the table. Jolee placed a glass of soda in front of Elizabeth as Christian approached Jensen.

Elizabeth watched her brother nervously, worried that Christian might say or do something aggressive, but all he did was set a glass of club soda down on the table.

"Sorry about how I acted back at Elizabeth's," he said begrudgingly, and Elizabeth suspected that Jolee had made him apologize.

Jensen glanced at Jolee, obviously thinking the same thing. But he nodded. "I would be pretty angry if someone upset my sister, too."

Christian shifted slightly, which Elizabeth found a little amusing. There was something rather funny about a tough, two-hundred-year-old vampire shuffling his feet sheepishly because his woman had called him to task.

But she was pulled out of her amusement when Jensen suggested that Christian and Jolee also join them.

"For a minute," Jolee agreed with one of her warm smiles. "We are still pretty busy."

Christian didn't look as if he wanted to sit, but he did. Jolee really was a powerful lady. She knew how to keep her arrogant brother in line.

For a moment, everyone sat, uncertain what to say, the uneasiness thick in the air. But gradually, again thanks to her sisters-in-law, everyone began to talk. Eventually, the conversation flowed rather easily, and Elizabeth found herself relaxing. She watched Jensen chat with her brothers, the awkwardness slowly disappearing. But while he made conversation, he also kept watching her, his gaze making her feel warm all over.

And for a moment, Elizabeth allowed herself to imagine what her life could be like with him. It was so easy to picture. He was all the things she'd believed she would have. But she couldn't let herself imagine too much. She still was what she was, and she was tied to someone else. Jensen deserved so much more than what she could offer.

Maybe because she knew her time with this man was limited, she found she didn't want their first official date to be spent with her family. Even though she was pleased that a truce had been reached.

Of course, before she could even figure out a tactful way to ask them to go, Christian rose.

"I guess we should let you two have a little time alone."

This was a time when a vampire's keen perception came in rather handy.

"Jensen and I were just discussing the pros and cons of club soda versus tonic water."

Mina nudged him. "You can talk about that another time. I think we are interrupting."

"No, we aren't," Sebastian said, genuinely confused.

"Sebastian," Mina took her mate's arm. "The band's nearly finished playing."

Sebastian frowned at her and then at the stage. Ren belted out the lyrics to a rocking '80s hit. Again, Sebastian frowned at Mina. "They still have at least a few more songs left."

Okay, it rather scared Elizabeth that Sebastian and Mina had followed this band enough that they seemed to have memorized the set list.

But Mina stood, her hand still on his arm. "Maybe they do, but I'm all finished listening."

She purred the words with an allure that Elizabeth wouldn't believe her uptight friend could pull off. But she did, very well.

Sebastian's eyes widened with realization, then he grinned. "Yeah—sorry, Jensen. Great talk, but we have to go."

He rose, tugging Mina along with him.

When Elizabeth looked at Jensen, he was smiling, too. They both laughed at her brother's overeager behavior.

"Your brothers are actually nice," he said, once they had stopped chuckling.

"Yes. They are. Do you have any siblings?"

Jensen shook his head. "No. Just me. My mother and father might have planned to have more kids. I'm not really sure. They were killed in a car crash when I was six."

Elizabeth reached across the table and touched his hand. "I'm sorry."

Jensen shrugged. "I don't really remember them. My granddad and grandmother raised me. They were really the only parents I ever knew. And in truth, losing my grandmother was harder than losing my parents. That sort of sounds terrible, doesn't it?"

Elizabeth shook her head. "No. Not at all. My parents died when I was thirteen. It was terrible, but it was far worse when I thought I'd lost my brothers. They were the ones who'd taken care of me after my parents died."

"How did you lose them?"

Elizabeth fiddled with the napkin under her drink. How

did she answer that? Somehow, telling him that she'd believed them all killed by an evil vampiress didn't seem like the best idea. Or an explanation that he would even remotely believe. She couldn't even tell him what happened to her. And these were the very reasons a real relationship was doomed.

But still she tried to find a way to explain. "I was—I thought that they had been killed, and because of that I got involved with a rough crowd."

Jensen studied her. He'd seen this before—her reluctance to talk about her past. But he wanted to understand. The whole story seemed almost fantastical.

"How did you believe they were killed?"

She hesitated again, and he got the feeling she was weighing how much to tell. He wasn't sure—he just saw hesitation there in her pale eyes.

"I believed that they had been murdered."

"Murdered?"

She nodded. Then she took a deep breath and the words just started to flow from her.

"I was attacked and left for dead. I was found, but it took me several weeks to recover. Once I did, I went back to my family home to find my brothers, only to find them gone. The property had been sold to a distant relative, and they were just—gone."

"Where did this happen?" The story truly *was* fantastical. And horrifying.

"In England. You wouldn't have heard about it," she assured him, as if she'd known that was exactly what he was thinking. It was just the type of sensational story that hit the media big in this country.

"So I ended up staying with the—people who discovered me. I was with them for many years before I left, realizing that I would never fit it. That I didn't want to fit in."

Jensen frowned, finding her words disturbing. Disturbing in part because of the things she wasn't saying. He started to ask more. He wanted to know about these people she had been with. Foster parents? A gang? What had she lived through, all the while believing she had to stay there, because she had no one?

But she spoke first, her question obviously shifting the attention from her to him.

"When did your grandmother pass away?"

"Nearly twelve years ago. Then it was just my granddad and me. That's part of why I came back here. To help him out."

"That's nice."

He shrugged. "He's my only family."

She studied him for a moment. "Why is that? I'd think a guy like you would have long since been married."

"A guy like me?" He chuckled. "I could say the same for you."

Her own smile disappeared, and again he got the feeling there was a lot more to that story, too.

"You know," she finally said, another smile curving her lips, but this one looked strained as if it was almost hurting her to smile. "I really am tired. Maybe I should head home."

For the first time, Jensen did notice the purplish shadows under her eyes. Immediately, he worried that the strange and sudden illness she'd had the other night could be returning.

"You do look tired. Do you feel all right?"

She nodded. "Just tired."

He stood, moving to put a hand on the back of her chair to help her rise. She allowed him to catch her elbow as she rose. Then his hand slipped to the small of her back. He half-expected her to pull away. There was a reticence to her. But she didn't move away from his touch—if anything, she leaned into it. Which made him feel a little better.

She didn't want to talk about her past, but she did want him. He'd learn about the past eventually. She just needed time to trust him. He had a feeling trust was a real issue for her. Given what she'd told him about her attack and the loss of her brothers, he could easily understand why.

Despite the speed of much of their relationship, he longed to go slow, too. That was all he wanted, he realized. To take all the time in the world to get to know her. Not much to ask, really.

Despite his wanting to know everything, the ride home was silent. She seemed lost in her own thoughts, while he was lost in thoughts about her.

When they pulled into her driveway and he parked the truck, he was rather surprised when she turned to him rather than just excusing herself with a quickly stated, *Good night.*

"I'd ask you in, but I think it might be a bad idea."

He'd agree with that. He knew he couldn't be alone with her and not want to touch her. And touching her would very quickly escalate to other things. She had that effect on him. But then he wanted to take forever to explore her body, too.

"I think you do need some sleep tonight."

She nodded.

"But I'd like to see you tomorrow."

She smiled, something akin to surprise in her eyes.

"You don't understand why I'd want to see you, do you?"

Only the slightest shake of her head was her answer. But it was still an answer he couldn't believe. Could she really have no idea how fascinating and beautiful and spellbinding she was? She'd had his attention from the very start, and he'd started to believe she always would.

"Well, I do want to see you. In fact, I'd like you to go to an anniversary party with me."

She straightened. "A party?"

"Yes, my receptionist at the office is celebrating her twenty-fifth wedding anniversary. And since she's talked of little else, I happen to know it's going to be a big to-do."

Jensen was sure he saw hesitation in her eyes again. But then she nodded, although her smile didn't quite reach her pale eyes.

"I'd love to go."

Chapter 16

Damn, they'd been together again. Brody had been sure that the other night had been the end. He'd been sure that he'd grab her tonight. He'd seen enough. He knew enough. And he would take her tonight. There was no doubt about that.

Initially, he'd been amused that his uptight, frigid little mate had found her horny side. But now, he knew more was going on here than he'd first realized. And he couldn't risk her doing something stupid.

The pack would not know what she'd done, and he'd make certain she didn't utter a word about her slutty side. She was still his ace in the hole. She was the one who would get him back what he deserved. Bring back his respect and his status.

There would always be someone who wanted to bring him down, but it sure as hell wasn't going to be his unfaithful mate and her weak, useless human lover. She was going to get Brody his life back, no matter what he had to do to her to make her cooperate.

Tonight, he was going to take her back where she belonged. By his side. Where the pack could see he was strong, in control, and superior.

* * *

Elizabeth rummaged through her bureau, looking for something to sleep in. She hadn't been making up excuses with Jensen. Exhaustion had just seemed to overtake her. She supposed it was all the drama of the night. There certainly had been a lot.

She almost laughed at the absurdity of it all. It was all rather funny and soap-operalike, except that she wasn't happy that her brothers had actually hurt Jensen.

Two vampires against one mortal.

"Bullies," she murmured as she tugged a t-shirt and some flannel boxers out of the drawer. She planned to give her brothers another piece of her mind, just for good measure. She wiggled out of her clothes and pulled on the new ones. Then she crawled into her bed, sighing at how wonderful the mattress felt.

She did feel oddly lighter that she'd talked to Mina, told her about some of her past. Maybe she could tell Jensen. Eventually.

For a moment, she considered forcing herself out of bed and going to her lab. She could get in a few more experiments before she fell asleep. She should do that—a cure was still her best, and only, chance to be with Jensen. But instead of moving to get up, her eyes drifted closed.

I wonder what I have to wear to an anniversary party, she mused, and that was her last thought before she sank into a deep sleep.

The house was dark and completely silent as Brody pushed open the back door. He wandered silently through the kitchen, the leathery pads of his paws only whispers against the worn hardwood. He made note of the place, of the hominess of the rooms.

Lizzie always did want a home. That was one desire she hadn't been able to keep locked away inside herself. And from the furniture to the decorations, she'd made a real home here.

Too bad tonight would be the last time she got to enjoy her little nest. Soon she'd be back with him and the pack.

He loped up the stairs, raising his nose, catching Lizzie's distinct scent. Relief filled him as he realized he still didn't smell the scent he had the other times. Maybe he'd been wrong about what he thought he'd sensed. Now, he only smelled the sweet, clean scent of Lizzie. A scent he remembered well. A pure scent that he'd worked hard to taint.

It was funny that you often looked to ruin the very thing you want.

How philosophical. He made a sound somewhere between a snort and a laugh, although in his current state it sounded more like a small growl. He stopped, motionless. His pointed ears twitched, moving just a little to hear all around him.

Still nothing but silence. But she was here. No doubt about that.

He padded down the hallway, following his nose. The scent brought him right to her. She was nestled in her bed, the covers pulled up to her chin. He remembered her smell, but he'd forgotten how truly beautiful she was. Even his keen eyesight couldn't tell him that from the distances he'd been watching her.

Then he frowned. He really was getting damned sappy here. Yes, she was beautiful—he'd hardly mate himself to a dog. A grin curled his lips back over his fangs at his own humor.

He stepped closer, nuzzling the covers with his snout, sniffing her scent in deeper. Oh yeah, he was going to be damned happy to have her back in his bed. Hell, he might just take her now, before they even headed back to the pack. Would she react to her dear old mate the way she had to her new, human lover? She'd better, or at the very least he'd make sure she fully remembered the experience.

But he wanted just one little taste while she was so sweet and unaware. One lick before letting her know he was there.

His long tongue lolled out of his mouth, then over her lips.

He then reared back and started to shift, something he normally did without much thought and with no side effects, but he stopped. He moved his tongue around in his mouth, realizing a certain taste laced his saliva. A taste he'd only ever heard of. A taste that he couldn't believe came from Lizzie, his mate.

He stared at her, his wolf eyes seeing her clearly in the dark room. Shit. It couldn't be. It wasn't possible.

But he knew what he'd tasted. Still tasted.

He nearly whipped back his large, black head and howled his rage. But instead, he stared at her, debating what had to be done now.

His only thought was to kill her. Just kill the whore. He took a step toward the bed, his teeth bared, his claws digging into the carpeting surrounding the bed.

He could just jump on her now and rip her throat out. She'd never even know who or what attacked her. But just as he got ready to leap, he stopped, spinning away from the bed. He silently paced the length of the bed, debating what to do.

Kill her. Kill her.

The words echoed through his head, an animal with only one thought. One desire.

But if he killed her, he'd be in the same position that had forced him to come for her in the first place. The pack was discontent with him. They didn't believe he was stable, grounded.

He stopped his pacing and eyed her. Grounded. An heir would give the pack the impression Brody had calmed down. A child and a wife. And Lizzie could give him both.

This was a setback, but all was not lost. Except she wouldn't stay. He knew that now. She would go back to the mortal. Especially now.

So he'd have to deal with the human. Brody looked back at his mate, sleeping so deeply she seemed barely alive.

The human would come for her, too. There was no deny-

ing the bond between them now. As unlikely and freakish as
it may be.

So he had to kill the human. That was the only answer.

Kill him, his wolf brain whispered. *Kill him.*

He wheeled around on all fours, moving like a vanishing
shadow through the house. *Kill him.*

Now, *that* he could do.

Jensen awoke, feeling as if something must have roused
him, though he couldn't say what. He listened, trying to see if
a noise had interrupted his sleep. He heard nothing.

Sitting up, he glanced at the clock. It was after three. He
wasn't even sure how long ago he'd dozed off, but it didn't
feel like he'd been asleep very long.

He listened again, still hearing nothing. It must have been
a reaction to a dream, he decided, shoving back the covers.
While he was up he might as well take a trip to the rest room.

He padded down the hall, aware that the bathroom light
was already on. Perhaps he'd heard Granddad get up or
something.

Still, Granddad leaving the light on struck him as strange.
Granddad was a child out of the Depression. He never forgot
to switch off a light.

Even though the light didn't seem like a particularly big
thing, he had the feeling something wasn't right. He turned
away from the bathroom and headed toward his grandfather's
room at the other end of the hall.

The door was ajar, which also seemed odd for this time of
the night. Jensen tapped on it lightly, and when he received
no answer, he pushed it open a little more so he could see the
old wooden four-poster bed his grandparents had owned for
as long as Jensen could remember.

"Granddad?"

A patch of light from the open door fell across the bed,
showing that his grandfather had been in bed. But now, the
covers were thrown back, the bed empty.

Jensen stepped farther into the room, a wave of fear filling him. Where was he?

Had his grandfather called to him, and that was what woke him from a sound sleep?

"Granddad?" he called, loudly this time. He walked farther into the room, scanning the floors to be sure the older man hadn't fallen down or something. The room was empty.

He rushed back to the bathroom. If he'd fallen on the tile, he could have easily banged his head. But after a quick scan of the bathroom, he realized his grandfather wasn't there, either.

Immediately he started down the stairs, two at a time.

"Granddad?" he shouted. "Granddad, where are you?"

Just as he reached the bottom step, a sound rang out—sharp, loud, echoing through the air. Panic filled Jensen as he dashed in the direction of the sound. The kitchen.

Once he reached the room, he saw his grandfather standing in the back doorway, a rifle raised to his shoulder aimed out into the backyard.

"Granddad," Jensen managed, although he felt a little breathless and he didn't think it was from the race through the house. "What the hell are you doing?"

His grandfather didn't answer right way; instead, he still trained the gun out the door.

Finally, he lowered the gun, then moved with surprising agility to close and lock that back door. He turned to Jensen.

"I just shot a black wolf."

Jensen stared at the old man. "What?"

"I just shot a black wolf. I got up to use the john, and while I was standing at the toilet, I noticed movement outside the window. Something large and black, crouching outside the house, watching."

Large and black. Crouching. Instantly, Jensen remembered what he'd seen in Elizabeth's barn.

"A wolf?"

Granddad nodded. "I couldn't see it too clearly from upstairs, so I went and got my gun and came down here to get a better look. When I got down here, it was on the back porch."

"A wolf?" Jensen repeated.

"Yes," his grandfather said, as if he thought he was the one who had to be mad.

Again Jensen just gaped at him. "And you shot it?"

"Just wounded, I think. I would have gotten him, if you hadn't started caterwauling. Startled me, and gave him the warning he needed." Granddad actually pursed his lips, peeved.

"Granddad, there aren't black wolves in West Virginia. It had to have been Tim McCormack's half-deaf old New-foundland."

Granddad's eyebrows rammed together as he scowled at Jensen. "You don't think I know the difference between a wolf and a Newfoundland? You forget, young man, that I was working with animals in these parts long before you were even a twinkle in your daddy's eyes."

Jensen took a breath, finding it hard to believe they were even having this argument. It was true that if anyone knew animals, it was his grandfather. But his grandfather also knew that there were no wolves in this part of the state. Had he somehow bought into the sensationalized stories in the newspaper of late?

"Could it have been a feral dog? A coydog, maybe?"

His grandfather shook his head. "I know what I saw. And I know what I shot."

Jensen nodded, for a moment believing his grandfather. He knew what he saw in that barn. Except he didn't. He had no idea. Maybe both he and his granddad had hallucinated this crouching black creature.

Maybe Granddad wasn't as lucid as he always believed. He was getting older. But that didn't explain away what he'd seen.

"Okay, well, maybe we should just head to bed."

His grandfather shook his head. "I think I'm pretty awake now."

Jensen couldn't argue that one. He didn't think he could get back to sleep now, either. Instead, he moved to the counter. "Coffee?"

His granddad nodded and wandered over to sit down at the kitchen table. Jensen noticed as he started to measure coffee into the filter, that his grandfather still held the rifle.

Whatever he thought he saw, it had shaken him. Just like it had shaken Jensen.

Elizabeth knew something wasn't right as soon as she woke. Nothing she could pinpoint, exactly—a strange scent, a funny feeling, but nothing that made her think, *Ah! That's it!*

But when she saw Jensen arrive at her door, she wondered if he'd somehow been transmitting a weird vibe that she'd managed to pick up.

"You look terrible," she said, opening her door wider to allow him in.

He stepped inside, then turned to her. "You look absolutely stunning." His gaze roamed over her, taking in her halter-cut black gown. His eyes lingered just briefly at the plunge of the neckline.

She immediately felt pleasure and regret mingle inside her. She was thrilled that he thought she looked good, but she should have tempered her comment to him a little more.

"Thank you. I shouldn't have said that," she said. "You look great." He did, in his black suit with his crisp white shirt and deep red tie. "You just look exhausted."

He smiled at that. "I am exhausted."

She gestured for him to sit down. "Are you sure you still want to go to this party? You look like you need a good night's sleep."

"And miss the chance to show off the most beautiful woman in West Pines?"

"Technically, I'm in Shady Forks," she pointed out. "But thank you."

"I think you have them both covered."

She smiled, then turned back to him. "Why are you so tired? What happened?"

She couldn't help wondering if the thing that upset him was indeed what she'd been feeling today. She had to admit the strange vibe she'd felt today was different from the other days. That endless restlessness. This was more the feeling . . . well, that something just wasn't right. She'd gone into town to buy the dress she was wearing, and she'd felt better while in town. But then she'd gotten back here, and things felt off again.

She really was starting to wonder if there was something wrong with the old farmhouse. First her uneasiness, then her uncontrollable desire for Jensen, and now just this lingering feeling of weirdness. Like a vaguely unpleasant smell that she couldn't locate.

"I'm really worried about my granddad."

She focused on his face, seeing the worry there.

"Is he sick?"

"I don't know. I think maybe. He was up last night shooting at something that he claims was a wolf."

His words gave her pause. "A wolf?"

"According to him, it was a huge, black wolf."

More uneasiness rose up in her, making it hard for her to pull in a full breath.

"At first I worried that he might have shot our neighbor's dog. They have an old Newfoundland. But when I walked around the yard this morning, searching for traces of blood, I didn't find anything. Which, I must say, I'm happy about. But it makes me think my granddad is having hallucinations or something. He is almost eighty."

"There was no blood?" she heard herself asking.

He frowned, shaking his head. "No."

But that still didn't ease her mind. Werewolf blood dried to powder in the sunlight, making it often impossible to track a werewolf. It also made it difficult to analyze the blood to get the DNA. Two ways werewolves had remained hidden to the human world.

"Did you see anything?" she asked.

He shook his head again. "That's what's making this all a bit hard. I really think he was having a hallucination. Maybe the onset of Alzheimer's."

But Elizabeth didn't believe Jensen's grandfather had hallucinated the creature. Or rather she feared he hadn't.

But Brody couldn't be here, could he? A black wolf. That was how Brody appeared in his shifted form. She glanced over to Jensen, realizing they'd both been quiet.

Jensen lounged on her sofa, eyes nearly closed, but from under his lashes, he seemed to be studying her.

What was he thinking? She couldn't tell.

"What are you going to do?" she asked gently, resisting the urge to reach out and touch his hand.

He opened his eyes, offering her a sweet, tired smile.

"I don't know. He's stubborn, and he won't let me take him to the hospital. I didn't even suggest it. He'd be so livid—well, I just know he wouldn't agree to go. And in truth, it's the first time he's acted so strangely."

"Maybe—maybe he did see something."

Jensen shrugged. "Maybe. But there are no wolves in this part of West Virginia. What could it be?"

She regarded him, getting the feeling he was asking her more than the question revealed. But it could be her own guilt.

"Did I mention to you how gorgeous you look?" he murmured again when she didn't respond, looking at her from under dark lashes.

"Well, you could again," she said with a smile. She picked out the fitted black dress with him in mind. Him and his reaction.

He leaned in and kissed her. Yep, that was the reaction she'd hoped for, and suddenly thoughts of possible werewolves fled her mind. Jensen had a way of making her forget a lot of things.

He tasted her slowly until she was curled against him, tasting him back with the same lazy thoroughness.

"We don't have to go," she told him again.

"We do," he said with regretful smile. "You haven't met Molly yet. She'd never forgive me."

She smiled, loving the fact that he was so concerned with his receptionist's feelings. But Jensen was that way. Just . . . good.

Again, she felt like a complete liar and fraud for being what she was. But she pushed the thought away. She did deserve this time with him. She did deserve a little taste of the life she once thought she'd have.

"Not to mention," he added, straightening up, "my grandfather is going to be there, and I want to keep an eye on him."

"Your grandfather will be there? Does he know—you're bringing a date?"

"Actually, no. He will be thrilled."

"I don't know . . ."

Jensen straightened even further. "What?"

"I'm just afraid that I'm not what your grandfather would want for you."

His frown deepened for a fraction of a second, then he smiled. "Are you kidding? Granddad will love you."

She raised an eyebrow to that.

"Oh, believe me. He will."

She wasn't convinced, so instead of meeting his gaze, she looked down at her hands.

Jensen reached forward and caught her chin, raising her face to his. He leaned forward and kissed her. Just a quick, sweet brush of his lips against hers.

"You are nervous about this, aren't you?"

She nodded just slightly. "I'm not exactly the girl next door."

She sensed, rather than saw, his stillness.

"Why would you think that I want that, anyway?" he finally asked.

She shrugged. She didn't know what he wanted. Well, no, she did believe he wanted her, but she just knew he wouldn't if he knew the whole truth.

"I don't want the girl next door," he said, his voice just a tad more adamant than it needed to be. "I want you. And I want to show up at this party with you on my arm."

She smiled, although she was sure the gesture was rather lame.

"Besides," he added, "I've already met your brothers. I have the scars to prove it. Now it's your turn to meet my family."

"Well, your grandfather can't be any more scary than that."

"See."

Chapter 17

Elizabeth seriously started to doubt her prediction as soon as they pulled up to the party. The inn where the party was being held was beautiful. An old Victorian with a huge veranda, nestled on the edge of a lake. It was truly gorgeous, and the kind of place that she had not stepped foot into for two hundred years. Her time with the pack had been spent at much less reputable establishments. And even during her time away from them, she hadn't gone to such classy places.

Now she wondered if she'd avoided them because she didn't know how to handle herself any longer. But she didn't reveal her fears, at least not when Jensen came around to her side of the truck and helped her down.

"Nice, isn't it?" he said as he followed her stare.

She nodded. "It's beautiful."

They started up the flagstone path to the veranda, and with each step she felt like weights were tied to her new high heels.

"Are you okay?"

She nodded, even as she found it hard to pull in a breath. She didn't know how to handle this. This wasn't where she fit in any longer. She wanted to, but she could tell this was going to be a disaster.

Jensen held the door open for her; warmth and the smells

of wonderfully prepared food, along with the sound of voices and laughter, bombarded her.

She stopped, feeling like she was so close to her old life. So close, yet so far, and so painfully inept. She stood there, unable to make her feet move.

"Are you sure you're okay?"

She didn't respond immediately—it was as if too many memories she thought long dead were barraging her just as the sounds and smells had.

"Elizabeth?"

She blinked at him, seeing his green eyes first, then the worry there. She tried to focus on him, knowing her behavior was more than a little strange.

"I—umm—it's—"

"Jensen!" A voice beside them caused both of them to look in that direction. A woman in her fifties with short, bright red hair and glasses several shades darker beamed at him.

"Molly," Jensen greeted the older woman, leaning in to kiss her cheek. "You look lovely."

"As do you," the woman said, hugging Jensen with a fondness evident in their brief embrace. "I'm so glad you came. And," she turned her eyes to Elizabeth, "I'm so glad you brought a date."

The older woman extended her hand.

"I'm Molly George, Jensen's receptionist. And," she lowered her voice, "his grandfather's before him. But don't tell anyone. It will give away my age."

Elizabeth accepted her extended hand, just as a tall man, slightly balding with a very warm smile, appeared beside Molly.

"I think the fact that this is your twenty-fifth wedding anniversary hints at your age, darling."

Molly elbowed the man, then smiled. "I could have gotten married at twelve, thank you very much."

"True," the man agreed. "Jensen. I'm so glad you made it."

"Wouldn't have missed it," Jensen said. "Herb, this is Elizabeth."

Jensen watched as Elizabeth smiled warmly at the Georges. She congratulated them on their anniversary and thanked them for the invitation via him.

Within seconds, her nervousness disappeared. Molly and Herb were absolutely charmed.

He gazed at her, studying her genuinely sweet smile and her elegance and her warmth, and he certainly understood why his friends were reacting the way they were. He was charmed by her, too. Besotted, really.

When Molly and Herb left to greet other guests, Jensen caught her hand, pulling her closer.

"I thought you were nervous," he said.

"I was," she admitted. "Then I remembered how much I love parties."

He smiled at that. And as he moved around the room, he realized he'd discovered another facet to Elizabeth, yet another one he wouldn't have guessed. She was a natural-born hostess. She could charm even the most antisocial person within a matter of seconds.

But as he stood back and watched her chat with the stodgy old Bob Turner, he couldn't blame any person in the room for being drawn to her. She had a vivaciousness, a verve that couldn't be ignored.

Hadn't he seen all of that simply by looking into her eyes from across a dark, crowded bar.

"So, Molly says you actually brought a date to this shindig."

Jensen turned to see his grandfather clad in his seersucker suit that he only dragged out for ritzy events.

"Yes. I did actually bring a date."

"Where is she?"

Jensen gestured toward where Elizabeth stood. "Right there."

Granddad's eyes widened, and he let out a low whistle. "Holy smokes."

Jensen laughed. "Yeah. I have to admit I've had that same reaction several times since meeting her."

"Well, let's go rescue her from Bob. That old codger has got to be boring her to tears."

They walked up to Elizabeth, then waited for Bob, who rarely strung more than four words together, to finish up a riveting story about his last fishing trip with his buddy, Joe.

Finally, when the story drew to an end, with no discernable point, Jensen jumped in to grab her away.

"Please excuse me, Mr. Turner," she said with another of her lovely smiles. Old Bob looked totally smitten.

"Elizabeth, this is my grandfather, Charles Adler."

Granddad offered her a hand. "Oh, just call me Granddad."

Elizabeth beamed at him. "Hi, Granddad. It's wonderful to meet you. Your grandson had told me all about you."

"Is that so," Granddad said, giving Jensen a pointed look that meant that might have not been a good thing. "He hasn't told me very much about you. But that's my grandson. Too damned secretive."

Elizabeth's smiled slipped ever so slightly, and Jensen immediately wondered if she was hurt that he hadn't mentioned her. But before he could decide, her smile returned, wide and beautiful.

"Well, we haven't known each other that long."

Jensen realized her words were true, but given what they had shared, it seemed far longer than a handful of days.

"So, you will come over to our house tomorrow morning. I make a mean brunch."

Elizabeth grinned at Granddad, then glanced at Jensen to read how he felt about the idea. He nodded.

"I'd love to," she said.

"You know, Granddad, it is customary to invite a person you just met. Not order her."

"Not if you are damned intent on having that person where you want them," Elizabeth pointed out.

"See?" Granddad said with a smug waggle of his grayed brows.

Elizabeth laughed at the older man, obviously as delighted by him as he was with her.

Definitely a good thing, Jensen decided. It was good to have the people he cared about like each other. He glanced at Elizabeth. He did care about her. A lot. Again, the handful of days thing just didn't seem to matter. He knew what he felt.

"Now, if you two youngsters will excuse me, I have a dance saved for me by Heddy. I believe I will go claim it."

Elizabeth waved as Granddad beelined to his lady friend.

"He doesn't seem confused," Elizabeth said.

"No. He doesn't," Jensen agreed. "The thing is, he hasn't—until last night."

"Maybe . . . Maybe he wasn't last night, either." Elizabeth seemed reluctant to say that for fear he might think she was mad, too.

"Why? Have you seen anything around your place?"

She shook her head. "No. But . . ."

She shrugged, although the gesture seemed more like she didn't want to say something rather than she didn't know what to say.

"I just hope he's okay," she said finally.

Again he got the feeling there was more she wanted to say, but instead she turned to watch the couples dancing in the next room.

"Do you want to dance?" he asked as he saw her expression become almost wistful.

The wistfulness turned to eagerness in the space of a heartbeat.

"I haven't danced for years."

"Well, neither have I, so let's go figure out how again."

She glanced back at the dance floor, then nodded.

They stepped out among the twirling couples, taking hold of each other much like awkward teenagers at a high-school dance.

After a few graceless turns, he pulled back slightly. "This isn't going to work."

Elizabeth's face fell. "You don't like it?"

"Oh, I like dancing with you, but I don't want to hold you like this." He pulled her closer, still cradling her hand in his, but he brought her close enough that they touched chest to thigh, and he slid his other hand down until it was pressed to the small of her back, just above the subtle curve of her bottom.

"That *is* better," Elizabeth agreed as she rested her head on his shoulder and allowed him to lead.

"I've never danced like this," she murmured, her warm breath touching the skin of his throat.

Nor had he. Dancing had never aroused him like this, that was for sure.

"My brothers would have had me sent to the abbey if they'd seen me this close to a man at a party."

Jensen found the comment a tad odd in a way he couldn't quite pinpoint. Abbey? Maybe that was a British thing—she had said that was where she was raised.

"Well, hopefully they won't take the same measures they did last night."

She immediately lifted her head and the hand that she had resting on his shoulder, moving it downward, stroking over his back.

"Are you still hurting?"

He shook his head. "Nah, it takes more than a couple of brawny brothers to injure me."

He didn't even want to think about what his back looked

like now. This morning it had been several interesting shades of blue and purple.

"Well, they are more than that," she muttered, then seemed to realize she'd said the words aloud.

He started to ask what she meant, when the hand that was carefully exploring his back sank lower still, rubbing the indentation of his spine, just above the top of his pants.

He pulled in a steadying breath. Who even knew that was an erogenous zone? But then again, anywhere Elizabeth touched seemed to be pretty damned erogenous.

"Maybe we should go outside for a moment," he suggested, realizing his black dress pants were suddenly feeling quite snug. He had images of one of his clients coming up to discuss their beloved pet with his anatomy and trousers doing a fair impersonation of a pup tent.

When she gave him a curious look, he moved his pelvis just a bit closer so she could feel him, hard and ready.

Her eyes widened, but then a naughty smile turned up her lips. "I think you do need some air. Cold air."

"Very cold air," he agreed.

Linking hands, they strolled toward the door off the dance floor, which led to the veranda at the back of the inn. But he didn't stop there. Instead, he headed off the porch toward the lake.

Once on one of the little paths, with the lake in view, Jensen stopped and pulled Elizabeth back against him.

"I don't think this is going to solve your problem," she pointed out, even as she rubbed against him.

"Nope," he agreed readily and captured her mouth.

She moaned as his tongue parted her lips and brushed teasingly against hers. His hands roamed down over her, loving the way her slight curves felt under the silky material of her dress.

"This is where I'm pretty sure that I'm being brought to the garden to be ruined."

Ruined didn't really describe what he wanted to do to her, but he couldn't stop kissing the curve of her jaw and the arch of her neck to ask her about the curious wording.

From her small, panting breaths and the way her body arced and wiggled against his, she didn't seem inclined to think it was a bad thing, either.

His hands caught the rounded globes of her bottom, and he pulled her up tighter to his body.

Then, suddenly, Elizabeth froze, her body going absolutely rigid in his arms.

Jensen lifted his head, expecting someone to be there with them, but as he looked around, he saw no one.

"What's wrong?" he asked, frowning down at her shadowed features.

"Did you hear that?"

He listened, then shook his head. "No."

She remained silent, and then in the distance he heard a faint howl. Long and eerie, but far away.

"It's a dog."

Elizabeth remained absolutely still. Again, a howl sounded—the sound echoing as if it were miles away.

"I—I want to go in." She pulled out of his arms and hurried back toward the inn.

"Okay," he said, confused, to her retreating back.

But once inside, she seemed to calm immediately, making him wonder if she had a phobia of dogs or something. But again he did think of his grandfather's claim of seeing that black wolf. And as the paper stated, Granddad wasn't alone. Hell, Jensen half-thought he might have seen one, too. His gaze returned to Elizabeth.

"Are you okay?"

She nodded, bobbing her head almost too adamantly. "I guess I got a little nervous."

"About the howling or about us getting caught out there?"

"Getting caught," she said, but he felt as if she was just

grabbing on to that choice. Maybe she was afraid of dogs, and unwilling to tell him.

"Do you want a drink?"

She nodded. "Just water."

He left her, heading to the bar with the intent to get right back to her. She had truly been shaken out there. He wasn't sure if it was the dog barking or if it had been something else.

"I didn't think you were here," a familiar voice said from behind him. Jensen turned to see Brian, shifting uncomfortably in his navy blue suit.

"Hey. Yeah. You know I had to come. Where's Jill?"

"With Melanie." There was no doubt from the way Brian said the words that he'd already heard all the dirty details of his less-than-illustrious date with Melanie.

But even knowing that his friend knew, he had no idea what to say.

"So did you bring the other woman?"

The other woman. He didn't like that. Elizabeth was not the *other* woman. She was the only woman. And he didn't want her somehow judged for his behavior.

Jensen only nodded, though, and gestured to Elizabeth where she leaned against the wall, watching the party, looking distinctly uncomfortable. It was almost impossible to believe that earlier, she'd appeared to be the belle of the ball. Now she looked like she just wanted to leave.

"Wow, I wouldn't have pegged her as the one you'd be here with."

Jensen frowned at his friend. "What do you mean?"

"She's just a lot different, that's all. Not to say she isn't gorgeous."

Jensen bristled slightly. He wasn't sure what his friend was trying to say—all he knew was he didn't like it. And he didn't like the way his friend was regarding her, either. Brian's eyes seemed to be roaming over her slowly, taking in every detail. And the details were many. Like the fit of her simple black dress, the way the waistband nipped in to show the subtle flare of her hips. And how the neckline came to a deep vee between her rounded breasts, hinting at her cleavage but still intriguingly modest.

"You know," Brian said slowly, his eyes narrowing, "I think she was the woman from the karaoke bar that night who threw a guy away from her."

Whatever comment Jensen had expected his friend to make, that wasn't it.

"Elizabeth?" Jensen had forgotten about that. Or rather hadn't thought about it. But she was strong. He knew that. And hadn't Brian said she growled? Jensen had forgotten the strange growls he'd heard that night, before the weirdness and her fever.

Brian nodded, giving his friend a rather astounded look. "That woman is one tough cookie."

Jensen turned back to look at Elizabeth. He knew she was a tough cookie, and he did remember—very vividly, in fact—what she'd looked like in her leather pants and jacket. But now, in her classic and elegant cocktail dress with her often heartbreaking eyes and timid smiles, he had a hard time relating her to the woman at the bar that night.

"Are you sure it was her?" Hadn't he considered it might be her, too? The description had fit. Yet, he was still surprised to hear it again. Somewhere along the way, he'd even forgotten Brian's story. He couldn't connect the woman he knew to that image.

Brian nodded. "Definitely. I remember those eyes."

Jensen looked in her direction again and saw her watching them. She glanced away when she saw him looking. Another thing the woman from the bar wouldn't have done. The change was curious, and Jensen realized he was no less intrigued.

In fact, he was more so.

"Brian, would you excuse me?"

Brian nodded. Jensen headed to the bar and asked the server for an ice water. Then he hurried back to Elizabeth.

"Here you go."

"Thanks." She accepted the glass, taking a sip. "How was your friend?" She sounded casual, but Jensen got the impression there was more to the nonchalantly stated question.

"He was fine. I should have introduced you."

She nodded. "Is he married to the woman who sang at the bar? The brunette?"

He nodded. "Yes, Jill. We actually grew up together."

"He was surprised you were here with me, wasn't he?"

Jensen considered lying outright, but he got the feeling she would know if he did. So instead he asked, "Why do you think that?"

"It was pretty evident on his face."

That was true—it had been.

"Well, he can't believe you'd be here with me," he told her, hoping that would soothe her obviously injured feelings.

"That isn't true," she said softly, looking down at her glass. "And he's right. You shouldn't be here with me."

Elizabeth could tell her words confused him, although how they could was a mystery to her. Just the look of surprise on his friend's face said it all. Said exactly what she'd been saying before she got caught up in the fantasy of being normal and human and able to fit back into a world she thought was lost to her.

"Your friend was wondering why you would choose me over the blonde from the other night." It wasn't a question, although she knew Jensen would respond.

"No. He didn't say that."

"He said something, though, didn't he?"

"He said you were gorgeous."

She snorted at that, not caring that the sound was more than a little inelegant.

"You are."

"Okay," she said, not believing him. "But that isn't what he said."

"Actually, he did say that, but he did also say he was surprised at me. My friends have this set idea of 'my type' and they didn't think you fit into that."

She started to tell him she'd been right then, but he cut her off.

"But I think I know myself a hell of a lot better than they do. Way better, actually. And you are absolutely my type."

He moved closer to her, placing one of his broad hands against her back. "I can't remember being this attracted to anyone. Ever." He leaned closer, obviously about to kiss her. But before their lips met, she saw something there. Something mingling with his yearning. An almost-melancholy.

She told herself to turn away from his kiss. She needed to stick to her guns. This wasn't right for him. Agreeing to date him was just greed on her part. She was using him, and in truth, she liked him far, far too much to do that.

But instead of pulling away, she leaned into him, her lips meeting his. She made a small noise, a desperate noise, and his arms came around her.

Neither of them seemed to remember they were in the middle of a party. All they were aware of was each other.

"Elizabeth?" he murmured against her lips.

"Yes?"

"I think we should get out of here. Not because you aren't the right type for me. Not because of anything my friend said. But because I want you so damned much I can't even think straight."

She stared into his eyes, feeling like she was getting lost in the darkest, greenest forest. She nodded. She wanted nothing more.

Neither of them spoke to anyone as they slipped out of the party. Jensen rushed her to his truck, handing her in. She had some pretty fond memories of this truck. Naughty as they were.

"What are you smiling about?" Jensen asked as he slid up onto the seat.

"Nothing." Her smile grew.

"I get the feeling you might be laughing at me."

She immediately sobered. "No. Definitely not."

"So tell me."

She glanced at him, another naughty little grin curling her lips. "I'm thinking that maybe our second date is going to end very well."

Jensen smiled at that. "Really?"

"Oh yeah."

Chapter 18

Jensen managed to get them home ten minutes faster than it should have taken, and with no major traffic incidents, with the exception of a few sharply made turns. But his rather reckless driving did seem a little adolescent.

Until he shifted the truck into Park and turned to the woman next to him. Then it just seemed like a really good plan, because soon, he was going to be holding this gorgeous woman very close to him.

"Sorry about the kind of crazy driving," he did feel the need to say.

She smiled. "I didn't notice."

He knew she was lying, but he appreciated her trying to make him seem less desperate.

"Did you want to come in? I have some tea or coffee."

He nodded, finding the question a little funny. Of course he wanted to come in. And he wanted more than coffee or tea. He wanted her. Now.

Instead, he opened his door, hopped down, and came around to open the door for her. He took her hand and helped her down, fighting the urge to tug her close. Instead, he linked his fingers with her more slender ones and started across the lawn.

Neither of them spoke as they walked into the house. Elizabeth steered them toward the kitchen. She released his hand as she walked over to the counter.

"No tea," she said after perusing her cupboards. "But I do have coffee."

"Coffee's great," he said, surprised after the times they had been together that he actually felt a little nervous at the prospect of it happening again. It made no sense, except that every time he was with her, he felt like he was in a little deeper.

Hell, he knew he was in deep. He wanted that—and that scared him.

She crossed to her counter and began to prepare the hot drink, bending forward to grab filters and then to fill the carafe with water. The angle gave him a perfect view of her perfectly rounded bottom against the silky fabric of her dress.

She moved to peer into the fridge.

"I only have milk," she said, glancing at him over her shoulder.

His eyes immediately moved up to meet hers, and he knew his expression was one of guilt.

"I take my coffee black."

She gave him a slight smile, then ducked back into the fridge. And this time he could have sworn she wiggled her hips a little as she searched.

He smiled. All of the Elizabeth he'd first met was not gone, which was definitely not a disappointment. Then again, nothing about Elizabeth was a disappointment. She was perfect. Although she often didn't seem to realize that.

She straightened and took the milk carton to the counter and opened a drawer to rummage for a spoon. He didn't wander closer, afraid that if he did, he'd have to touch her.

She turned to him, leaning against the counter. The only sound was the hiss and pop of the brewing coffee. They just looked at each other, not speaking, just wanting each other.

The coffee hissed loudly, indicating it was done. She smiled at him, the sight making his body tighten with desire. She turned back to the counter and filled two mugs. Then she strolled toward him, holding out one for him.

Their fingers brushed lightly, teasingly, as he accepted it.

"It's a really nice night," she said. "Would you like to go sit on the porch swing?"

Now that seemed like an innocent enough thing to do. The kind of thing that parents had allowed their dating teens to do for generations. Surely that was safe.

"That sounds like a great idea."

She led him back to the large porch attached to the front of the house. On one end, a wooden swing cushioned with floral pillows swung slightly in the breeze.

He waited for her to sit, then settled beside her, trying to keep a little space between them. The swing creaked as they rocked in a slow, steady rhythm. Even that made him think of what he'd like to be doing with and to Elizabeth at this very moment.

He closed his eyes just briefly, trying to push the idea out of his mind. Then he took a swallow of the hot, richly bitter brew.

"This is nice," she said, sounding far calmer than he felt.

"Yes."

They swayed back and forth, the sound of the breeze in the trees, the low squeak of the swing. All of it should have been lulling, calming. But all Jensen could feel was the heat radiating from Elizabeth's body. The smell of her—the rich, spicy scent. All he could think about was how much he wanted her.

But he had to stay cool.

"Jensen?"

"Mmm," he said, then took a sip of his coffee, trying to focus on that rather than his own damned libido, which was in overdrive, and had been all night long.

"I think . . . I think we should . . ."

He glanced at her, and she leaned forward and kissed him. It was a quick kiss, not at all like the long, slow kiss they had shared outside at the anniversary party. But somehow, it was far more telling.

"I know I told you that I was ashamed of my behavior when I first met you. And I still can't explain it, but the truth is . . . I just want you far too much to do this slow thing."

He stared at her. Holy monkey.

"Elizabeth . . ."

She placed her fingers up to his lips, the gesture designed to shush him, but the touch reminded him so much of the very first time she'd touched him.

"Tonight," she said, her finger a cool and pleasing pressure on his mouth. "Tonight you let me experience something I thought I'd lost."

He didn't understand. He had no idea what he'd let her experience.

"I'm . . ." She shook her head. "I'm just crazy about you."

She sighed, like saying those words had been so hard for her. And maybe they had. He could understand that. There was something between them that was confusing and overwhelming and . . .

He leaned in and kissed her. This time the gesture wasn't quick, but slow and thorough and filled with everything he was feeling. He stopped long enough to take her coffee cup and place it on the floor beside his. Then his hands were back on her, caressing her. His lips found hers again.

She moaned and arced into him. Their lips played over each other's, velvety-soft skin creating a gentle friction that ignited Jensen's desire as sure as flint against steel.

He pulled her closer until she was halfway onto his lap. The swing squeaked under them and shimmied under the sudden movement.

He touched the bare skin of her shoulders, her smooth flesh cool from the night air.

"Are you too cold?" he murmured against her lips.

She lifted her head, her eyes wide. "Are you kidding?"

He chuckled, then kissed her again. She tugged at his tie,

loosening the knotted material; then her fingers moved to the buttons, working them until her hands were stroking over his chest.

His lips moved from her lips to her throat, then to the creamy skin exposed by the vee neck of her dress.

Her hands continued to touch him as he explored the swell of her breasts with his lips and his tongue.

Quickly their exploring grew more frantic, until both of them were panting, their movements jerky and excited.

"Stand up," he muttered roughly, the command gruffer than he intended.

She didn't seem to notice. She simply did as he asked.

Jensen reached for the fluttering material of her skirt, lifting it so he could see her hose and the small, lacy panties underneath. His fingers moved to them, slowly rolling them down her long legs, until she was bared to his touch. He stroked her. Feeling her heat, her moisture. Then he pulled her onto him, so she straddled him.

"I'll take my time next time," he told her in between kissing her lips. She nodded, seeming to share the same need.

Her finger went to his belt, then his pants. Soon he was freed, and she positioned him to enter her.

But once he was deep inside her, neither of them felt the need to hurry. They rocked together, their bodies undulating, their eyes locked as they watched each other.

A slow swing into total bliss. And Jensen knew he was lost. He loved this woman.

She lifted her head from his shoulder, her eyes holding his. And for a second, he nearly said the words aloud, but then her gaze broke from his, her pale eyes wide as she stared out at the darkened lawn.

"What?" He followed her stare, his eyes finally adjusting to see what she saw.

"We have an audience."

He nodded. "Why, yes, we do."

They both watched as two deer moved farther onto the

lawn. Munching on bits of still-green grass, watching them back.

"Maybe we should go inside," he suggested.

"Yes," she agreed, scrambling off his lap. "I suddenly feel like dinner theater."

Jensen laughed. "Yes, and what I have in mind next is for your eyes only."

She grinned in return, but her eyes returned to the deer. Jensen got the feeling the sight shook her a little, and he wondered why.

Brody paced back and forth at the edge of the woods, watching the couple as they rose, not even bothering to adjust their clothing, and disappear inside. The two deer that had wandered onto the large lawn remained stock-still, except for their ears. He growled low in his throat, his teeth gnashing, and they took off across the lawn in the opposite direction.

Those stupid animals had some sense, unlike Lizzie and her mortal, Brody thought.

He was going to kill them both. The animal in him demanded that kind of revenge for what that mortal had done to his mate.

He stopped his pacing, to stare at the house and to rest. The shot that old man had taken at him had hit almost dead-on. Even now, he knew the bullet was still lodged under his ribcage. It had come dangerously close to his heart. He didn't need a doctor to tell him that. And it still hurt like hell. That old bastard was going to die, too. Slowly.

He eased down into a position like the Sphinx, his paws out in front of him, his pose upright. This pose didn't ease the pain much, but it was better than the pacing. And he had to give himself time to heal a little. Staying in his wolf form would help him heal. For some reason, the werewolf form healed much faster than the human.

He growled again. See, even the human form of a werewolf was weaker. And full humans were weaker still. That lowly mortal who Lizzie had mated with was going to be damned easy to kill.

He just needed to heal more before he tried. He couldn't risk Lizzie discovering him and going into her werewolf form. Brody was the far stronger wolf, but wounded like he was, Lizzie might have a fighting chance. And he wasn't risking it. He wanted to see that human torn to shreds. And he wanted Lizzie to see it happen. Then she would know better than to go looking for a mate elsewhere. But then he was going to kill her, too. Unless she agreed to his terms. All of them.

He ducked his head, trying to lick the place where the bullet had entered him, but he couldn't reach it. Being able to tend it would also make it heal quicker. But for now, it appeared he'd just have to be patient.

And there was no reason not to be. The deed was already done. Nothing that happened between Lizzie and her mortal tonight would add to that.

Oh, she was going to pay for every indiscretion. But he did need her. She was his only chance to get back into the pack. As much as he hated it, he needed her.

"Hmm," Granddad said, looking up from his crossword puzzle. "I didn't think you'd both be showing up for brunch. I sort of thought one of you would already be here to actually help me."

Jensen smiled at his granddad, knowing the old man was probably thrilled he hadn't come home last night, old matchmaker that he was.

Elizabeth, on the other hand, blushed to a brilliant shade of red.

Jensen pulled her tight to his side, charmed and amazed that this woman could be the wild lover she'd been last night and then be so easily embarrassed this morning. He loved how mercurial she was. It fascinated him.

"I can help you," she said, trying to pull out of his embrace to go to the counter already laden with the makings of a huge meal.

"Nonsense," Granddad said adamantly. "You are the guest. Jensen can help me. I've taught him how to cook with the best of them."

Elizabeth looked like she wanted to argue, but then she admitted, "It might be best if I do stay out of the way. I'm a pretty horrible cook. Which is strange, because I love to eat."

Jensen smiled. Most women wouldn't admit that. And he'd seen Elizabeth's appetite—she did like food.

Her admission caught Granddad's attention for a different reason, however. "Do you want a lesson?"

Elizabeth's eyes widened at the prospect. "You would be willing to show me?"

"Sure. Nothing to cooking, really."

"That's not true," Elizabeth said with a frown. "Cooking is a real talent. I try, but I'm a disaster."

"Well, you haven't tasted my cooking," Granddad pointed out. "I might be, too."

"But I have tasted Jensen's, and if you taught him what he knows, you've got to be quite a chef."

"Jensen, you got yourself a beauty and a charmer in this one." Granddad nodded his approval, then directed Elizabeth over to the counter.

Deciding his granddad had just stolen his woman, at least for a while, he settled down at the table to read the newspaper. Which turned out to be impossible. The interaction between his grandfather and Elizabeth was far too entertaining.

"Just break it into here?" Elizabeth held an egg as if she thought it might spontaneously explode in her hand. She waved it gently in the direction of a mixing bowl.

"Yes. Right in there."

She hesitated, then tapped the shell delicately on the rim. The egg barely cracked. She tapped it again, this time with more force and the egg cracked totally, bits of shell going into the bowl with the yolk and white.

"Oh no," she said, sounding so endearingly disheartened that Jensen had to smile.

"Not a problem," Granddad said, his tone kind, just like he'd been with Jensen all through his childhood.

Granddad showed her how to pick out the shells and had her break another egg and another until Elizabeth could crack an egg like a pro.

Elizabeth smiled at Jensen as if she'd conquered the world. Jensen couldn't help but grin back. He suddenly saw her right here every morning. The image should have scared him, but it simply felt—right.

Before long, Elizabeth was serving platters of pancakes and omelets and bacon.

"This looks great. I would say you're a natural." Jensen snagged a piece of bacon off the plate.

"Who knew?" she said with another triumphant grin.

She waited until Granddad joined them before she sat down.

Granddad passed Elizabeth the platter of pancakes. "Go ahead—taste how good your cooking is."

She smiled and plunged a fork into the golden cakes, scooping up two. She added them to her plate, then moved to take some of the omelet and then some of the bacon. She topped all of that off with some hash browns.

Jensen watched her add a generous amount of real maple syrup to the pancakes.

She paused as she saw him watching her. Her cheeks colored a rosy pink as she self-consciously set the syrup down.

"Sorry," she murmured. "I don't know how to cook, but I know how to eat."

Jensen's smile broadened even more. He really did find it refreshing to hear a woman say that. But rather than tell her that, he reached for the bottle of amber syrup.

"I like to eat, too."

He doused his own pancakes with nearly as much as she'd used. Then he dug in, trying to show her that he had no problem with her eating habits.

She picked up her fork, toying briefly with the crispy edge of the pancake. Then she cut into it, scooping a small portion into her mouth. Her eyes closed with appreciation as she slowly chewed the food.

"Good, huh?" Granddad said, a slight curve to his lips as he also watched her. He looked nearly as entranced as Jensen.

She opened her eyes and nodded. "Delicious."

"And you made them."

"With your help," she pointed out.

Granddad shrugged. "I just directed, you did the work." He took a bite of the omelet. "And you did a damned fine job."

Her smile broadened, but then she was lost to the lure of her food.

The conversation was easy and natural as they demolished the brunch, all of them doing their fair share to clean the plates.

Granddad leaned back, tossing his napkin onto the table. "I bet that is the most action this table has seen in years."

Jensen nearly choked on a sip of coffee. Elizabeth shifted, again toying with her silverware and making no eye contact.

Granddad straightened, his far-too-observant gaze straying from Jensen to Elizabeth, then back to Jensen. He remained silent for a moment, obviously trying to decipher what had changed the comfortable atmosphere of the room. Finally he stood.

"Jensen, you haven't showed Elizabeth around the house. Why don't you do that, while I clean up."

"I'll clean up," Jensen said. "You and Elizabeth cooked. I'll do the dishes."

Granddad shook his head. "Nope. I've got it. You two go find something fun to do."

Jensen considered arguing further, but the set of his grand-father's jaw told him it would be wasted breath.

He turned to Elizabeth. "Would you like to see the house?"

Elizabeth was sure that her face was still bright red from his grandfather's table comment. She'd wanted to crawl under the table as images of what she and Jensen had done on that table flashed through her mind. She knew from Jensen's star-tled look that his mind had gone in the exact same direction.

Fortunately, Jensen's lovely grandfather had sensed the sudden tension and had given them an out.

"I'd love to see the rest of the house," she said, managing to keep her voice even. Although she was starting to feel like, when things went well, something always happened to re-mind her of what she was. Of who she was. She just didn't know how this could work.

Jensen stood and waited for her to rise as well. Then he steered her toward the kitchen door.

Elizabeth stopped and glanced at the older man. "Are you sure you don't want some help?"

He shook his head, already rinsing bowls and placing them in the dishwasher. "I've got it. You two go."

She nodded. "Thank you for the cooking lesson."

"Thank you for getting my grandson to stop acting like a zombie."

At that comment, Jensen caught her fingers and tugged her from the room.

She followed, but her mind was on that last comment.

"This is the living room, which I think you saw briefly the night you came over here."

"Why were you acting like a zombie?"

Jensen laughed slightly, but the sound seemed strained to her ears. "My granddad has a strange sense of humor."

Elizabeth hadn't found his sense of humor odd. And the comment hadn't been said as a joke. But it didn't appear that she was going to get an answer from Jensen.

"This is the den." He flipped on a light, and stepped back to let her peek inside. She got the vague impression of dark wood, books, and a marble fireplace.

"Nice," she said, her thoughts still on why Jensen had been a zombie. What had happened to him? The idea that something had caused him to stop living, stop being the vivacious, happy person she knew, bothered her deeply.

He led her to the stairs.

"Just ignore the walls here."

"Why?" she asked, then realized the answer. The wall, all the way up the staircase, was scattered with pictures. Mostly of Jensen. From a baby to . . . a picture that looked like it may have been taken fairly recently. A picture of him with his grandfather, both of them in thigh-high wading boots, holding up a large fish.

But what captured her attention were the pictures of him as a child. She stopped in front of each one, taking in the way his cocky smile was already established, even at four years old. Of course, it grew more handsome, more irresistible with each passing year.

"Look at you in this one," she exclaimed, leaning in to study a picture of him at about nine years old, dressed in a white lab coat with a surgeon's mask tied around his neck along with a stethoscope, and a plastic toy doctor's bag in his hand.

"Were you already practicing to be a vet?"

Jensen stared at the picture for a moment, then offered her a lopsided smile that, while it contained his usual charm, didn't seem to reach his eyes.

"Yes. Although I think I was already practicing my plan to get all the girls to play doctor."

She turned to face him, cocking an eyebrow. "Really?"

"Mm—hmm. Want to come to my bedroom and play?" He leaned in and kissed the side of her neck, his tongue darting out to taste the sensitive skin.

She pulled in a hitched breath, desire zipping through every nerve-ending of her body.

"Jensen," she managed to murmur. "Your granddad."

He lifted his head, listening. "I can hear him in the kitchen." His lips returned to her neck, then moved up to nip her earlobe.

Again another zing of need whizzed through her, and again she breathed out brokenly.

"Come on," he said, his soft words tickling her ear. "I'll show you my bedroom."

She smiled. "You are bad."

"Only with you."

For some reason, his words gave her pause—a feeling she couldn't quite place blotted out some of her desire. Fear, maybe, or worry. Was she making him bad? Was her past somehow affecting him? Making him not act like the person he really was?

Jensen didn't give her much of a chance to consider that idea. He led her right to one of the doorways along the upstairs hallway. Once inside, he closed it soundly behind them and pulled her back into his arms. This time, his lips captured hers fully, the supple softness of them brushing and teasing until she lost all thoughts but opening for him and tasting him back.

"This is my room," he finally murmured against her lips.

"It's nice," she said, her lips curving against him. He kissed her again.

She wasn't even aware that Jensen was walking her backward until her thighs hit something and she sat down on his bed. She laughed up at him, feeling quite naughty herself. He grinned back, then followed her down, his lips tasting her again as his weight pinned her down.

They lay on the bed, kissing, their hands exploring each other over their clothes.

"You know," he said, pulling back to look at her, "this bed has seen a lot less action than the kitchen table."

"Really?" She tried not to laugh. "I'm sorry."

"Well, I was thinking you could rectify that for me."

She gave him a dubious look. "Jensen, your grandfather is right downstairs."

"Yes. But I happen to know that he's going golfing in . . ." He glanced at the digital alarm clock shaped like a football on the nightstand. "About ten minutes. So if we are just quiet . . ."

He started to kiss her again, but this time she placed a hand in the center of his chest to stop him. "I don't know."

He smiled in that way she found utterly irresistible. "I'll make it worth your while."

She laughed. "I have no doubt about that." She couldn't help wiggling against him. God, he made her so hot. He truly was the sexiest man she'd ever seen.

He tensed against her wiggle, and she expected him to kiss her again, but instead he pushed off the bed and headed to the door. He turned the lock, then strode back to where she lay sprawled on the bed.

"There. I think we're safe."

She didn't know about that, and she was still rather embarrassed that Jensen's sweet granddad was probably very aware of what they were doing up here, but then, he was also aware that she and Jensen had spent the night together. And she didn't think the older man thought they'd just been talking then, either.

He started to crawl back onto the bed, when there was a sharp rap on the newly locked door. Both of them froze, even though they were completely clad, and not even in the process of doing something sexual.

"Jensen?" It was his grandfather.

Jensen glanced at Elizabeth, then climbed off the bed. Elizabeth sat up and straightened her clothes. Jensen smoothed down several tangled locks of her hair, then went to the door.

When he opened it, it was his granddad who looked decidedly awkward. He held out the cordless phone.

"A horse emergency," he explained quietly.

Jensen accepted the phone. "I'll be right back," he told Elizabeth.

She nodded and waved for him to go.

Jensen stepped out of the room, saying hello.

Granddad gave Elizabeth a smile that still looked as if he felt a tad uncomfortable interrupting them.

"Did you want help now with the kitchen?" she asked, hoping to dispel the awkwardness of the moment.

"All done," he assured her. "I'm actually meeting a friend for golf. Will you be all right waiting for Jensen?"

She nodded. "Absolutely. Have a good time."

He nodded in return. "I'm sure I'll see you later."

"Yes."

After he left, and she heard him climbing down the stairs, she rose from the bed. For the first time, she really looked at Jensen's bedroom, the bedroom that he obviously had during his childhood. And from the looks of it, not much had changed. The walls were covered with pennants from sporting teams. A baseball bat and mitt sat beside his bureau, probably untouched since his high-school days.

She wandered over to the bookcase near the windows, seeing college textbooks mixed in with books he probably read in high school. *Heart of Darkness, Billy Budd, Collected Works of Shakespeare. The Hardy Boys.*

She smiled, imagining him lying in that bed at all of eleven or twelve reading about Joe and Frank Hardy.

She picked up one of the books, flipping the pages, the scent of old paper wafting out from the covers. She put it back.

She strolled around a bit more, then returned to the bed, lounging back against the headboard. She was tired, she realized. But that made sense. She'd gotten very little sleep last night. Both she and Jensen had been insatiable.

She smiled at the memory. He was a talented man.

She glanced at the clock, wondering if it was far too early

in the day to sneak a nap. She chuckled aloud at the football clock. Then her gaze dropped, noticing a picture frame placed facedown on the nightstand.

Almost reluctantly, she reached out and picked up the picture. It was Jensen with a pretty blonde. From the look of them, it was probably taken a few years ago. There was a fullness to Jensen's face that was gone now, hinting at his youth.

But it was the blonde that Elizabeth couldn't stop staring at. She was very pretty with long, very pale hair. Her eyes were a guileless sky blue, her smile truly happy. Jensen had his arm around her, but something in their stance spoke of a more intimate connection than the pose showed.

Elizabeth stared at it a moment longer, then put it back the way she'd found it.

She pulled in a deep breath, trying not to think about that picture. Trying not to question why the relatively innocuous photo had shaken her.

She leaned her head back, staring blankly out at the room. Who was that girl? Had she been someone important to Jensen? Obviously, he still had the photo on his nightstand. But why was it facedown?

As she wondered, she noticed something on the top shelf of his bookcase. A book, or rather what appeared to be a photo album, pink. Very out of place with all the other books on the shelf.

Even as she told herself not to, she pushed off the bed and walked over to reach for the book.

Chapter 19

It was a photo album, obviously hand-decorated with red hearts and white lace.

She hesitated; again telling herself she should put it back. This was Jensen's private property. But her hands didn't seem willing to listen.

She flipped open the book, her eyes slowly scanning the pictures and the captions and the little decorations added to the pages. She turned another page and another, until she had seen the whole book. And though mainly filled with photos, the book told a very vivid story.

The story of a boy and a girl who had been madly in love. The story of two people who planned to be together forever. Proms, parties. The beach with friends, graduation, heading away to college. And every picture stated one thing very, very clearly.

Jensen had loved the girl who made this book. It was clear in every single picture. There in his dark green eyes. There in that cocky smile.

And the girl had loved him just as completely.

Whoever came up with the adages that pictures don't lie and a picture is worth a thousand words had known what they were talking about.

She flipped through the album one more time, even though it hurt her. Although it had no right to—she knew that. But it did.

She was carefully placing the book back where she'd found it as Jensen walked back into the room. She spun to face him, but he didn't seem to note the guilt in her demeanor.

"Sorry about that. One of my patients has a sick mare. I think I'm going to have to go out to his farm and check the horse out."

"Okay," Elizabeth agreed, feeling the need to get away from Jensen for a little while. She felt shaken by those pictures, which she knew was unfair. Of course Jensen had had a life before her. She was being ridiculous.

"Why don't you come with me," Jensen said as he went to the closet and pulled out a large black bag.

That suggestion pulled her from her shaken thoughts. "Oh, I don't think that's a good idea."

"It's fine. I think I know what's wrong with the horse. And if I'm right, it won't take long at all. Then we can sneak back here and show my poor neglected bed some action."

He grinned at her, a sweet, teasing smile.

"I don't think so."

"Why not? The beauty of being a vet is that my patients don't mind who I bring along with me."

She raised a dubious eyebrow. "You might be surprised."

A werewolf was definitely a guest most animals did mind tagging along. A lot.

"Are you afraid of horses?"

The question startled her. She was so focused on them being scared of her, she didn't realize Jensen would think it might be vice versa.

"No. I used to love horses." She'd once had the prettiest, sweetest-tempered mare. She realized that was the first time she'd thought of Sunny in decades. Although she had wondered, when she'd first changed over, what happened to her dear horse. She needed to ask her brothers what happened to her.

"Used to? Did you get injured by one?"

"No. I . . ." Another thing she couldn't explain, not fully, not totally honestly. The open smile of the blonde in the pictures appeared in her mind. "I just haven't been around them for a very long time."

Jensen caught her fingers, pulling her toward the door. "Then you should come with me."

He hurried her down the stairs and to his truck as if he knew she would argue. Once she was deposited onto the seat and he was inside as well with the engine running, she did try to change his mind.

"Animals tend to be very skittish around me."

Jensen gave her a disbelieving look. "Yeah, so I've noticed."

"Why do you say that?"

"Because you have owls and skunks hanging out in your barn while you work. Because deer come right up to your porch. And if I recall correctly, a mouse was on your kitchen counter this morning, like it was your pet."

"That was all very, very unusual." Okay, even he found those animals' behaviors odd, and he didn't have the whole story.

But horses seemed to be particularly sensitive to werewolves. She didn't know why.

"I'll just wait in the truck. I think that's the best plan."

He looked like he wanted to argue, but he only nodded.

After a few more turns, he pulled the truck up to a white farmhouse with black shutters. A man came out to meet them before Jensen could even hop out of the truck.

"Lee, is the horse worse?" Jensen asked, reaching back into the truck for the black bag.

"'Bout the same. I'm just coming out to tell you that Missy just called, and she can't get the old station wagon started. She's over in Hillsboro with the kids, so I'm going to have to head over there. Are you okay to tend Ginger without me?"

"Sure. Go on. I have Elizabeth with me if I need someone to help hold her."

Lee, a man in his late thirties with salt-and-pepper hair and a lined, leathered face, nodded at her and tipped his worn cowboy hat. "I appreciate you coming over here on a Saturday."

"Not a problem," Jensen said. "Go on. I'll handle the mare."

"She's being more than a little ornery. Be careful. I really do hate to leave."

"It's fine," Jensen assured him, not seeming the least bit worried about the owner's warning.

Lee thanked him again and then loped toward a beat-up pickup truck that seriously looked like it had no more hope of starting than the mentioned old station wagon. But the ancient vehicle did start, rumbling grumpily as Lee turned out onto the main road.

Jensen started toward the barn, and she remembered his past mention of getting kicked in the head by a horse once. Although she really didn't believe she could be the slightest bit of help—in fact, she might just make matters worse—she had to call after him.

"Wait!"

Jensen stopped, turning to look at her.

She opened the door and jumped down from the truck. "I want to go. I don't think I'll be much help, but at least I can call 911 if this crazed horse injures you."

Jensen shook his head. "Elizabeth, if the horse is really going to make you nervous, then you don't have to go."

"Whatever. You dragged me here. I'm going."

Jensen waited for her to join him, and laughed at her disgruntled mutter.

As they approached the barn, Elizabeth tensed, her steps slowing. All she needed was for this poor horse to go totally wild and really hurt Jensen. Still, she felt she had to be there. Jensen shouldn't be alone with an animal that was unpredictable.

She thought of her behavior that night that she'd started to change, the night that she still believed she could stay away from this man. He'd been as close to a feral, dangerous animal as he could get. Thank God she'd somehow controlled herself. Even now, she shivered at what could have happened if she'd totally shifted.

Jensen pushed open the large barn door and headed straight to the last stall.

"Have you been here before?" she asked, casting a wary glance at the few horses that bobbed their heads over the stall gates. They sniffed the air, their large nostrils flaring and twitching as she passed. But none reacted with fear.

"Yes. And I know that Lee puts his sick horses in the last stall. It has a little more space than some of the others."

He stopped at the stall he mentioned, opening it slowly. Before he stepped inside, he spoke to the horse low and even. Most of his words were reassurances that he wouldn't hurt the ailing animal, but it wasn't the words the animal would react to, it was his tone.

He also kept his movement slow and fluid. Nothing to jar, nothing that would threaten. He set down his bag and then carefully reached for the animal's nose. He touched it, murmuring more quiet reassurances.

Then he turned to Elizabeth. "I really think she'd be okay for me to look at alone, if you are nervous."

"No," she said, keeping her voice low, too. "I'm okay." In fact, she was fascinated, watching him work. His gentleness, his calmness soothed her, too.

He left the horse and went to his bag. When he unzipped it, the horse shifted a little, reacting to the sound.

Jensen stopped and again talked quietly to the animal, although this time the horse didn't seem to respond so readily. She pranced just a bit, her ears pulling back.

"Shh," Jensen said, easing open his bag and pulling out two syringes. "Shh, big girl. I'm just going to take a little blood and then give you a shot of something that will make you feel better."

The horse pranced more, and Elizabeth thought her huge brown eyes were getting a wild glint to them.

Jensen continued to talk calmly as he readied the syringes. The horse seemed to respond a little, but when Jensen rose, though he also kept that movement fluid, the horse pranced back, her nostrils flaring, a huffing noise escaping her.

Jensen didn't back away, but he didn't move forward, either. "Elizabeth," he said, not looking at her but keeping his eyes trained on the animal, "I think I might need you. But if she gets too agitated, I'll just have to wait until Lee gets back."

Elizabeth hesitated, afraid that she was the problem. She didn't believe approaching the horse would really help.

Still, she could see that Jensen did need help. And if she agitated the horse more, then he'd leave with her and wait for the owner.

Carefully, she stepped into the stall, the hay under her feet making her approach noiseless. She stopped a few feet from the animal, suddenly a little scared that she might get trampled.

The horse whipped her large head in her direction, eyes definitely hinting at wildness, maybe only the kind of madness that accompanied illness, but Elizabeth still had to fight to keep from backing away.

Instead, she held out her palm to the animal. The mare's nose flared, then twitched; then, to her utter amazement, the horse stepped forward and nuzzled her palm.

She rubbed the velvety nose, remembering how much she'd loved petting Sunny. The horse stepped closer, seeming to want more from her.

She stroked up her forehead and back down. She murmured to the animal, telling her how pretty she was. How good. All the while, the horse nuzzled her back.

"Okay. Done."

Elizabeth blinked and turned to gape at Jensen. He was moving back to his bag to drop the empty antibiotic syringe and blood sample into his bag.

"You already did it?" She blinked again. "She didn't even react."

Jensen grinned at her. "She was too busy adoring you."

As if in agreement, the horse nuzzled her hair, the brush of her velvety nose making Elizabeth giggle.

Jensen looped his medical bag on his shoulder, then moved to pet the horse, who didn't even acknowledge the touch. He stepped out of the stall and waited for Elizabeth.

Elizabeth whispered good-bye to the sweet horse. Then she stepped outside, too. Jensen secured the gate.

"You should have told me you're a horse whisperer," he said as they left the barn.

"I didn't know I was." She was shocked at how the horse had reacted.

"Well, I think I'm going to have to get you on payroll. You'd sure save me lots of injuries from kicks and bites."

She was sure the horse's reaction had been a fluke. Like the other animals. Although how many flukes could she have?

"Well, I just need to drop this blood sample off to the lab I use in West Pines—then I'm yours for the day."

Elizabeth smiled at his offer, but again she wondered about the blonde in the photos. He'd sure looked like he was hers. Totally hers.

It wasn't even fair to wonder about that woman and what had happened. After all, she'd been far from open with Jensen. She had more secrets than he could ever have. Whoever the blonde was, she hadn't been who Brody was to her.

She was practically married. There hadn't been any vows, there was no ring, but in many ways what she'd agreed to in mating with Brody was even more binding.

Jensen talked to her about what he thought was wrong with the horse—likely an easily treated infection. Elizabeth nodded and made the appropriate responses, but still her mind swirled around who the blonde had been.

Jensen pulled up to a medical lab that handled his animal bloodwork, too. He labeled and enveloped the sample and put it in the dropbox.

"Okay," he said as he slid back into the truck. "What should we do now? I must admit I'm feeling a little disappointed that we didn't get to play doctor."

Elizabeth smiled—she knew he could play vet with her anytime.

"What's going on?" Jensen asked, turning slightly in the seat to face her. "You have been preoccupied since we left the horse."

She didn't answer, afraid if she opened her mouth questions that she had no right to ask would pop out.

"Before we left the house," he added. "On the ride to Lee's, I thought you were just nervous. But now, I think something was bothering you. Still is."

She shook her head. "No. It's just . . . who is the girl in the picture by your bed?"

Jensen straightened as if her question physically hit him.

"I'm sorry," she said immediately. "I shouldn't have asked."

But Jensen was already shaking his head. "No. I forgot that picture was there. It was just an old—girlfriend."

Elizabeth could tell from the hesitation in his answer there was more to it. Was she the one who got away? Did he still love her? She didn't have a right to know. She didn't.

"I also saw the photo album that I guess she must have made." God, what was she doing? "You look like you were pretty serious."

Jensen didn't respond for a moment. His eyes remained focused straight ahead as if he was studying something of great interest outside the car.

Finally he cleared his throat. "Yeah. We were pretty serious. Very serious, and she, umm, died."

A strange mixture of pain and jealousy raced through her. He'd loved that woman and she'd died. It was horrible. Yet all she could think was that he wasn't over her. He still loved her. And if she were alive, Elizabeth would not be in this truck with him.

She made a slight noise, appalled at her own selfishness. Her endless selfishness. She was jealous of a dead woman, yet she was the one with a mate. At least Jensen was unattached, even if it wasn't of his own will.

God, she needed to get away. She needed to sort out all the crazy thoughts swirling in her head.

"I—I think I should maybe go home."

She expected Jensen to argue. To tell her more about the blonde. But instead, all he did was nod and turn on the ignition.

Neither spoke as he drove toward her house. She wanted to, but now, when it seemed very necessary, her wayward mouth wouldn't work. It seemed her body was never in control of itself.

Jensen still didn't say anything as he pulled up to her house and shifted the truck into Park. This time he didn't turn off the ignition, she noticed. Her uncooperative mouth might want to talk to him, but it was more than obvious he didn't want to talk to her.

She opened her door, also noting for the first time that he didn't jump out to open it for her. Not that she could expect that when he so obviously wanted to flee.

She slid out of the vehicle and nearly had the door shut before he said, "I'll see you later."

It was a feeble promise, as far as promises went, but she grasped on to it like a lifeline.

"Yes. Call me later."

He nodded, although his face was grim. No cocky smile. No twinkle in his green eyes.

Still, she held on to his words, praying they were true. She couldn't lose him. She couldn't.

She smiled, knowing the gesture was as weak as his words. Then she closed the door.

She didn't even get inside the house before he shifted the car into Reverse and backed out of her driveway, escaping her in a spray of gravel.

Chapter 20

Jensen pulled into his driveway and sat there. *Just go back.* Images of Elizabeth's uncertain expression haunted him. The wary way she'd looked at him as she'd gotten out of his car. The way she'd seemed almost desperate when he said he'd see her later.

She was confused by his reaction. Hell, *he* was confused. When she'd asked about Katie, it was almost as if she'd brought another world into their relationship. A world that she wasn't a part of, and he didn't want her to be.

But why shouldn't Elizabeth know about Katie? She had a right to be curious. He was curious as hell about her other men. She'd never mentioned any, but he did wonder.

He turned off the engine and got out of the truck. As the door slammed, the sound loud and jarring in the afternoon air, he felt like that sound was just punctuating a huge mistake.

He shouldn't have taken her home. Taking her home wasn't the problem, it was the fact that he'd left her there. Watching him go, from her porch. Confused and hurt.

And understandably so. She didn't even know what she'd asked that was so wrong. And she hadn't asked anything that was wrong. She'd asked a curious and totally valid question.

He was the one who couldn't answer her.

He stepped into the house, nearly groaning that his grandfather sat at the kitchen table working on one of his many crosswords.

"Hi. Where's Elizabeth?"

He could count on his granddad to focus right on the one thing he didn't want to talk about.

"She went home. She was . . . tired."

Granddad nodded, then wrote in another word.

"She seems like a great girl, Jen."

Jensen nodded. Yes, she was. And perhaps one that he might have lost, just because he couldn't deal with his own past.

"She's very fond of you. You can see it all over her face."

Jensen would have liked to think he wasn't selfish and so needy that his grandfather's words could fill him with satisfaction. But they did.

Maybe Elizabeth would forgive him for his reluctance to talk about Katie. But he could tell from the look on her face that she'd believed the reason he wouldn't talk was because he still loved Katie.

Even a week ago, he would have agreed. He would have said that he absolutely loved Katie and wouldn't fall for another. Now, he wasn't so sure.

Actually, he *was* sure. He had fallen in love again. That was absolutely what he felt for Elizabeth. So why had his inclination been to run from her questions?

Because, you fool, you don't want her to see what an utter failure you are. You let Katie die, for God's sake.

How did he tell the woman he was falling for that he'd played a part in his first love's death?

"You know, I get the feeling that Elizabeth is just a really good person." Granddad's comment was offhanded, and as was his way, he still answered the crossword clues as if he hadn't even spoken.

Jensen crossed to the counter, leaning against it. Debating what he needed to do.

"I don't think I'd let a woman like that one get away."

Jensen stared at his grandfather, bent over his puzzle. What did his grandfather know about any of this? He didn't know what had happened that last night with Katie.

Hell, she wouldn't even have been driving if they hadn't had that stupid fight. Such a stupid, stupid fight. And who had paid for Jensen's stupidity? Katie. Katie had. With her life.

He didn't say anything as he left the kitchen, hurrying up the steps to his bedroom. The room that had been his since he'd moved in with his grandparents. So much of his childhood was still apparent in this room, and in truth, he didn't even notice it anymore.

He picked up the picture of himself and Katie as they were preparing to leave for college.

Once he'd looked at that picture every single night, wondering "what if." What if things had turned out differently?

He had to admit that since he decided he wanted to be with Elizabeth he hadn't given the picture a thought. Like the sports pennants. Like the old science project he'd made in ninth grade, still sitting on his bookshelf, gathering dust.

The idea that he could just forget about Katie didn't make him feel any better. He stared at the picture, remembering everything about that day.

His grandmother's roses were still blooming, and the sweet smell had scented the air. He and Granddad had to wrestle all their luggage around, trying to find the right combination to make it all fit like a huge—and heavy, thanks to Katie's suitcases—3-D puzzle. But they had made it all fit. Katie had apologized for all her stuff, but she didn't offer to leave anything behind. Not because she was greedy, but because she was sure everything she'd packed was a necessity. She was leaving West Pines for good. Or so she thought.

He remembered the tape Katie had made to listen to in the car while they drove. Songs that were important to them and to their friends. And he remembered they had laughed, a lot, giddy with the prospect of moving on to a new part of their lives.

No. He'd never forgotten anything about Katie. If anything, he'd relived his time with Katie over and over, afraid he'd forget something.

"Jensen?"

Jensen started, looking up from the photo to where his grandfather leaned on the door frame.

"I know you loved Katie. I know you still love her. And I also know that if she'd lived, you two would be together now. But she didn't. And you can't stop living, too."

Jensen stared at him, not saying anything. Not knowing what to say.

"And letting go of Elizabeth isn't the tribute that Katie would have wanted."

Jensen nodded.

Granddad crossed over to him and clapped him on the shoulder, then turned to leave the room. But he paused again in the doorway.

"Just for the record, I really like Elizabeth."

Jensen nodded again. He really liked her, too. But that wasn't the issue. Would she really like him if she knew the truth about him? About how selfish he could be?

Elizabeth's eyes popped open, a feeling of disorientation filling her. She'd fallen asleep. She blinked around, realizing that she must have dozed off on her sofa.

She lay there for a moment, still trying to get her bearings. Then she remembered her last conversation with Jensen. Or the lack of conversation, and his hard expression as he'd driven away.

How had she managed to fall asleep? Her mind had been racing when she'd lain down. But given that she couldn't recall lying there for more than a few minutes, she must have fallen asleep almost immediately. Maybe sleep had been her way of dealing with emotional distress, although it never had been.

But it definitely seemed to be now, because all she wanted to do was curl back up against the cushions and fall back into oblivion.

Instead, she eased up to a sitting position, her limbs tired and heavy as if she was struggling through water. Obviously, the nap had done very little to ease her weariness.

But she didn't give in to the exhaustion that urged her body to lie down. She pushed up to her feet and ambled across the floor, feeling every bit of her hundred and eighty-nine years.

Love isn't supposed to make you feel old.

The thought barely registered in her brain, when she stumbled to a halt, sagging against the doorframe into the kitchen. But this time it wasn't her exhausted body affecting her. It was her own thoughts.

Was she really in love with Jensen? How was that even possible? They'd hardly had what anyone would call a conventional relationship. In fact, had they even shared enough to constitute a relationship?

She pushed away from the wall and tottered to the refrigerator. She opened the door, her stomach growling loudly, as if it had a mind of its own.

She really was a mess. Here she was, debating the fact that she could be in love with a man. A human. A person whom she could never have. Even if he wanted her, which didn't seem likely now. And she was also thinking she was starving. Something was seriously wrong with her. But then, she'd known that for a while.

She grabbed a container of yogurt and headed to the counter to get a bowl and a box of granola.

Fixing her snack, she tried to get her jumbled thoughts into some semblance of order.

"What do you really expect to happen with Jensen?" she

asked aloud, as if she expected some greater power to answer for her.

Of course, the room remained silent. Except the quiet skitter of paws as her apparently pet mouse scurried out into the middle of the room.

"As if my life isn't weird enough," she said to the small rodent, who reared up on his back feet and watched her, no fear whatsoever in its small, black eyes.

Elizabeth shook her head, then sat down at the table to eat. As she scooped the first spoonful of the concoction into her mouth, she started to list what she'd want to happen versus what could feasibly happen.

"I want Jensen," she admitted to herself and the mouse. "I—I do love him."

Saying it aloud, she almost cringed. Loving him was such a bad idea. A doomed, painful, and utterly unobtainable desire. Yet, she couldn't seem to tell her heart any of this.

"It isn't a real choice. Just let things end. Just let him go."

She knew her words were the right ones, but she also knew she couldn't do it. She knew she had to see him again. Somehow, in such a short time, Jensen had become as necessary to her as water and air. Surely, feeling this way wasn't normal. It certainly wasn't healthy. And the truth was, Jensen might have decided he wasn't interested in her. If his reaction to her questions were any indication, he wasn't close to being over the blonde in those pictures. Maybe bringing her up had shown him how strange his relationship with Elizabeth was. Maybe he truly did see that Elizabeth wasn't his type.

And she wasn't thinking about the two biggest problems, both of which could very well never be overcome. She was a werewolf. And she was mated.

"You cannot love him. Just let him go," she murmured.

"Now, *that*, sweet Lizzie, is the best idea I've heard in a long while."

Chapter 21

Elizabeth whipped around in her chair, staring at the speaker. She nearly fell as she scrambled upright, backing away, hardly able to believe her eyes. But she'd known he would come for her one day.

"Brody," she managed, trying to keep the fear from her voice.

"Yes, it's me. In the flesh." He raised a black eyebrow and stepped farther into the room.

Elizabeth automatically stepped back.

"I can see you are glad to see me."

"How . . . why are you here?"

Brody smiled, his grin revealing his white, even teeth. His teeth were the best feature of his broad, harsh face. When she'd first met him, she'd told herself that any man with a smile like his couldn't be all bad. She'd been wrong. There was very little in Brody that was good. He was too selfish, too hardened to have much goodness inside him.

"Well, I couldn't very well let my mate leave me forever."

He strolled to her table, taking a seat as if he owned the place. He lifted her bowl of yogurt and granola, sniffing it. He grimaced, and pushed it away.

Leaning back and crossing his trunk-like arms over his barrel chest, he regarded her.

"And you've been a very bad mate, haven't you?"

She froze, fear immediately spiking through her, making her panic. But she swallowed, willing herself to remain calm. Brody could sense her fear. A werewolf could sense fear, but Brody fed off it. He liked to cause fear in others.

"I don't know what you are talking about."

He raised his thick, black brow again. "Really?"

She shook her head, determined to hold her ground. She'd done it many times before, and in truth, she'd often walked away from their clashes, while not necessarily the victor, at least unscathed. This time she knew it was very important she didn't submit.

He relaxed even more, regarding her with his brown eyes. So brown they often looked black, empty.

"Let me refresh your memory. The front seat of a pickup truck. An old man's kitchen table. On that creaky, wooden swing out there on your front porch."

Bile rose up in the back of Elizabeth's throat, but she swallowed back her nausea. Oh God, Brody had watched them. Had seen it all. And while his wrath frightened her to the point that she was nearly shaking, it was the idea that he'd witnessed moments that should have been just hers and Jensen's that distressed her. That he was somehow tainting them with his presence. That was what sickened her.

But she managed to pull herself up to her full height. "It's nothing more than what you've done," she said with false bravado, amazed it sounded believable, even to her ears.

"So you were just extending a little payback, eh?"

She nodded, trying to look angry rather than scared.

He quirked his lips, seeming to consider that information. For a moment, she thought he was going to accept her explanation. After all, Brody had cheated on her almost from the day that she'd agreed to mate with him. Not the natural behavior of a mated werewolf, but he'd never been conventional in any of his werewolf traits. Including his fidelity. And in truth, she'd been more than happy for him to go to other females. She'd mated for survival, not happiness or love.

But her hope that he'd just accept her reason was quickly dashed as he rose and stalked toward her. She backed away, but soon felt the handle of the refrigerator sharp in her back.

He cornered her there, blocking her escape with his massive body. He was about the same height as Jensen, but he had a good fifty pounds on Jensen's lean, athletic build. Brody was like a tank. And he was a bully. And Elizabeth knew she was having a hard time keeping the fear out of her eyes.

"Now, darling, I appreciate that you think turnabout is fair play. But that isn't the way I see it."

Elizabeth raised her chin, meeting his eyes. "Is this another of your random alpha male rules?"

He laughed, the sound low and dangerous. "Random alpha male rules? Now, baby, you know I never had any of those. These are just Brody's rules. And the number one rule is that Brody's mate does not cheat. Especially not with a human."

His eyes roamed down her body, making her skin crawl. "You let yourself be tainted, woman."

She didn't disagree with that, but it had been Brody who'd done the tainting, not Jensen. Jensen had made her realize what she could have had. If she hadn't been so scared and pathetic.

She started as he moved, but she was surprised that he actually released her and paced away from her. She used the moment to shift away from the fridge, sidling closer to the back door.

He turned back to face her and she froze.

"The truth is that I could let that go. After all, from what I saw, the human seemed to teach you a trick or two." He grinned, the lascivious gleam in his eyes nearly making her shiver with revulsion. But she didn't. She remained absolutely still, doing nothing to draw him back to her.

He began to pace again, and for the first time, she realized

his movements seemed a little jerky, as if something was hurting him. She watched his movements, trying to figure out what
was wrong as she edged past the back door to the counter,
spotting the knife holder. Even if she ran out the back door
now, Brody would catch her in a heartbeat. She needed a
weapon.

"But . . ." He spun toward her, his dark eyes moving over
her again. She remained motionless, barely even pulling in a
breath. But her frozen posture didn't save her this time. He
darted, and before she could even prepare for his impact, she
found herself pinned to the wall, his huge, hard bulk holding
her there. She tried to pull in a breath, but couldn't.

"But," he repeated with one of his deceptively attractive
smiles, "I can't let go what I've tasted on your skin." To
punctuate his words, he leaned forward and licked her, his
tongue moving up her cheek like a hot, slimy slug.

This time she couldn't suppress a violent shudder.

He shifted back to look at her, and this time there was no
smile, lascivious or otherwise. This time his mouth was set in
a grim scowl. His black eyes burned with disgust.

"Oh, Lizzie, you have sealed that human's death."

His words seemed to knock the breath out of her. Jensen.

"Why?" she asked, not understanding what was motivat-
ing him. What had he tasted? When? She just didn't understand. "What does the human matter? We are over, anyway."

Brody nodded, his expression stating that he clearly didn't
believe her. "So I heard you say."

"He isn't important. And—and I shouldn't have been with
him. I just did it to—to hurt you." She knew she was grabbing at straws, but she couldn't let Brody go after Jensen.
Jensen would be dead before he even realized what hit him.

"To hurt me?" He clearly didn't believe her. But she should
have known that given the chance, Brody would take advantage of the situation.

"If that's the case, then I guess you'd want to show a little of that passion to me." He didn't wait for her to answer as he smashed his mouth down on hers.

Elizabeth struggled to suppress the wave of nausea rising up inside her. Instead, she tried to keep her lips relaxed as he battered them with his rough, painful kiss.

She tried to keep her movements unnoticed as she reached behind her for one of the knives. Her fingers brushed the wooden handles and she eased one out of its slot.

"Baby, I'm just not feeling the passion I saw with the human. You were getting freaky with him." He bit her bottom lip hard, as if to demonstrate the freakiness he wanted from her.

"Oh," she said, smiling sweetly even as another swell of nausea filled her. "I can be pretty freaky."

She didn't hesitate but drove the blade straight into his side. The knife slid in easier than she would have guessed, and he instantly jerked away from her.

Staring down at the steak knife, he let out a low growl that was more wolf than human. "You bitch."

Elizabeth didn't wait for any other reaction. She raced to the back door, flying down the steps, adrenaline coursing through her and adding to her speed. But once she reached the woods, she paused.

She glanced back at her house. She didn't think Brody had exited yet. So she took a moment, concentrating. She'd be able to get to Jensen faster if she changed into wolf form. She never willingly shifted, but this time she knew she had to make the change. She had to get to him before Brody did.

Pulling in a calming breath, she let it happen. The shift hurt, but once it was done, the pain would be forgotten. And since it wasn't quite the full moon, she would be able to think like herself. Only the full moon made her all wolf.

After a few pained moans and cracking of joints, she rose, then started running, her paws carrying her over the ground, eating up the distance between her and Jensen.

*   *   *

Jensen pushed aside Katie's scrapbook. It was the first time he'd opened the book since Katie had died. Pain still filled his chest as he looked at the pictures. He wished things had gone differently. That Katie was here. He'd still give his own life for that to be the outcome of that night. But she was gone. And he'd mourned her. He still mourned her.

But he also mourned the look on Elizabeth's face as he'd driven away earlier today.

He glanced at the window. It was dark. Where had the afternoon gone? Had he really just sat here staring at pictures, trying to sort out his feelings?

Yeah, he had. And he wasn't that much closer to an answer. But he did know that he had to go to Elizabeth. He couldn't go to Katie. But he could go to Elizabeth.

He got up from his bed, shoving his feet into his shoes. He walked over to the closet to grab a coat.

As he started to shrug on the leather jacket, he heard the back door slam. Then he heard the muffled voice of his grandfather shouting something.

Tugging on the coat, he hurried down the hall and took the stairs two at a time. What the hell was his grandfather yelling about? As he reached the living room, he heard a gunshot.

Shit, not again.

He ran out into the kitchen, and sure enough his grandfather was again on the back porch. Again he had his old rifle in his hand, aiming out at the darkened dooryard.

"Granddad," he cried, just as another shot rang out. But unlike the last time, this time he heard a sharp yelp.

"Granddad! What the hell are you doing?"

His grandfather didn't answer him, but loped down the steps, rifle still poised to shoot.

Jensen followed him out, not sure what he would find. But pretty damned sure it was going to be the McCormacks' Newfoundland in a pool of blood.

He reached his grandfather, who scanned the ground, obviously looking for a trail of blood.

"I know I got it this time," he stated, not looking up from his search.

"Granddad, I'm starting to really worry about you."

"Don't worry about me. Worry about that damned wolf."

Jensen shook his head. This was really becoming a very strange obsession. A worrisome obsession. But he did find himself also scanning the ground for blood or pawprints.

Sure enough, he spotted prints in the damp driveway. Of course, he couldn't be sure without really studying them if they were canine or some other animal.

Dog, he guessed, but he did find himself following them. His grandfather veered the other way, and Jensen hesitated to call to him about what he'd discovered. He was truly afraid he was going to find someone's family pet, shot and dying. And given what Granddad had done for the last fifty years, Jensen knew he'd be devastated if he'd killed a domesticated animal.

No, it was best for Jensen to follow the trail himself, and if there was some poor animal injured, he'd handle it.

The trail continued toward the old woodshed behind the garage. He moved forward slowly as he realized the tracks seemed to lead right up to it. He approached slowly, afraid that the hurt animal might charge out of fear. But as he got to the building, nothing appeared. He glanced around, checking the door to see if it was open. The double doors were locked. He started to walk behind the shed to see if he could pick up the trail, when he heard a whimper. He stopped and listened.

Then he saw it. A large, black form in the waning light. Collapsed on the ground. He stepped a little closer. He saw the flash of pale eyes.

Again he heard a sound, although this time the sound didn't seem like an animal. It had an almost human quality to it.

He took another step forward, frightened by what he was

seeing. Suddenly very frightened, when something came at him from his right, launching him into the air. He landed on the ground with a hard thud.

He rolled onto his back, scrambling to get his bearings and rise. But before he could manage to even sit up, the thing pounced onto him, pinning him to the ground with tremendous weight.

He stared up at the creature, not really sure what he was looking at. Between the darkness and his own disorientation, he just couldn't tell. But he knew whatever it was, it wasn't a human form. And it wasn't any animal that he was familiar with in this region. It was too large to be a dog. And it was indeed black, or dark enough to blend into the night.

The animal growled low in its throat, the sound as eerie as it was terrifying. Jensen could feel its breath on his face. He braced his hands on its neck, trying to push it away from him. Muscles bulged under its fur. Tendons and large bones made the animal like a living tank, immovable.

The creature growled again, and lunged at him, his jaws going straight for Jensen's throat. Teeth began to clamp onto Jensen's skin, although oddly, it didn't hurt.

Shock, Jensen realized, even as it dawned on him that he was going to die. Then a shot rang out, deafening in its nearness. The creature on him jerked, and Jensen realized it had been hit. The creature rolled off of him, growling ferociously.

Jensen didn't waste any time; he levered himself up on his arms, using both his hands and feet to scramble backwards away from the thing. It lunged at him again.

Jensen shoved at it, struggling to get out from underneath the crushing weight. In this position he was truly helpless.

"Goddamned thing," he heard his grandfather yell, and he heard the faint sound of his grandfather reloading his rifle.

This time when the shot rang out, the animal jerked back off of Jensen. It made a noise somewhere between a yelp and a growl, the sound almost unnatural.

Jensen saw the glint of black eyes, staring at him as if it was considering lunging again, but then it spun and raced off into the night.

Jensen fell back onto the hard, damp ground, panting, his heart racing so hard he truly thought he might pass out.

"Jensen? Are you okay?"

He nodded faintly, then realized his granddad probably couldn't see him. "Yes. I'm just winded."

Granddad knelt beside him, his hands moving over him as if to check for any broken bones or open wounds.

Jensen struggled upright. "I'm fine. You scared it off before it could do any real damage." *Such as rip my throat out.*

He sat there for a second, badly shaken. That had been the weirdest damned thing he'd ever experienced. Rubbing a shaking hand over his face, he tried to calm his heart rate.

"I think it's gone. And I think I wounded it again."

Jensen looked up at his grandfather's silhouetted figure. "You think that was the same thing that you shot the other night?"

"Do you really think there are two of those things out there?" Granddad countered.

Yes, he did. He struggled to his feet. He knew there were two. And the other could be right behind the shed, waiting.

"Give me the gun," he told the older man. "And wait inside."

For once, Granddad didn't seem to need to be told twice. He handed the rifle to his grandson.

Jensen headed toward the woodshed, listening closely. For some reason the breeze through the branches, the leaves under his feet, seemed much louder than usual. Not to mention the scents of damp earth, dead leaves wet from the earlier rain, and the hints of gasoline from his grandfather's ancient sedan. All of it seemed so intense, so pronounced. Obviously because his senses were already in overdrive from the earlier incident. Now everything had him more aware, more on edge.

He glanced around, easily seeing the garage and the wood-shed behind. He blinked, wondering why he could see them so easily now, when earlier he'd had a hard time even making out that animal that was only inches from his face.

Because he wasn't panicking now, he reasoned, even as his heart pounded against his rib cage. He lifted the gun. Then a sound stopped him. He froze, listening.

It was a faint moan. A feeble sound, yet filled with pain. He glanced around, trying to pinpoint the source. Another small groan, low and distinctly feminine.

He zeroed in on the woodshed. The sound had definitely come from the same place where he'd seen the other one. He paused, debating whether he should wait for his grandfather to get his other rifle. It there were two of those things . . . But he didn't wait—he strode in the direction of the shed. When he got closer, a familiar scent wafted around him.

Elizabeth.

"Elizabeth?" he called, opening the doors and looking inside. His grandfather's ride-on lawnmower was parked in the middle of the space. Several rows of wood lined one wall; the other was littered with gardening tools and other lawn equipment.

She was here. He knew it. He shut the doors and walked around the shed. He reached the back and spotted her—half-sitting, half-lying against the side of the building—right where the thing had been.

"Oh my God." He rushed forward, stopping short of touching her. She moaned again, but otherwise didn't respond. He wasn't even sure if she was conscious. He stared at her, unsure what to do. He knew what he'd seen back here, and it hadn't been Elizabeth. Yet here she was now.

What was happening?

She groaned again, the sound so pained, and this time he couldn't stay away. This was Elizabeth. And she was hurt.

He set down the rifle and lifted her against his chest. He

ran toward the house, barreling up the back steps and into the kitchen. Granddad started as he entered, then rose.

"Dear God. Is she all right?"

Jensen shook his head. "I have no idea. I found her out by the woodshed."

He hurried through the kitchen, taking her to the sofa. Carefully, he placed her on the cushions. She moaned again, something obviously causing her pain. He inspected what he could see. Her face was free of scrapes. Her arms, too. Then he noticed a wet, dark spot barely visible on her blue shirt. He looked down at his own hands, and saw they were covered with dark red. Blood.

He peeled back her t-shirt, easing it upward until he could see the wound—round, red, and ragged—in her right shoulder.

Not a wound that could have been made by an animal. Definitely a gunshot wound.

"I shot her." Jensen heard his grandfather say, his voice a little reedy and confused. "How did I shoot her?"

Jensen didn't answer. He didn't know. Given what he knew now, he found it hard to believe that his granddad could confuse Elizabeth for what he saw out there. He knew what he'd seen and there was no mistaking that creature for a human.

"Maybe it ricocheted or something." Even as he said the words, he didn't believe them. "But she definitely needs to go to the hospital."

Jensen started to lift her again, his panic at the paleness of her features making him a little rough.

This time she cried out—the jarring pain roused her. She blinked up at him, her gaze dazed although she gradually managed to focus.

"Jensen?" She started to lift her arm to touch his face, but she winced and let it drop back to her stomach. Still she gazed at him as if he were a figment of her imagination.

"You are alive," she murmured. This time she did touch him, using her other hand. "You are alive."

Her pale eyes welled with tears.

"Yes, sweetheart, I'm fine." He wondered if she'd seen the attack. She must have, since it was the only reason for her emotional reaction.

"He was going to kill you."

She had seen that attack.

"It's okay. Granddad shot him. It's okay now."

She stared at him for a moment, then let out a sigh of relief. "He's gone, then?"

"Yes. Gone for good."

"Good. Good."

Her eyes drifted shut for a moment, and he was afraid she'd fallen unconscious again. Although given how painful her injury must be, it might be a blessing.

Carefully, he attempted to lift her again. Her eyes snapped open.

"Please, Jensen, no." Her plea nearly broke his heart. She was in a lot of pain. That was clear in her eyes.

"Sweetheart, I have to get you to the hospital."

Her eyes widened and panic, true panic, filled them, just as they had the night of her fever. "No! No!"

She struggled, trying to sit up.

He gently held her down, trying to stop the worst of her struggling. "Elizabeth, stop. You are going to hurt yourself even worse."

She did stop, but her eyes still pleaded with him. "No hospital. Promise me."

He hesitated, taking in her pale skin and the sweat dampening her hair. She was in serious pain. Instead of answering her, he carefully slid an arm under her shoulders and lifted her. She moaned.

"Sorry, baby," he whispered, then he carefully lifted her shirt to see if the bullet had gone straight through her shoulder. There was no exit wound.

He eased her back down.

"Elizabeth, I have to take you to the hospital. The bullet is still lodged in your shoulder. It has to be removed or it could get infected. It definitely won't heal properly. Not to mention there could be damage to the bones and the nerves. You have to go."

"No," she said adamantly. "You can get the bullet out."

He shook his head. "No, Elizabeth."

"You are a vet. You can take care of me better than anyone at the hospital."

Jensen frowned at her reasoning, a flicker of panic seizing him. A vet? What was she telling him? But he pushed the thought aside, scared of how pale she was. She did need help.

"Elizabeth," he started, his voice coaxing, but she cut him off.

"If you take me to the hospital, I'll leave the first time you turn your back."

He stared at her, believing her.

He nodded. "Okay. But I'm going to move you upstairs."

She nodded, and this time she didn't make a sound as he lifted her. Probably another attempt to show him she didn't need a hospital.

He brought her up to his bedroom. Granddad followed close behind, remaining silent.

He settled her on the bed, then turned to Granddad. "I need my bag. Could you get that for me? My bag is in my truck."

Granddad nodded and left the room.

Jensen turned back to Elizabeth. "Okay, sweetheart, I'm going to have to get rid of your shirt."

She nodded. "Nothing you haven't seen before."

He laughed at that. "Well, I have to admit I like it a lot more when I'm looking for other reasons."

"Me, too," she murmured.

He lifted her, working the t-shirt upward and over her good shoulder and her head; then he carefully eased it off the injured arm.

He gently settled her against the mattress, and pulled the sheet up over her chest. Her skin was burning hot, he realized. As hot as it had been that night at her house. This time, he worried that she already had an infection coursing through her body.

He left her just long enough to grab towels from the linen closet. When he came back into the room, the sight of her, almost gray against the white of his sheets, shook him. Her pallor shook him badly. What if he couldn't do this? What if she died like Katie had?

He closed his eyes briefly, trying to get control of his doubts, of the absolute fear gripping him.

When he opened his eyes, Elizabeth was watching him. She offered him a small, pained smile.

"I must look really bad."

He immediately shook his head. "No. No."

He sat down beside her, careful not to jar the bed too much.

Granddad hurried back into the room carrying a tray, which was actually a cookie sheet, and Jensen's medical bag.

Jensen thanked him, then searched his bag for a scalpel, long-handled tweezers, gauze, and antibiotics to pack the wound with once he had the bullet out.

Elizabeth watched him set everything out on the tray. She didn't react to the use of the cookie sheet. If the makeshift operating room concerned Elizabeth, she didn't show it.

He reached back into his bag for a topical anesthesia and a syringe. He tried not to let her see the syringe, but she did, again watching with no noticeable concern.

"Okay. I'm going to numb the skin around the wound before I give you the shot of a more powerful anesthesia."

"Okay," she said, closing her eyes. Somehow that made it easier for him to work. He hated looking into those pale blue depths, seeing complete trust there. It unnerved him.

He swabbed around the area, and then prepared the syringe.

"Okay, this will hurt a little." He pierced the tip of the needle into the fragile flesh of her shoulder, hating to do it, but knowing it would be better than rooting around for the bullet without it.

She flinched and made a small hiss, but otherwise remained still.

"Okay, done. Now we'll wait for that to numb up."

She opened her eyes and offered him another feeble smile. "Not too bad, vet."

He smiled at that. He looked around to see Granddad watching from the doorway. He smiled his encouragement, too.

"Okay." Jensen tested the area. "Is it numbed?"

She nodded.

"Okay. He reached for the tweezers. As he got the instrument closer to the wound, he hesitated. Even with the numbing agent, she was going to feel discomfort, and it killed him to have to cause her any pain. But if he didn't, she'd likely get an infection that could literally kill her.

He eased the instrument into the bullet hole, gently probing. Elizabeth made a slight gasp, but remained still. Her hand moved to his leg, her fingers bracing into the denim of his jeans.

"It's okay. I'll find it quickly. We'll get this over with as fast as possible."

He continued to soothe her, telling her she was doing great. That it would be just a few seconds more. And Elizabeth seemed to listen to him, taking comfort in his reassurances.

Finally he connected with something hard. He allowed the tweezers to open and clamped onto the solid mass. Gently he pulled and the item came out easily. He held up the tweezers to find a gray bullet there. Silently, he thanked God.

"That wasn't so hard," she murmured with another smile. He smiled back.

"Well, I had a great patient."

Quickly, he packed the wound and bandaged it. Then he got her some pain meds—really designed for dogs and cats, but they would take the edge off her pain.

Once she was bandaged, medicated, and covered in several thick blankets, he left the room briefly just to clean up his instruments and change his own bloodied clothes.

Jensen quickly cleaned up, placing his items back in his bag; then he stripped off his soiled clothes to pull on a t-shirt and a pair of sweatpants.

When he got back to Elizabeth she was asleep. Her skin was still pale, but no longer gray. And when he touched her forehead, her skin was cooler. She still had a fever, but it wasn't raging.

He pulled a chair to the edge of the bed and sank down onto it. He had to admit he was exhausted, but there was no way he was leaving her tonight. He didn't understand what happened out there, but he knew he had to stay with her.

If anything, he felt more protective, more possessive of her now than he had before. Even as his mind swirled with confusion, with crazy thoughts that simply couldn't be real.

He leaned forward and rested a hand on her belly, not sure why he needed to touch her there, but he did. And he felt great relief, because he knew she was safe. He'd kept her safe.

Elizabeth opened her eyes and realized her whole body ached as if she'd done an aerobics marathon. She blinked, not immediately recognizing where she was. Then she saw the football alarm clock and felt the burning itch in her right shoulder.

She struggled upright, searching the room for Jensen. As if he knew she was looking for him, he stepped into the room, wearing only a pair of low-slung jeans, toweling off his short, mahogany-brown hair.

"Hey," he smiled, dropping the towel to his side as he saw she was awake.

She smiled. "Hi."

He threw the towel onto a chair, which was already draped with a quilt and a pillow.

"I don't think you should be up," he said, walking over and touching her forehead. She knew her skin was cool from the relieved expression on his face.

"I feel okay," she assured him.

He nodded, cocking one eyebrow as if to say he knew she had to be lying. But she did feel all right. The healing wound itched like crazy, and the lead from the bullet made it burn a little, too. But overall, she felt great.

Jensen's fingers moved to the bandage covering the bullet wound. Carefully, he removed the gauze to inspect it. Surprise creased his brow as he frowned at the injury.

"It looks really good. I . . ." He gently touched the edge where the skin already looked fully healed. "I can't believe how good it looks, actually."

She imagined that was true. The wound would mostly be gone by tomorrow, and how would she explain that? Maybe she should have made him leave the bullet lodged in her shoulder. Lead really interfered with a werewolf's healing process. Silver would eventually kill, lead just made a big mess.

"I've always been a fast healer," she told him weakly.

"I can see that." He shook his head as he inspected it again, then replaced the gauze. He eased her back on the pillows. "But I still don't think you should be up yet."

She smiled, relaxing like a good, obedient patient.

He smiled back, but then the smile disappeared.

"Do you remember last night?"

Some of it. But how did she explain?

"There was a large, black animal out there last night," he said, his voice oddly distant as if he still couldn't really believe what he'd seen. She couldn't blame him. Werewolves were hard to believe.

"You did see it?" he asked.

She shook her head. "No." But she knew what he saw.

And he'd seen her as a wolf, too. She knew it from his dazed look.

She started to sit up.

"Elizabeth, I really think you should lay back. You look pale." Again he nudged her down among the pillows. She allowed him to, because she had no idea what else to do. And frankly, she was surprised he would touch her.

Oh God, this couldn't be happening. Please, please don't let this be happening.

"Elizabeth, I'm going to get you something to drink. And maybe some food. You've got to be hungry."

For the first time since she could remember, she couldn't imagine being able to swallow a bite.

But apparently Jensen took her dazed stare as consent, because he tucked the blankets around her, then left the room with the promise of something delicious.

She watched him go, unable to grasp what she knew was the truth. He'd seen her. He'd seen Brody. And somehow he'd survived. That much she was thankful—God, *more* than thankful—for.

She closed her eyes, swallowing back wave after wave of nausea.

Even if he could accept the truth, how could she throw him into the middle of this? Brody wouldn't stop. Not for long.

She pulled a breath in slowly through her nose, then blew the air out from between her lips. She did it again, and again.

All she needed was to hyperventilate on him. He was the one who deserved to be overwhelmed.

It was . . . one day until the full moon. She had to tell him before then. He had to be prepared. He was going to hate her, but he had to know the truth.

Out of the corner of her eye, she saw the picture frame containing Jensen and the blonde, still facedown where it had been.

She picked it up, staring at the pretty face of the blonde. Her straightforward smile and clear blue eyes. She'd never have hurt Jensen. She'd have been the perfect mate—*wife* for him. She'd been exactly what she'd appeared to be. A nice, sweet girl who loved Jensen.

"Her name was Katie."

Elizabeth's head snapped up. Jensen stood in the doorway with a huge plate loaded with toast and eggs and bacon and sliced fruit.

When she just gaped at him, he seemed to think her shocked look was somehow related to the large quantity of food.

"Granddad is feeling a little guilt, so he had this waiting to go for when you woke up."

She nodded, having no idea what to say to him. Tears choked her, but she managed to hold them back.

Jensen crossed to the bed and set the tray on her lap. She glanced at it, but then her gaze returned to him.

God, what did she say?

Jensen pulled up the chair, his expression one of heart-breaking understanding. An expression she so didn't deserve.

"I'm so sorry I hurt you yesterday."

Elizabeth frowned, then shook her head. What could he possibly be apologizing for? She was the one who needed to apologize. She was the one who'd deceived him. Put him in terrible danger.

"I didn't want to tell you about Katie, but probably not for the reasons you think. In fact, definitely not for the reasons you think."

She stared at him. Had it only been yesterday that they'd talked about Katie? Now, that seemed like ages ago, and she felt like she had even less right to know about it.

If anything, she wished Katie was still alive and that Jensen was with her now. Far from here, happy and safe.

"Katie and I were high-school sweethearts," he said

slowly. "We started dating our sophomore year. We left to-gether after high school so I could attend Cornell. You saw in the picture. Katie didn't have money for college, so she took classes and we planned she'd go full-time once I finished. We were . . . we were serious. Engaged."

Even though she couldn't put Jensen's fate out of her mind, Elizabeth had to listen. She did want to know. She loved Jensen, she wanted to understand everything about him. Even though she knew that he would soon hate her.

"Katie had a rough home life. Raised by a single mother, who wasn't the best parent, she couldn't wait to leave West Pines behind. She craved a new life. So, after my second year of college, she was not pleased when I told her that I thought I'd like to move back here and take over my granddad's prac-tice." He shook his head as he remembered, obviously dis-gusted with his behavior.

"But I was determined to do just that. She overheard me talking about my plan with some friends at a campus party. She was angry, because she felt like I'd betrayed her in a way. I was her escape route—she didn't want to come back here. I knew that, yet I wanted what I wanted. We ar-gued."

Dread filled Elizabeth again. She knew this story didn't have a happy ending, and she didn't want him to have to live it again. She started to reach for him, but he stopped her.

"Please let me tell you."

She still wanted to say no. She didn't deserve to know. Not when she hadn't told him so many truths about herself. But instead of stopping him, she nodded.

"I left the party to cool down, which I did. I don't think I'd changed my mind, but I was calmer. So I decided to head back to the party to talk to Katie.

"As I approached the party, I saw a car off the road. The front end was crushed, wrapped around a tree. I pulled over and ran to the car."

He shook his head again, his eyes distant like he was back there on that roadside.

"I couldn't believe it when I got to the driver's side and saw Katie there in the driver's seat. She was pinned, the engine block pushed back and crushing her legs."

This time Elizabeth did touch him, gripping his hand. Feeling sick for him. For that memory that had to be burned forever into his brain.

He squeezed her fingers back, then continued, "I couldn't get her out. And I knew from the color of her skin, she didn't have long. She was totally gray. I remember that. And I remember I just kept chanting, "I'm sorry. Oh, I'm sorry," over and over again. But she never heard my apology. She never revived, and I could do nothing but hold her through the shattered window."

"Oh, Jensen," Elizabeth leaned forward and touched his face, his hair.

"I knew she'd hated this town. That she wanted nothing more than to leave and never look back. But I let my own dreams destroy hers."

"It isn't your fault," Elizabeth assured him. "It was an accident."

"I shouldn't have been so selfish."

His words hit her, reflecting her own feelings.

"You weren't being selfish. You wanted something different. It could have been talked through, worked out. She was the one who chose to drive while she was upset. You can't take that burden." Elizabeth caught his face between her hands, forcing him to look at her. "I can't tell you why it happened. But I know it wasn't your fault. We all make mistakes, but the accident was not your fault."

He stared into her eyes, then he kissed her. All his pain, all his guilt and regret in his harsh kiss. And she let him take his anguish out on her, feeling terrible anguish of her own.

Finally, his mouth gentled and he caressed her ravaged lips

with so much tenderness that her eyes welled with tears. When he tasted the saltiness, he pulled back.

"Elizabeth?" His eyes roamed her face, trying to understand her tears.

She again held his face so she could look in his eyes.

"You mustn't believe it was your fault. Please do that for me. You are too good and kind to carry that kind of guilt any longer. And Katie knew that. Why do you think she was in love with you? She knew. She did."

Chapter 22

Jensen wasn't sure of that, but when he looked in Elizabeth's beautiful eyes, he wanted to believe it. For her as much as for Katie, he wanted to believe.

He nodded slightly, and she pressed her lips softly to his, a whispering, sweet kiss.

When they parted, they just stared at each other, both of them visibly shaken. But even as painful as it had been for him to tell her about Katie, he did feel somehow purged. Elizabeth now knew him. She understood.

And he wanted to know her. Whatever she was hiding, and he knew she was hiding something. She had been from the moment they met.

He offered her a weak smile. "You are squishing your food." He gestured to the tray she still had on her lap. They'd gotten butter from the toast and a bit of egg on the sheets, but overall the meal still looked edible.

"You try and eat," he told her. "I'm going to go down and get a cup of coffee." He needed a moment to gather himself after that. And to figure out how to get her to talk in the same candid way.

He looked at Elizabeth, also realizing half the reason he was so shaken was because he loved her. He loved her madly. He needed a moment to deal with exactly how much.

"Do you want some?"

Elizabeth shook her head.

"I'll be right back."

She nodded, and again he noticed her eyes looked a little glassy from tears. He should stay, he realized, but he just needed a moment.

He glanced at her again, then left the room.

Elizabeth set aside the tray and scrambled as quietly as she could from the bed. She had to save Jensen. She had to stop Brody. And she only had two choices. She had to contact her old pack—they could control Brody. And she had to pray that Dr. Fowler had figured out her serum. That was the only way to free herself.

She crept over to Jensen's door and locked it. Then she tiptoed to the window, and carefully and quietly pulled it open. Looking out, she gauged that she could easily climb out onto the porch roof and then jump. At least she could in her wolf form.

She pulled in a deep breath. Then she willed herself to shift. She made a slight growl as her cells snapped and reformed. As her joints popped and reshifted.

Once in her wolf form, she paused, listening for Jensen or Granddad. She could hear them in the kitchen, although she didn't listen to what they said. No time to eavesdrop.

She leapt through the window out onto the roof, then jumped down to the ground, her thick wolf muscles and bones easily taking the jar of hitting the ground. Without looking back at the house, she ran for the woods. She knew Jensen would come looking for her, but hopefully, by the time he did, she'd have contacted those she needed to. And maybe, just maybe, the serum could cure her.

Brody growled, the sound rough and raw. But goddamn he hurt. Between the two bullets still lodged in him, one in his side and the other in his shoulder, and the stab wound that was nearly healed but just pissed him off, he was a hurting unit.

He lay in the far stall of Elizabeth's barn, where he planned to wait until that stupid bitch returned. And she would have to eventually.

He needed to get these bullets out of him. The lead was making him weaker. But he couldn't leave now—not that he had anywhere to go. He couldn't go back to the pack. Not without her. He was taking her back.

And then, once the pack saw he deserved their respect, he was going to kill the bitch.

She'd long since lost her usefulness, anyway. In fact, given her current state, she was a damned detriment.

He licked his wounds as well as he could. Oh yeah, she was going to die. And he still planned to kill her real mate, too.

Jensen knocked on the door to his bedroom for the third time.

"Elizabeth?" He tried the door handle again. It was definitely locked. He jiggled the handle. "Elizabeth?"

Worry twisted in his chest. Had she tried to get dressed or something and passed out?

He paused, debating what to do, when suddenly he was hit with an absolute certainty that she was gone.

He tilted his head, wondering at the strange knowledge. But it was a certainty. No doubt about it.

Without another thought, he shouldered the door open, the wood cracking loudly under his blow.

Even though he already knew what he would find, his gaze went from the empty bed to the open window. The blue tieback curtains fluttered in the breeze, the only traces of Elizabeth her faint scent on the sheets.

* * *

Elizabeth ran up the stairs to her bedroom. She threw open the door to her closet, rooting through the darkness until she found a large knapsack. It was times like this when having only a motorcycle to ride was a real hindrance.

She unzipped the canvas sack, debating if she would have enough room for everything she needed to bring. After a second, she realized she was just going to have to make it work.

Slinging the empty bag over her shoulder, she rushed back down the steps. She checked her messages, praying Dr. Fowler had called. No.

She grabbed her cell phone and dashed out the front door. The sun had gone down quickly, casting the yard in an eerie grayness, not quite light and not quite dark.

She picked up her speed, realizing that it wouldn't take Jensen long to figure out she was gone and where she'd come. In fact, she was shocked he wasn't here yet. Truck almost always beat four paws.

But he hadn't been here, she could sense that. Tugging open the barn door, she didn't bother with the overhead light and hurried right to her makeshift lab.

As she reached for the flap of plastic, she paused. Something wasn't right. She glanced around, her eyes adjusting easily to the darkness. She lifted her nose, breathing in deeply. All the scents were normal. Old, moldy hay, weathered wood, musty . . .

Then she paused. There was no musky scent of the skunk. No smell of the owls.

She looked up to the rafters. The owls were gone. What did that mean?

"Well, hey, Lizzie."

Elizabeth spun to see a dark figure lumbering toward her, the movements unnatural, awkward. But she recognized the voice. She tried to focus, realizing her best bet was to shift.

But before she could change, Brody was on top of her, his weight driving away both her focus and her breath. She tried to struggle, but his sheer size made it virtually impossible, even with her preternatural strength.

"There's no point fighting," he said, his breath hot on her face. "But if it's a fight you want . . ."

The last thing she remembered was a thundering blow to the side of her face.

Chapter 23

Jensen wheeled into Elizabeth's driveway, the tires skidding as he braked sharply to a stop. He jammed the gearshift into Park, and jumped out of the truck without bothering to turn off the ignition.

Again, even though it wasn't possible, he sensed that she was here—or had been here. How she could have beaten him was a mystery. Even with the time wasted, while his grandfather grilled him about how an injured woman could have escaped from his second-floor window.

Which *was* a mystery, he had to admit. Although there were a lot of implausible, mysterious things about her. But she had escaped. And she had been here.

He paused at the fact that he kept thinking *had been*. She had to be here—where else would she go?

He ran up to the house, not bothering to knock.

"Elizabeth?"

He checked the kitchen, then bounded up the stairs. Before he even checked the second bedroom, he knew the house was empty. Again, he didn't question how, he didn't waste his time.

He raced back downstairs, heading to the only other place she could be. The barn.

But he hadn't even stepped into the old building before he realized she was not there, either.

Shit. Where was she? He knew she'd been there. Her smell still hung faintly in the air.

Again he wondered how the hell he knew these things, but he also had the very unnerving feeling that he didn't have time to question them.

Elizabeth was in terrible trouble. Images of that beast from last night flashed in his mind.

He ran back to his truck, ramming the gearshift into reverse, a spray of gravel flying as he whipped the truck around and raced to the only other place he could think to look for her. Leo's.

Jensen strode into the bar, scanning the room for long, dark hair and pale eyes. She wasn't there. Again, that certainty filled him. Along with complete fear. He needed to protect her, and he didn't even know where to find her.

"Jensen?"

He turned to see Christian approaching him.

"Hey. Have you seen Elizabeth tonight?" He knew the answer already, but he had to ask. Her trail couldn't just disappear.

"No." Christian immediately looked very concerned. "Why? What happened?"

Jensen tried to find the best way to start. Given what he'd already experienced of Christian's temper, he decided it wasn't wise to mention the shooting. In fact, he had no idea where to start. Jumping out his bedroom window didn't sound particularly great, either.

"Hey, Jensen, where's Elizabeth?" Sebastian strolled up, only to stop a few feet from him, eyes widening as if he'd just witnessed something shocking about Jensen's appearance.

He suspected he looked pretty damned frazzled. He sure as hell felt frazzled. Hell, he was scared. Bone-deep scared, and he couldn't even say why, exactly.

"What's going on?" Sebastian frowned.

"I can't find Elizabeth. She disappeared from my house

and when I went to hers, she was missing. And I have a really, really bad feeling about it."

"That's not good," Sebastian stated, looking worried himself.

"No, it's not," Christian agreed. "Did she say anything to you before she disappeared?"

"No. She didn't. Do you have any idea where she might have gone?" Jensen again got a strange vibe, but this time not from the brothers. He glanced at the door in time to see three large biker-types walk through the door. He instantly recognized them from the other night. Jensen noticed that Christian and Sebastian also watched them as they approached the bar.

"Interesting," Sebastian said.

"Do you know them?" Jensen asked.

"No," Sebastian said. "But I'm willing to bet they might know Elizabeth."

Jensen frowned, wondering why that would be the case. But at this point, he was willing to go with any idea the strange brothers had.

Still, he couldn't help asking, "Why do you think they would know her?"

But the brothers didn't answer; instead, Christian headed back to the bar to take their drink orders. Jensen walked to the bar, too, but took a bar stool one seat down from the biker guys. The one closest to Jensen was liberally tattooed in an image of a full moon with clouds and a moonlit landscape.

For some reason, Jensen found the image enthralling.

"Stop staring at him," Sebastian hissed as he took the stool beside Jensen.

Jensen started, but did as Sebastian said, realizing it was probably a very bad idea to stare at a guy like that.

Christian returned to the bikers, placing mugs of beer in front of them. The men just nodded their thanks.

"Chatty," Sebastian commented quietly.

Jensen nodded. Yeah, they needed to be a lot more forth-coming if they had any hope of getting any information. He frowned. As if these guys would know anything about Elizabeth.

"Why, again, do we think these people know Elizabeth?" Jensen was really wondering about these brothers.

"Because they are—wearing—biker clothes. And Elizabeth—used to—travel with a biker—crowd."

Jensen stared at Sebastian. That was the most ridiculous and far-out explanation he'd ever heard. Something was definitely not right here.

"There have to be hundreds of thousands of bikers roaming the U.S. Why do you think these three might know her? And even if they do, know her whereabouts?"

Sebastian cast a quick look over at the couples. "There aren't many roaming around quite like these guys."

Before Jensen could ask what that meant, Christian returned to the trio.

"How are the beers?"

Again, the men offered noncommittal replies.

"So, are you just traveling through?" Christian kept his tone conversational as he wiped down the bar.

"Yeah," the one with the tattoo said, then took a long swallow of his beer.

"That's good." Christian nodded, obviously trying to think of a new angle to get these guys to talk.

"We don't get a lot of your type—this time of year."

One of the men, Jensen wasn't sure who, grunted.

"This is a waste of time," Jensen muttered to Sebastian.

Sebastian didn't answer; instead, his expression was far away, as if he was concentrating very hard on something. Just as Jensen decided to repeat himself, Sebastian glanced at him.

"No, I think we are on the right track."

Jensen frowned. "Why would you think that?" Boy, these guys were nuts.

"Because Christian is making them nervous."

Jensen glanced back over to the bikers. One sipped his beer, the other two stared straight ahead, looking far more bored than nervous.

"Yeah, they look really shaken," Jensen stated dryly.

"Shh," Sebastian hissed, giving him a look like he was the one who crazy.

What the hell were these brothers seeing that he wasn't? Jensen wondered. This was the biggest dead-end he'd ever seen. And even if he could see what the brothers saw in these bikers, Jensen knew they just needed to search. He knew deep in the pit of his stomach that Elizabeth was in real danger.

He frowned at his own train of thought. How did he know that? After all, Elizabeth had a track record of running away. And he had just revealed how he'd failed Katie. Elizabeth knew he'd never told that to anyone but her. That was enough to get her panicked. She might have just run from *him*. Period.

He considered that for a moment, then shook his head. No. She was in trouble, and she needed him. Now.

"I'm just going to go look for her," Jensen said suddenly, standing. But Sebastian caught his shoulder, his grip tight.

"No. We don't know where to look. There's no point going without a plan."

Jensen gaped at him. "This is the plan?" Then he realized his voice was getting a little too loud. He lowered it to hiss, "Question random bikers?"

"Trust me. It's a better plan than you know. And eventually, you will know why." Sebastian glanced at the wall behind the bar.

Jensen followed his gaze and he realized that Sebastian was looking at a calendar. What the hell was going on here?

Christian appeared, placing two beers on the bar in front of them.

"These guys are uncomfortable," he murmured.

"I know," Sebastian agreed.

Again Jensen looked over at the group. What the hell were they seeing, because he just saw a group relaxing with their drinks.

This time, he couldn't stop from saying what he'd been thinking. "Are you two totally nuts?"

"Shh," Sebastian hissed again, flashing a subtle look toward the bikers.

"I'm sorry," Jensen said quietly, but not keeping the irritation out of his voice. "But I don't follow this line of thought at all. Why would they know her?"

The brothers looked at each other, then back to him.

"You are just going to have to trust us on this one. But we want to find Elizabeth as badly as you do."

"Then let's go look for her, and stop wasting time with this ridiculous plan."

"All right," Christian said, keeping his voice low and calm.

Sebastian's head snapped toward Christian. "You're kidding, right? The ridiculous plan would be to just go out and search."

Jensen glared at Sebastian.

"Give me a few more minutes with these guys, and if I get nothing, we'll come up with a new plan."

Jensen started to hesitate, finding no reason to waste any more time with this strategy. But arguing wouldn't do any good. Plus, Christian had such a reasonable way of talking that it almost seemed silly to disagree with him. Almost.

But Jensen felt himself nodding.

Christian nodded in return, then headed down the bar to the bikers.

Jensen sat down again, staring at the beer in front of him. He almost wanted to take a drink, but he knew this wasn't the time to start drinking. Elizabeth needed him clear and levelheaded.

Sebastian didn't have the same thoughts. He sat back down and downed half of it.

"Can I get you anything?" Jensen heard Christian ask the bikers.

One of the men asked for another beer, the other two said they were fine. Christian strode away to get the order. When he returned, setting the beer in front of the men, he lingered.

"You know, I just have to ask, because we do have a regular here like you folks. Elizabeth is her name. You wouldn't happen to know her, would you?" Again, Christian kept his tone casual as if the answer didn't much matter to him. Certainly the bikers wouldn't know the woman in question was someone as close to Christian as his sister.

The one with the moon tattoo shook his head, not even giving the idea a thought. "Nope. Never heard of her."

He clearly was not interested in small talk.

Jensen started to stand again, and again Sebastian caught his arm to get him to remain seated.

"He knows her."

Jensen frowned at Sebastian. "He said he didn't."

"He's lying."

Jensen's frown deepened, but he remained on the bar stool.

"That's right. She usually goes by Lizzie, actually," Christian added.

Sebastian chuckled quietly. "Oh, that got their attention."

Jensen watched the bikers, seeing nothing that indicated they were anything but bored with Christian's comments.

"She actually hasn't been here in a while—"

"You know," the one with the tattoos said suddenly. "I'm not really sure why you are talking to us."

Christian shrugged, still remaining calm. "Just that she was like you. You know."

"Well, we don't know her." And for the first time, Jensen also seemed to sense they were lying. The brothers were right.

"Sorry to bother you," Christian said. "I just thought maybe—well, you never know. It is a small world, as they say."

The tattooed man reached into the back pocket of his jeans and pulled out a black wallet. He tossed down a fifty—more than enough to cover their bill. Then he stood, and the other two followed suit.

"We don't know her," the man stated, then strode toward the exit, the other two close behind.

The brothers and Jensen watched them leave and as soon as the door slammed shut behind them, Christian stated, "I'm going to tell Jolee that we are leaving."

"I'll ask Mina to help her with the bar."

Jensen frowned, not understanding anything that was going on—even though he did know they needed to follow those men. But he accepted it. Hell, he hadn't understood anything since they got here.

And at least they were doing something, even if it was just going on a wild-goose chase.

Chapter 24

Within five minutes, they were loaded into Jensen's truck and headed toward the mountains.

"How do you know they headed this way?" Jensen asked.

"I just know," Sebastian said, staring ahead as if he was somehow tracking them in his mind.

"You know," Jensen said slowly as he turned onto Route 219, "I don't really get you guys, but since you seem so definite, I'm trusting you."

"We're your best bet at the moment," Christian told him.

Jensen pressed down on the accelerator and the truck picked up speed.

Throughout the night, Sebastian or Christian would tell Jensen where to turn until they were high up on the narrow, twisting roads of the Blue Ridge Mountains. Jensen had stopped questioning them about their strange navigational skills. He somehow felt that they were on the right track, too. He couldn't say why or how, but he felt as if they were getting closer to Elizabeth.

"Who would bring her up here?" Jensen asked after they turned onto yet another winding road.

"I'm not sure," Christian said.

"She hasn't told us a lot about her past since we were reunited," Sebastian said, then winced as if he realized he might have said too much.

"She told me that you were separated for years and just recently found each other again. I also got the feeling her past wasn't good."

The brothers nodded.

"Yeah," Christian said. "And she hasn't told us a lot about what happened in those years. So I don't know who might want her back." Now it was Christian's turn to look as if he'd said too much.

"Wanted her back?" Jensen found that wording curious, not to mention Christian's expression. "Was she really with a biker gang or something?"

"Or something," Sebastian said. "We really don't know the details. Now, I wish I'd pressured her more to talk about it."

Jensen wished the same thing. But he never guessed someone would want to hurt her. Maybe he should have. He should have protected her and he failed. But he did have the feeling now that they were on the right track. They were getting closer.

"We are going to have to stop soon," Christian stated.

"What?" Jensen frowned quickly in his direction, then looked back to the narrow road.

"I know it doesn't make much sense, but Sebastian and I have to get inside before the sun rises."

Again, Jensen cast a quick frown in their direction. "Why?"

"We can't be out in the sun," Christian said. "Our skin can't tolerate the sun's rays."

"What? Like vampires?" Jensen said in disbelief.

"Yeah," Sebastian said with a slight smile. "Exactly like vampires."

Jensen glanced at them, sudden wariness filling him. They weren't joking, were they? He thought of the creature outside that woodshed. Then finding Elizabeth in its place.

"Jensen, our skin will blister and burn," Christian said in his sensible, calm way. "It's really dangerous for us. I know you want to keep going, but we can't. And I don't think you should go without us."

"Okay. I think I saw a sign back there for a motel in another few miles or so. Let's hope it's open this time of year." Jensen glanced at the mountains, realizing the sky just above was really starting to lighten. He pressed harder on the accelerator.

Fortunately, the motel was open and they had vacancies. While Christian and Sebastian took their room key and headed to their cabin, Jensen registered. By the time he finished and got his own room key, the rays of the sun were brushing the treetops like long fingers grasping everything in their reach. Elizabeth's brothers had been wise to hurry to their room.

His room was right beside theirs. He knocked just to be sure they had made it there okay.

"Yeah?" Christian called through the closed door.

"Are you all right?" Jensen asked.

"All set. Don't go anywhere without us," he answered.

"Like I can. You and Sebastian seem to be my navigational system."

The door jerked open a crack, although Jensen couldn't see who'd opened it. The hotel room was pitch black, not a single light on.

"We're serious," Sebastian's voice said from behind the door. "You are going to need us."

Jensen nodded, even though he wasn't sure Sebastian could see him. "Okay. I'll wait." He hesitated to leave the door. "But I get a strong feeling that Elizabeth is in real danger."

There was silence on the other side of the door. "I know you do. And that's why you are going to need us."

Jensen agreed with that as he went to his own room and fell onto the bed. He had no idea where to look for her. Hell, he didn't even understand how her brothers did. Their reasoning made no sense to him.

He shut his eyes, knowing he was going to have a long day of waiting ahead of him. God, he hoped Elizabeth was okay.

He was scared.

"You know, Lizzie, when I first saw you, even the way you were—half-dead—I remember thinking you were something. You were special. You were put on this earth to be an alpha's mate."

Elizabeth remained perfectly still, even though her position, crouched in the corner, was starting to make the muscles in her thighs ache. Still, her animal instincts told her to remain motionless, quiet, and let him rant.

He'd been raging now for nearly two hours. He'd raved about the pack and about the elders having no idea what they were doing. He fumed about the pack not knowing what was best, what was the inevitable. Of course, she hadn't been able to figure that out from his blathering tirade, either. He was making little-to-no sense.

But there was one thing she was certain of—Brody was not the same man she'd left so long ago. He was leaner, nothing more than bow-tight muscle, skin, and bone. And he was even more feral than he'd been.

He'd always been edged with an incivility. A wild, hungry streak that made him dangerous. But the look she saw flashing in his eyes now went beyond even that. It was as if he was more animal than man. And that made her very nervous.

"You always knew that I was destined to be the alpha."

Elizabeth didn't argue, although that was never true. The pack knew he was too dangerous to be alpha. Too much of a loose cannon. What did the pack think of him now?

He stopped his rant and glared at her. She swallowed, scared of the hatred she saw in those dark depths.

"You could ruin this for me," he growled, his voice low, eerie.

She took in a calming breath, then asked in an even tone, "Ruin what?"

He started pacing again, and she thought he wasn't going to answer.

"The pack, that group of stupid bastards, banished me."

Elizabeth gaped at him. She couldn't help it. The pack had always had issues with Brody. His unpredictability. His propensity for violence. But it wasn't as if the rest of the wolves were much better. They'd all been rough and wild. Traveling as a biker gang, causing trouble wherever they went.

What had he done to merit being banished? The ultimate punishment for a werewolf. Wolves—even werewolves—were natural pack animals.

She'd left the pack, but the truth was, she'd never belonged with them to begin with. And she'd been lucky enough to find Dr. Fowler and his followers to be her social link.

She watched Brody pace, his movements stiff and a tad awkward. She could see he was in pain, which meant Jensen's grandfather had connected with a bullet. And the bullet had to still be lodged in his body.

Could she escape? Was she fast enough to get away? Not that she even knew where she was. She glanced at the door across the room, a straight shot in the barren cabin.

"Don't think about it," Brody growled, and Elizabeth looked back to him to see he was guessing her thoughts. "Or I will kill you."

She didn't doubt him. His rage was clear on his face. But why was he blaming her? What did he want from her?

This time she had to ask.

"Brody, why did you come for me? How can I help you?"

His eyes roamed over her, and he sneered. "I don't know that you can. Not in the state you are in now."

She didn't understand what he meant. The state she was in?

His boots pounded the wood floor as he approached her, and she fought the urge to curl up. To protect herself.

He grabbed her arm, his fingers biting into her flesh. Roughly he dragged her to her feet.

"So here's the thing, Lizzie. I do need you. You give me credibility with the losers in the pack. They know you are above them. And since I'm your mate, that puts me above them, too."

She started to argue. The pack hadn't ever respected her or her noble upbringing. Only Brody had ever believed that. But she held her tongue. She had a feeling that the only thing that was going to save her was letting him continue to believe that.

"But you know we have a tricky situation here, don't we?"

She had no idea what he was talking about. But apparently her confusion was the wrong reaction, because he squeezed her arm, bruising her skin with his powerful grip.

She cried out. He really was crazy.

"So here is the deal," Brody said, his mouth close to her ear, his fingers still biting angrily into her arm. "We're going back to the pack, and you are going to pretend we made up. All nice and lovey-dovey. And we are going to pretend that brat you're carrying is mine."

At his words, all the air left her lungs. A wave of light-headedness made her weave; the only thing keeping her on her feet was his cruel hand gripping her.

Brody laughed, obviously seeing her confusion. "You didn't know, did you?"

She didn't react. She was too stunned. A brat? A baby? She was pregnant. She couldn't be. It wasn't possible. Yet, she suddenly knew it was true. She was carrying Jensen's baby.

Jensen sat up, having faded in and out of a doze. But now he had the strongest, clearest sensation that Elizabeth was in real danger.

He slipped off the bed and went to the window. The sun was still bright. Maybe two hours to go before it set. To the right, he noticed the moon, a pale, ghostly orb barely visible against the clear blue sky.

As he looked at the celestial body, he suddenly saw flashes of Elizabeth. In a cabin. Crouching on the floor. Her arms crossed protectively over her stomach as if she was sick or in pain.

Without thinking about it, he crossed to the nightstand and picked up the keys to his truck. He couldn't wait for Elizabeth's brothers. He knew something was very wrong. She needed him now.

He considered knocking on Sebastian and Christian's door to tell them he was leaving, but then decided against it. He had the feeling they would try to talk him out of going.

But there was no talking him out of this. He had to go. The compulsion to get in his truck and drive was overwhelming.

He slid into the truck and put the key in the ignition. Then he paused, his hand on the gearshift. *What are you doing? You have no idea where she is.*

But for some reason, that rational thought disappeared from his head. He put the truck into reverse and wheeled out of the parking place. He pulled up to the road and paused for a moment, looking both ways. Where was she?

"This is nuts," he muttered to himself; then another vivid image filled his mind. Elizabeth staring up at someone, her eyes wide and full of fear.

He blinked away the image, his attention turning to the road. Left. He needed to go left. The tires squealed as he turned in that direction.

At the first intersection, he automatically flipped the directional signal to indicate he was turning left again. By the time the light changed and he was heading deeper into the woods, he stopped questioning how he knew where he was going. He just did. Just like he knew Elizabeth needed him.

"I planned to kill you. I mean, you're knocked up with a human's brat. And you are a cheat. Not to mention, an abandoner. Certainly all good reasons to kill you."

Elizabeth tried not to move as he strode closer to her. Yet, she couldn't keep from tightening her hold on herself—and the life growing inside her.

"But then, after a while I calmed down." He crouched down, so he could look into her face. "You know, being shot can really cloud a person's judgment."

He stood again, although she didn't look up at him. She just held herself, trying to think of what she could do to escape.

"Anyway," he continued, "I decided to keep you. You are still my best bet to get back into the pack. And this time to show them that I should be the alpha. The pack leader."

Even though she knew she should just remain silent, she couldn't. This was insanity. "How do you think I can do that? The pack will never allow you to be leader."

Instead of getting enraged, as she thought he would, he smiled, although the curl of his lips was cruel, sinister-looking.

"Yes, they will. And you will help me. Because if you don't, I will kill your human. And his whelp."

Fear filled her, a small noise escaping her at the idea of either Jensen or the baby being hurt. But what Brody was asking of her couldn't be done. The pack would never accept him as their leader. He was delusional. And his delusions were making him very dangerous.

"How—how do you know I'm pregnant?" How did this lunatic know, when she had no clue.

"I tasted it on you. The change of your hormones."

When she just stared at him, he grinned again and added, "I was in your room the other night, and just couldn't resist taking a little taste of you."

She tightened her hold around her midriff, and he laughed.

"Good thing I did, too. The brat is a great bargaining chip, isn't it? And I'll be even more appealing to the pack if I return an expectant father."

Rage flared in Elizabeth. "There is no way in hell I'm going back with you, much less allowing you anywhere near my child."

She immediately realized her mistake. Brody's smile vanished—then he took a lightning-fast step toward her. The back of his hand connected with her cheekbone. Stars flashed before her, blotting out everything else.

"You'll do whatever I say," he growled, "or everyone you love will pay."

Chapter 25

Jensen saw another vivid image of Elizabeth, this one making him growl low in his throat. Fury rose up inside him, but he struggled to stay calm and focused. He was close now.

In fact, he was very close. Without questioning his actions, he pulled the truck onto the soft shoulder of the narrow mountain road.

He shut off the engine and hopped down onto the deserted road. Woods surrounded him, but he knew she was here. Very close.

He started up the rise, his steps certain. He kept going until he spotted a small cabin, barely visible through the trees in the waning light.

That was where she was. He knew it as surely as he knew his own name.

But instead of rushing toward the building, he moved stealthily, patiently. He had to go in carefully. In his visions, he hadn't been able to see her captor, but he had the faint impression of a large man. Lean muscles, large bones. And cruelty. But he knew that from what he saw of Elizabeth. He'd seen bruises on her cheek. Blood on her lips.

More rage spiked through him. This man would die for what he'd done to Elizabeth.

As he got closer to the cabin, he heard voices. He stopped, tilting his head. He was closer, but not near enough to hear anyone clearly. Yet, he could hear Elizabeth's captor without even straining.

"So let's get this straight. You help me, and I'll let the human and the brat live."

Jensen frowned. The human and the brat? What was he talking about?

"The plan is pretty simple, isn't it?" The voice sounded like it contained a sneer.

Jensen stepped closer.

"Isn't it, Lizzie?"

Jensen heard a small noise that he knew must be Elizabeth, but he couldn't make out what she said. If anything. Her response sounded like little more than a whimper.

Jensen suddenly felt her pain, both physical and mental, and he knew he had to get in there. He had to protect her. The urge was so strong, he hurried toward the cabin, giving up on the stealth attack. She needed him, now.

But as he grabbed the doorknob, her captor's words stopped him again.

"So do you agree, Lizzie? You will come back with me? You will be the perfect mate? Or I will carry out my threat. You know I will."

Jensen listened closely.

"Yes" was Elizabeth's quiet, heartbreaking answer.

"We will change soon. If you pull anything stupid like trying to escape, I will kill you. And then go back for the human. And the old man, too."

Jensen's muscles tightened at her captor's words, most of which he didn't understand, but he did understand this guy was very dangerous.

He turned the door handle, gripping the old metal knob slowly and carefully. Make no noise. Surprise was his best strategy.

He eased the door open, trying to peek in. To get an idea where the captor was. He couldn't see the man, but he could see Elizabeth. And she saw him. Her eyes widened, and she opened her mouth to call out to him. But before Jensen could react, the door jerked violently open, hauling him into the room.

Elizabeth let out a squeal and pushed up to her feet, getting ready to run to him. Without thinking, he straightened, quickly getting his bearings, and took a step toward her. But before he could reach her, a large arm clamped around his neck. He choked as the strong arm squeezed. Again Elizabeth cried out, but all Jensen could really register was her face. Her eyes wide with horror. The bruises on her cheek, her tangled hair.

Rage replaced the disorientation of the attack from behind. He dug his fingers into the arm holding him, using it for balance. Then he shoved backwards, using all his body weight.

The large man behind him stumbled, surprised by Jensen's move. They both toppled to the ground. Jensen used the opportunity to break free. He scrambled to his feet and ran to Elizabeth. Instead of grabbing her, he just placed himself between her and her captor, for the first time seeing who he was up against.

The man was already on his feet, which brought him to Jensen's height, but he was much wider. Shaggy, dark hair shrouded his rough, large-boned features and empty, dark eyes. He looked more animal than human.

Which he is, his mind told him. He didn't understand the thought, but he accepted it. He braced himself, expecting the huge man to come after him.

Instead, the man tilted his head, surveying Jensen. "How brave, human. But very stupid."

Elizabeth made a noise, but Jensen didn't hazard a look at her. He couldn't let this animal have an opportunity to attack.

But obviously, the hulk didn't feel the same way. He glanced at the window out at the darkened woods, then he laughed, the sound as coarse as he was.

"Well, this is going to be a pathetic fight."

"Please," Elizabeth begged. "Jensen, just run. Please." Then she spoke to the animal. "Brody, he doesn't even know what's going to happen. He can't fight. Please. I will go with you. I will help you."

"Help him what?" Jensen asked. And what was going to happen?

The hulk stepped toward them, and Jensen steeled himself and made sure Elizabeth was behind him, blocked.

Just as Jensen thought the man would reach for him, he stopped, standing right in the shaft of faint moonlight that came through the window.

Jensen frowned as the man just stood there, watching them. His face blank. His eyes unreadable. Suddenly his face contorted, twisting into a horrific mask of distorted muscles.

Jensen opened his mouth to ask what was happening, but no words would escape. All he could do was watch him in amazed horror.

Before Jensen's eyes, the man's body began to twist and alter, muscles warping. Loud cracks echoed in Jensen's ears and he realized it was the man's bones.

Dear God!

"It's okay," Elizabeth whispered from behind him, although her voice sounded strange, thick and slurred. And filled with pain.

Jensen's eyes darted from the man, or whatever he was, to Elizabeth. A dismayed noise escaped him as he saw Elizabeth. She was doing the same thing, her face distorting.

"Elizabeth!"

She grimaced, her eyes intense as if she was trying to control the incredible changes that were happening.

"Please just run. Please!"

"What?" This was insanity. It was unbelievable. But yet, wasn't it the very thing that he'd been toying with in the back of his mind? That Elizabeth was . . .

"We are . . . werewolves."

Jensen looked back to the man, who was now on his

hands and knees. His skin looked as if it was bubbling, his muscles shifting, his bones rearranging.

"This is real," he murmured. He knew it. He could feel the truth in himself.

"Yes. I'm so . . . so . . . sorry."

Jensen looked back to Elizabeth to see her fall to her knees. He knelt beside her.

"You . . ." A cry of pain escaped her, but she dropped her head, managing to calm herself. "You . . . have to go. Now!"

He shook his head. "No. I can't. I can't."

"Brave," the creature in front of him growled, the words barely intelligible. "Brave and stupid."

"Jensen—he will kill you. Please." Elizabeth's features had changed, but her pale eyes were the same. Begging him.

"No," Jensen said. "Make me like you. Give me a chance to fight him."

Elizabeth shook her head, her hair now a mane. "No. No."

Suddenly, the creature near them growled, the sound loud and eerie. Jensen stood, backing away from the animal, the large and black and deadly wolf.

Elizabeth, now fully changed, stepped in between them, snarling at the other werewolf. Her wolf form was larger than her human form, but she was still smaller than Brody.

Jensen watched, stunned by what he was seeing. Then something triggered in him—the need to protect his woman. The need to protect his . . . Brody's words returned. *Brat.*

Elizabeth was pregnant.

Before he realized what he intended to do, he rushed in between the snarling wolves, just as they reared up to lunge. The impact was like two battering rams pounding into him, knocking him to the floor. The wolves fell apart, both obviously stunned by his move.

Jensen looked at Elizabeth, praying that even in wolf form she understood that he wasn't going to leave her.

"Make me like you," he shouted. "Do it."

Elizabeth's pale wolf eyes blinked. Then she did as he asked, her paw coming up to score the skin of his shoulder. The impact of the scratch was instantaneous. He fell back, the shallow wound burning like hell. He was vaguely aware of the two wolves again lunging at each other. Elizabeth working to keep Brody away, while Jensen changed.

Time elapsed and distorted, just as his body did. And the next thing he knew he was changed, moving on all fours, leaping into the fray. Going for the huge one. Attacking the male that would hurt his mate.

The fight wasn't long. Even as big as the one wolf was, he wasn't a match for the two of them. Soon Jensen had Brody on his back, his fangs at the male's throat.

Then time seemed to shift again. As did reality. Soon, the whole cabin was teeming with wolves, all of them snarling and nipping and circling Jensen and Brody.

Then time and reality lapsed again.

When Jensen woke, he was on the floor of the cabin. Elizabeth lay beside him, her body curled protectively around his. She lifted her head as soon as she felt him rouse.

She regarded him with wide, worried eyes. Then they filled with tears.

"Jensen, I'm so sorry."

Jensen sat up, frowning around him. The cabin was empty, though signs of struggle remained. "Where is he?"

"Brody is gone. Members of my old pack came and took him. They'd been tracking him. They will deal with him."

Jensen's frown deepened as he touched Elizabeth's face, brushing aside her tears. "Then why are you apologizing?"

An inelegant sob escaped her. "Because I made you into a monster."

He considered that. "I asked you to. And I have a hard time believing you are a monster."

"I'm a werewolf!" The cry was followed by another loud sob.

He nodded, giving her an indulgent smile. "Yes. And so am I. Because I want to be. Because I love you."

She stared at him, tears rolling down her cheeks. "God, I love you, too." She flung herself at him, and all he could feel was love as he held her tight. He supposed what had happened last night had been beyond weird and should have terrified him, but it didn't. Not in the least.

What he felt was right and natural. Elizabeth was his mate. And she was having his child.

He leaned back to assess her, looking for any signs of injury. "Are you okay? Is the baby okay?"

She blinked at him, managing to smile through her tears. "Yes. We're fine."

He hugged her again. God, he loved this woman. Fur and all.

"You know, I think we have bigger problems," he said, managing to speak, even though his emotions threatened to choke him.

"What's that?" she asked against his shoulder.

"The fact that we have no clothes."

Elizabeth made a noise, the sound between a laugh and another sob. "Yes, that's just one of the problems with being a werewolf."

He kissed her, his hand moving down over the smooth curve of her back.

"Or not," she added, her hands moving over him in return.

They kissed and touched for several moments, until Jensen broke the kiss to peer at her.

"Are your brothers really vampires?"

"I'm afraid so."

Jensen considered that. "Well, we should probably ease Granddad into all of this."

Elizabeth laughed.

Chapter 26

Elizabeth stepped into the barroom, her arm looped through Rhys's. The chairs, which she, Mina, and Jolee had draped in white cloth and satin bows, were lined up in straight rows. White lights twinkled from the rafters and along the walls, replacing the usual colored ones. And up on the karaoke stage was an archway, also draped in white with flowers and greenery. Underneath, waiting for her, stood Jensen.

He looked sinfully handsome in his black tuxedo, his green eyes watching her, that lopsided smile curving his beautiful lips. Granddad stood beside him as his best man, a smile on his lips and affection clear in the eyes so like his grandson's.

"Ready?" Rhys murmured.

Elizabeth nodded.

They started down the makeshift aisle as all her friends and her family watched her, smiles on all their faces. Christian looked impossibly handsome. Sebastian winked and grinned. She grinned back.

"When I imagined giving you away, it wasn't quite like this," Rhys said, although he smiled, too.

Her grin widened.

"That's funny," her gaze left her brother and locked with Jensen's, "because this is exactly how I imagined it."

When they reached the altar, Rhys hugged her tight and

then handed her over to Jensen. The two men shook hands, and Elizabeth's eyes welled at the sight.

The rest of the wedding was a blur for her. She was too caught up in the perfection of the moment, of having her family there to see this wonderful event. And she was especially lost in Jensen. The man of her dreams. Her werewolf mate.

When the ceremony was done, they mingled with their guests. A buffet was set up along the bar and Jed served drinks.

Jensen talked easily with her brothers. Friends chatted and ate and drank. And again, Elizabeth feared she might cry.

Jensen glanced at her from across the room, obviously sensing her emotions. He excused himself to join her.

"Are you okay?" he asked.

She nodded, smiling through her tears. "Just being a ridiculously happy and hormonal, pregnant bride."

He chuckled and looped an arm around her to pull her close.

"You go right ahead," he told her, kissing her gently.

Just as their kiss would have deepened, someone cleared his throat as a cue.

They turned to see Brian standing there, smiling. Jill stood at his side, looking embarrassed, and Elizabeth knew it hadn't been her idea to speak to them at that very moment.

"Sorry to interrupt," Brian said, looking anything but sorry, and Elizabeth was quickly learning that Jensen's best friend was a big tease. "We just wanted to congratulate you both. We are so happy for you."

Jensen released her to hug his old friends.

Then Brian hugged Elizabeth. Jill followed.

"You are just what Jensen needed," Jill said as she squeezed her, and again, tears filled Elizabeth's eyes. Jill's words meant so much. Jensen's friends had accepted her.

When they parted, Jensen tugged her back against his side, his large body feeling so right against hers.

Music began to play, and Brian asked Jill to dance. They excused themselves to head to the dance floor that Christian had set up near the altar.

Jensen used the moment alone to steal another kiss.

"Excuse me, kids."

Elizabeth blinked away from Jensen, slightly dazed by the kiss. Then she realized who stood in front of her.

"Dr. Fowler!"

The older man, in his usual tweed suit, nodded to her. "Congratulations, Elizabeth."

She stepped forward and hugged Dr. Fowler, pleased to see him. Then she introduced Jensen to her mentor.

"I'm sorry I haven't been in touch," Dr. Fowler said. "I was in Europe for several weeks, working with a group of," he dropped his voice slightly, "weresheep."

Jensen made a noise, and Elizabeth knew he was trying to contain a chuckle. The variety of were-creatures still surprised and amused him.

"But I did get the chance to study your serum." The older man gave them a distinctly disappointed look. "And I hate to tell you this, Elizabeth. But as far as I could see, the only cell transformation I saw would only manage to change your pheromones so that you are no longer threatening to other animals."

Elizabeth stared at him for a moment. "You mean, I've just managed to get other animals to like me?"

Dr. Fowler nodded.

Both Jensen and Elizabeth were silent for a moment. Then Jensen started laughing.

Dr. Fowler looked confused.

"That's actually a good thing," Jensen explained. "Because I'm a veterinarian and I happen to want to keep on being one."

Dr. Fowler still looked confused, but nodded. "Well— good, then."

But Elizabeth couldn't share Jensen's happiness quite yet.

"Did the changes in pheromones also allow Jensen and me to mate?"

She hated that that might be the case. It somehow made her feel like their love had been manufactured.

Dr. Fowler shook his head. "No. Jensen is your true mate, that's very clear. It's rare, but there are reported cases of humans and werewolves being natural mates. That is the case here."

Elizabeth smiled, feeling even luckier for finding this wonderful man. She kissed Jensen on the cheek.

The doctor talked for a while longer, then the older man left to speak with Elizabeth's brothers.

When Elizabeth looked at Jensen, he was grinning.

"What?" she asked, smiling back.

"This is a great day. I have the love of my life, my soul mate, a baby on the way, and I'm going to be the best damned vet in the county. Once you give me some of your serum."

Her smile slipped slightly. "And you are a wolf."

He considered that for a moment, then shrugged. "I can definitely think of worse things. And by being a wolf, I have you. For a long, long time."

"Forever," she vowed. They kissed.

"I love you," he said against her lips, and she was enveloped in his passion.

For the first time, Elizabeth was glad she was a werewolf. Nothing beat an alpha male as a mate.

Here's a peek at HelenKay Dimon's
YOUR MOUTH DRIVES ME CRAZY.
Available now from Brava!

The world spun beneath Annie until her feet landed on the cold tile floor of the shower stall. Strong arms banded around her waist, holding her in place.

Every cell in her body snapped to life. The lethargy weighing her down disappeared with the screech of the shower curtain rings against the rod. A rush of water echoed in her ears as steam filled the room.

"Here we go," the stranger said to the room as if the nut chatted with unconscious people all the time.

He balanced her body against his. Rough denim scratched against her sensitive skin from the front. Lukewarm water splashed over her bare body from the back, making her skin tingle and burn.

A gasp caught in her throat as her shoulders stiffened under the spray. A scream rumbled right behind the gasp, but she managed to swallow that, too.

"This should help." He continued his one-sided conversation in a deep, hypnotizing voice.

He seemed mighty pleased with himself. And since he had stepped right under the water with her, a bit ballsy for her taste.

"This will feel better in a second," he said to the quiet room.

He wasn't wrong.

Firm hands caressed her skull, replacing the frigid ocean

with bathwater. He rinsed and massaged and rinsed again. The sweep of his hands wiped away the last of her confusion. With that task done, his palms turned to her arms, brushing up and down, igniting every nerve ending in their path.

His chest rubbed against her bare breasts until heat replaced her chill. With thighs smashed against his legs, the full-body rubdown sparked life into body parts that had been on a deep-freeze hold for more than a year.

"Better?"

She didn't answer him. Wasn't even sure she could speak if she wanted to.

"Open your eyes and say something."

The husky command broke her out of her mental wanderings and sent a shot of anxiety skating down her spine. This was the part of the program where she ran and hid . . . and then ran some more.

Naked. Alone. Strange man. Yeah, a very bad combination.

"I know you're awake." He sounded pretty damn amused by the idea.

The jig was up. Okay, fine, she got his point.

Not knowing if her rescuer counted as a friend or foe, she played the scene with the utmost care. Only a complete madman would attack a vulnerable woman who didn't know her own name. If her stranger fell into that category, she'd scream and make a mad dash into the kitchen for the nearest sharp knife. The nearest sharp anything.

She groaned in pain that was only half false.

"Your eyes are still closed," he said.

Yeah, pal, no kidding.

"You aren't fooling me."

Well, she could certainly try.

His hands continued to massage her sore flesh with just the right amount of pressure to bring her blood sizzling back to life. If he kept this up, her eyes wouldn't open. She'd be asleep.

She couldn't remember the last time she slept through the

night. Actually, she could. It had been fifteen months, fifteen months of searching. The path led to Kauai. To the yacht. To flying over the side and into the water. To being in this shower.

"We can stand here all night for all I care," he said.

Nothing that extreme. Maybe ten more minutes.

He chuckled. "Doesn't bother me."

Lucky for her she found an accommodating potential serial killer.

"Because I'm the one with clothes on," he pointed out.

Her eyelids flew open.

Turn the page for a look at Susan Johnson's story,
"School for Scandal",
in the PERFECT KISSES anthology.
Available now from Brava!

Finally, just as she was about to despair of finding her sister, she saw Harriet and the notorious James Bell near one of the far windows overlooking the street. The viscount was leaning back against the narrow wall of the alcove, floor to ceiling French doors to his right, the ballroom to his left, and Harriet in his arms.

Her face was raised to him as though waiting for his kiss.

Taking his cue, he did exactly that. He kissed her.

For so lengthy an interval that Claire was able to approach them unheeded.

"If you'll excuse me," Claire said, keeping her tone severe even as she grappled with the powerful impact of the viscount's outrageous beauty. "My sister is not allowed at entertainments such as this. Come, Harriet. I'm here to take you home."

The viscount had looked up lazily when Claire had first spoken, but had neither moved, released Harriet, nor altered his expression. "And you are?" he finally drawled, his heavy-lidded gaze surveying Claire from head to toe before coming back to rest on her face.

"I am Claire Russell, Harriet's older sister and I must *insist* that you release her immediately. It is wholly inappropriate for her to be in attendance here. As you well know, Harriet," she added, turning to her sister.

"Auntie said I could come," Harriet mutinously retorted, her pretty mouth pursed in a pout.

"Our aunt was no doubt mistaken about the style of entertainment." Claire refused to admit that her aunt would stoop so low in order to snare a man like Ormond. Although, from the viscount's sudden amused expression, she rather thought he already knew.

"Why don't I have a servant see your sister home," the viscount graciously offered, pushing away from the wall and easing Harriet back a step. "I'll take you riding in the park tomorrow, poppet," he added, smiling to assuage Harriet's frown. He lifted his hand in a negligent gesture and was immediately acknowledged by a footman, the man seemingly materializing out of thin air. "There, now, my sweet," the viscount said, brushing Harriet's cheek with his finger. "Jordan will see you home. And I shall call on you tomorrow at four."

Harriet glared at her sister. "You are ever so vexing, Cleery. Do go away," she pettishly said. "I *am not* a child you can order about!"

Ormond nodded at his footman and a look of understanding passed between them. "Now, now, don't chide your sister," the viscount calmly murmured. "She's merely concerned with the—ah . . . environment. And on second thought, I believe she's right."

"I appreciate your understanding," Claire replied, coolly. "Come, Harriet." Fully expecting to be obeyed, she turned to go.

"If you don't mind, Miss Russell." The viscount seized her arm with a quickness that belied his fashionable languor and pulled her back. "Perhaps you might stay a moment. We could discuss the—er—situation. Go now, poppet," he urged since Harriet gave no appearance of obeying her sister. "I'm sure your sister is anxious to ring a peal over my head." He smiled at Harriet to allay the sudden suspicion in her gaze. "I shall set this all right and tomorrow you and I will ride in Hyde Park. Would that please you?"

"Oh, very well," Harriet grumbled with the petulance

common to women who were widely admired for their beauty. Ormond couldn't possibly be interested in Claire anyway unless he was a devotee of blue-stocking women which she very well knew he wasn't. And riding with him in Hyde Park tomorrow for all the world to see would be ever so delicious. She shot a fretful glance at her sister. "Cleery ruined everything tonight anyway."

"Indeed," the viscount said with a faint smile. His lashes lowered almost infinitesimally and taking his cue, Jordan stepped forward to escort Harriet home.

And a moment later, Claire found herself alone with the man reputed to be the most handsome man in England.

Nor could she honestly deny the designation.

In truth—any woman, not just an innocent like her sister—would be hard pressed to withstand his brute virility. His dark, sensual gaze seemed to offer ravishment and pleasure in equal measure while his muscled form was conspicuous even beneath his fine tailoring and indolent pose.

Quickly taking herself to task, she sternly reminded herself why she had come to this debauch: To save Harriet from disaster. To allow herself to be even fleetingly captivated by a flagrant libertine like Ormond was inexcusable.

Overcompensating perhaps for her injudicious thoughts, she addressed him with rare hauteur. "We really have nothing to discuss, my lord. I certainly have no intention of ringing a peal over your head. I doubt it would do any good. May I only state, firmly and clearly, that I do not wish Harriet to become involved with a man such as yourself." Her duty done, once again she turned to leave.

And once again he stopped her, clasping her wrist lightly. "And what kind of man might that be?" he asked with a teasing smile.

She shook off his hold. "I need not explain the particulars to you, sir. Your reputation is one of long standing. Surely you know what you are."

"Would you like tea, Miss Russell?"

And finally here's Diane Whiteside's
THE NORTHERN DEVIL.
Coming next month from Brava!

"I must remarry and quickly," Rachel announced.

Marriage to someone else? Well, he'd always known it would happen one day. But it seemed more wrenching now that he'd carried her and known the softness of her in his arms, and the sweet smell of her in his lungs.

"There is no time for a protracted struggle against Collins, here in Omaha. It is vital that he be immediately cut off from all revenues, especially as my trustee."

Lucas immediately came fully alert, recognizing her sharpened tone. "Why is it so urgent?"

"He means to trap William Donovan at the Bluebird Mine and kill him."

"*Murder* Donovan? Why, that bast—toadstool!"

She nodded agreement. "But if he's no longer my trustee—"

His mind was racing, considering the implications. "Then he can't give orders to the men at the Bluebird Mine in your name."

Her pacing brought her less than a foot from him. She stopped with a small gasp and pivoted, swishing her train out of his way. Did she glance too long at him over her shoulder? But if so, she wasn't behaving like a woman who knew how to flirt.

"Yes. Elias bought the mine several years ago from an old

friend, who needed to raise cash. He also sold an interest to Donovan, as part of a bigger deal."

"So Humphreys, the mine's manager, has always answered to Boston."

She sank down onto the settee by the coffee tray. "Exactly. I'll need to personally tell him that I've remarried so he won't help Collins in any way."

Every protective instinct in Lucas revolted. "No! You won't go anywhere near the Bluebird, not if there's about to be a murder attempt."

She raised a haughty eyebrow. Ah, that was more like the woman he was acquainted with—who enjoyed challenging his mind, not his loins.

He relaxed, ready for a pleasant round of debate.

"Mr. Grainger, it's critical that an innocent man's life be saved. That's far more important than any polite folderol about not sending women into danger. I'm certain that once Mr. Humphreys understands I've remarried, he won't assist Mr. Collins, and all will be well."

A Nevada mine supervisor would fall into line like a sheep when she crooked her finger? Appalled at her optimism, Lucas opened his mouth to roar objections but she was still talking.

"No, what I need your help for is to find another husband. Immediately, before Mr. Collins can take legal steps to regain my custody."

Lucas frowned. Rachel Davis and another man—in her wedding bed? Someone certain to be honorable, polite, and respectful even in the bedroom.

He growled, deep in his throat, and began to stride up and down the carpet.

Like hell, anyone else was climbing into her bed if she was willing to accept a marriage of convenience!

But marry her himself?

He swallowed hard.

She was right: The best way to protect Donovan's life,

given Collins's malice, was for her to marry. He owed Donovan a blood debt that his life alone would not repay—but his honor would. Marrying Rachel would even the scales.

Did his old vow never to marry carry any weight against saving Donovan's life?

He grimaced and spun on his heel. No.

But Rachel was his friend. She wasn't looking for love, just protection and companionship. They could build a solid union together on that basis.

But in marrying her, there'd be the necessity of siring children. For the first time in his life, he'd have to hope that his seed would set fruit. Fruit that could grow to become a little child, vibrant and alive, beautiful, intelligent, happy to see him. A true family, in other words, and his oldest dream.

He began to smile.